A Deadly Affair

ANGUS BRODIE AND MIKAELA FORSYTHE
MURDER MYSTERY

CARLA SIMPSON

Cover art by Dar Albert at Wicked Smart Designs

Published by Oliver-Heber Books

0 9 8 7 6 5 4 3 2 1

Prologue

WHITECHAPEL, **London**

10 January 1889

Her eyes were wide open, lips parted as if she would have said something, or perhaps smiled one last time.

She was young compared to the others, pretty, with her dark hair fanned out about her. But there were no words, not even a startled scream.

There was only the cruel mockery of the gaping wound at her throat—the macabre smile the killer had given her—as a pale hand moved slowly through the water as if waving farewell.

One

THE MORGUE, BOW STREET POLICE STATION, LONDON

"ARE you quite certain that you're up to this?" I gently asked my housekeeper. "I will do this if you cannot."

Not that I was in the habit of identifying dead bodies. My housekeeper, Alice, had been with my family since my sister and I were small children, after my first experience with viewing dead bodies. She was in fact like family.

We had lost our mother first to consumption. Then, our father a year later. Not from some illness, but from a self-inflicted gunshot wound.

Only later we learned that his decision to take his own life was due to *losses* that included the only home we had ever known and what little remained of the Forsythe estate.

It was sold off to pay our father's gambling debts, a dark shadow for two young children to live with, save for a small inheritance from our maternal grandfather and the somewhat eccentric kindness of our great aunt, Lady Antonia Montgomery.

Aunt Antonia had never wed, though not for lack of suitors, but for lack of any man who could possibly keep up with her rather adventuresome spirit. Nor had she any experience with children. That, however, did not prevent her from taking on two orphaned children, ages six and eight years at the time.

She saw it as another great adventure, without the usual inconvenience of child-bearing, as she later explained it. In the two of us, she had a ready-made family that suited her somewhat unconventional maternal instincts quite well. It was quite a challenge for her.

No two children could have been more different than Linnie and me, as we were often reminded.

"Linnie is so feminine and delicate, while Mikaela looks as if she might have sprouted in a hedgerow," our governess once commented, no doubt due to my rather unruly dark hair and equally unruly nature. She was promptly dismissed.

One might have opinions, but as far as our aunt was concerned, one should keep them to oneself or risk her wrath.

That observation, however, was not entirely unwarranted. I would much rather have spent a day adventuring about the rough and wild countryside of our aunt's estate in the wilds of Scotland, rather than at lessons I found to be tedious and incredibly boring. Perhaps it was that earlier experience of viewing dead bodies that had imbued me with a more pragmatic view and the habit of questioning everything about me.

I had been the first to find our father in the stables with a good portion of his head missing, blood soaking the hay where he had fallen. I had not been frightened by it, merely curious the way children can be in finding something they have no experience with or understanding of.

I simply chose to close off the traumatic experience —our aunt's physician called it—with a detachment that prevented me from becoming hysterical or mentally undone.

Linnie was far different, and had not seen death up close, and had no understanding of it.

She was quiet by nature, even shy, while I much preferred climbing trees and successfully—most of the time—walking on rocks across a stream, or wielding a make-believe sword while she read Chaucer or Shakespeare, or painted her pictures.

"*Mikaela Forsythe, wild gypsy,*" Aunt Antonia called me with a knowing smile after she brought us to live with her. For it was nothing for me to bring home some poor creature that I'd found in the forest of her country estate with the hope of making it a pet.

"*Whatever shall become of you?*" She pretended to lecture me on the proprieties of a young lady who did not go about exploring in the forest and return with a torn dress and mud-spattered shoes, or no shoes at all.

As childhood passed, we attended the finest finishing school, with art and music lessons which I considered to be dull and quite boring, while Linnie excelled in both.

Now Lady Litton, my sister had made a brilliant marriage. For my part, I had been pushing the boundaries of propriety and had set off on a series of adventures across Europe to the Far East, writing about those adventures with my character, Emma Fortescue, to surprising success.

Now the world had been turned upside down once more.

Linnie had been missing these past several days along with her maid, Mary, who was Alice's daughter. In all that time there had been no word from her. She had simply vanished.

Then, just this morning, we received word from her

husband, Sir Charles Litton, that a young woman's body had been found, pulled from the river in a part of the city where no respectable girl or woman would dare go.

The first information received from him had mentioned a brief description provided by Chief Inspector Abberline of the Metropolitan Police. It described the young woman, approximately twenty years of age with dark hair, and wearing the clothes of a servant.

My initial relief that it couldn't possibly be Linnie was replaced by the very real possibility that the young woman *was* known to us.

Aunt Antonia had provided her private coach, along with Mr. Munro, who managed her household. Together, we made the trip across London to the Bow Street police station.

Now, Alice tearfully nodded, a handkerchief clutched in her hand. She suddenly seemed very old and very small. as if she might disappear inside herself at any moment.

She nodded and whispered, "I have to know..."

Mr. Munro stood with us, one at each side of her, he with that stoic Scot bearing, his crisp blue eyes hooded beneath the arch of dark brows.

It struck me that we formed quite an odd group—the tall Scot, the diminutive Irish woman, and me, bound together by this horrible circumstance. I tightened my arm about Alice's shoulders, then nodded for the police surgeon to continue.

"Water usually has an adverse effect on body tissue," he explained. "However, we're most fortunate that the Thames is quite cold this time of year. The body is well preserved and there has been very little deterioration."

Deterioration? As if the man was describing fruit or fresh cod at market. And, as for his observation that the situation was most *fortunate*? That raised the question as to what could have possibly been *unfortunate.*

It was a ridiculous choice of words, with little thought for the poor woman who stood beside me.

The surgeon looked up then, his expression what could only be described as curious with an amount of excitement. He obviously performed these tasks far too often, given the crime that ravaged the East End and with the recent murders of other young women.

I suppose one developed a certain detachment for such things. However, I saw no reason for such detached analysis.

"If you please," I made no attempt to disguise my irritation. Beside me, Alice softly moaned behind the handkerchief and swayed unsteadily. I feared that she might go down.

The surgeon, who greatly resembled Ichabod Crane with his gaunt features and disheveled hair, cleared his throat as if he had merely been interrupted from some dissertation before a gallery of medical students,

"Do continue, Dr. Bond." Chief Inspector Abberline, who was also present, instructed him.

He stood apart, his expression unreadable as the good doctor pulled back the sheet that had been draped over the examination table.

It was done with great ceremony, much like a magician drawing back a curtain to reveal that the person behind the curtain had disappeared. Except that poor Mary Ryan still lay there, her lips tinged blue, with an assortment of bruises that had turned blue as well, and the gaping wound at her throat.

"My sweet girl!" Alice let out a startled gasp, swayed, and would most certainly have gone down had Mr. Munro not tightened his arm about her.

"These things are never pleasant," Abberline commented, as he now came to stand at the other side of the table.

"However we do need to know if you are able to identify the body."

This was directed at poor Alice, her eyes tightly closed, a hand pressed over her heart, the other clasping the handkerchief to her pale face.

It wasn't merely unpleasant, I thought, it was horrible and frightening, and I wasn't about to put her through any more of this.

I nodded to Mr. Munro and he escorted Alice from the room, towering over the tiny, grief-stricken woman, as I stepped closer to the examination table.

Horrible and terribly sad, I thought, as I looked down at the body of poor Mary Ryan. Yet, I was struck by something the doctor had spoken of about the coldness of the river this time of year.

There was no wasting away of the body as of yet, as I had seen once quite by accident on an adventure to India some years earlier.

A man had drowned in the Ganges, his body bloated, flies doing what flies do. The stench drifted on the air among the flotsam and garbage usually found there, as he bobbed against the shoreline in the hot, humid weather that day.

This however, was very different. I could almost believe that Mary was simply resting, soon to waken, and laugh at us all with her quick wit at being so serious. Except for the bruising on her arms and the ghastly cut at her throat.

"And you are?" the chief inspector inquired, his gaze directed at me, a thick brow arching over that brown gaze.

His tone was very much like that of the local official who had questioned Aunt Antonia over the circumstances of our father's death. Then, as now, there was no care or warmth of sympathy for those who had lost a loved one. He was simply performing his duty.

I introduced myself.

"Her name is Mary Ryan," I explained. She was a maid in my sister's household."

And now she was dead. And *yes*, we would accept responsibility for the body, and make the necessary arrangements. It was the least we could do for poor Mary, and her mother.

That ghastly slash mark at her throat, similar to the other murders in Whitechapel, offered little else other than the method of her death and dozens more unanswered questions. Not the least was—what was Mary doing in that part of London?

Abberline wrote down her name, along with mine, in a small note book.

"What information do you have regarding the attack?" I asked. "Were there any witnesses?"

Was she simply the next victim of the crazed madman who had stalked the East End for over a year?

What was Mary doing there? And where was my sister?

"INSPECTOR ABBERLINE IS AN IMBECILE!"

It was something I entirely agreed with.

I had returned to my aunt's residence at Sussex Square. I thought it the best place for Alice under the circumstances—familiar surroundings with people she knew, rather than my town house.

There, it was just the two of us and my frequent excursions would have left her much alone at a time when she did not need to be left alone.

"Of course, Alice may remain as long as necessary," Aunt Antonia had replied when we arrived, and gave instructions that she was to be given one of the upstairs rooms and allowed to rest. All the while the household staff whispered and gossiped amongst themselves.

"The chief inspector will make the *usual inquiries*," I added, and made no attempt to disguise my sarcasm.

"The perfect embodiment of a public official," Aunt Antonia commiserated, then motioned to Mr. Munro.

"Please have Mr. Symons bring luncheon," she requested, as I stood at the window in her front parlor and stared out at the leaden sky that had settled over London. It much resembled a shroud that lent itself to the somber events of that morning.

"Miss Mikaela?" he inquired.

I shook my head.

I would rather have preferred a drink, preferably my aunt's twenty-year whisky from her estate in Scotland, regardless of the time of day.

I thanked him for his assistance earlier that morning. More than once, through the difficult affair of identifying Mary's body, I had feared that he might have to carry poor Alice to the coach. I was grateful for the way he had taken charge of providing information where Mary's body was to be taken.

Officially, Munro managed my aunt's household along with her other estate in Scotland. This also included the country house outside of London, and her chateau in the south of France.

Unofficially?

I, along with the gossips of London society, had often wondered what other duties might be included. However, I respected my aunt far too much to question the other aspects of their relationship. After all, who was I to criticize?

"*I shall live my life as I choose,*" she had once commented when, as a child, I had overheard the gossip.

A lesson to live by. Raised in such an environment, I was of much the same opinion.

However, Aunt Antonia had admonished me more than once about the dangers of my headstrong ways and my *adventures* as she called them. Yet, she had confided at the time that were she younger, she would have been inclined to go off *adventuring* herself.

It was no wonder then, raised with that influence, that I was still unmarried. I was a spinster according to the society pages, where my name occasionally appeared along with speculation that there might be a forthcoming engagement.

There had been three, to be precise. It had come to my attention that one of the gentlemen had inquired about Lady Antonia's substantial estate. May the devil take them, I said at the time, and refused them all. My opinion had not changed.

There had been no comment then from my aunt regarding my continued status as an unmarried woman. Nor had there been a wringing of hands over what was to become of me. There was, as always, only her unfailing support.

"The man is an ass. 'Tis his loss."

That particular gentleman had eventually wed a very sweet, docile creature with a substantial inheritance. When I received the news, I had happily taken myself off to Egypt, where I traversed the Nile, joined a caravan where I slept with a knife under my blanket courtesy of Mr. Munro, and had encountered the Bedouin in the desert.

Afterward, I returned briefly for Linnie's wedding, then immediately departed to Europe on my next adventure, including an escape from my travel party to the Isle of Crete.

It was a grand adventure for my next novel. I had hired a guide upon the recommendation of friends. For days on end we explored Greek ruins, ate at small street cafes, and shopped in open-air markets. Then my guide, a strikingly handsome young man, suggested that I might want to see the island of Crete before returning to England. We set off, leaving the rest of my party at the Acropolis and other sites.

The day we arrived on Crete was warm. The water was an incredible shade of blue, and there was a great deal of ouzo. In the moment it seemed perfectly natural to swim naked in the sea. When in Greece...

There was a bit of a dust-up among the others in my travel party when they finally arrived. Word had somehow made its way to Aunt Antonia regarding my *conduct*. Afterward, when I had returned, she had dismissed the entire episode. She had simply inquired if the water off the Isle of Crete was as warm as she had heard.

"*They,*" obviously referring to the ladies I had traveled with, "*have most certainly never had an invitation to swim naked in the Aegean!*"

And that was the end of the matter.

Now, my aunt's butler, Mr. Symons, had arrived, silver tray in hand with a crystal decanter filled with that glowing amber refreshment that Aunt Antonia preferred—her version of *afternoon tea*. It was a rather fine single-malt whisky.

Mr. Symons was followed by one of my aunt's maids who carried a wrapped bundle.

"What have you there, Annie?" my aunt asked at the girl's obvious hesitation.

"Beg pardon, ma'am. These are the clothes Mary was wearing."

"Oh, yes, I quite see," my aunt replied.

The clothes had been provided after the surgeon's examination at the mortuary. I'd had them wrapped in brown paper and said nothing to Alice at the time.

"I'll take them," I told her. "Alice may eventually want them."

"I'll see that they're placed in the coach." Mr. Munro took the wrapped bundle from the girl and left to see to the matter, as my aunt poured two tumblers.

"So, Mary's death is *'under investigation',*" Aunt Antonia commented, when we were left alone to discuss the matter.

"And what of Lenore's disappearance?"

I took a healthy drink and closed my eyes as it warmed its way into my stomach.

"The Chief Inspector was completely unaware," I replied.

A brow lifted at that. It was a sign I had learned as a child that had the power to send servants fleeing, or her solicitor or some other person seeking the door.

"The wife of a peer of the realm and member of Parliament has disappeared, and he knows nothing of it?" Aunt Antonia inquired.

"Charles has made inquiries of his own through private sources." I repeated what he had told me when we were first informed that Linnie had disappeared.

It was obviously an effort to prevent any gossip that she had gone off without a word to anyone. Instead he had put it out among their circle of acquaintances that she had taken herself off to the country for a few days.

"You and Lenore were to go to Brighton together, as I recall," Aunt Antonia commented.

We had made plans to go, just the two of us months earlier. I had hoped it would lift Linnie's spirits after suffering the loss of her first child several months earlier.

She had been devastated at the loss, and I had put off my next trip abroad to be with her. But that was some months ago, and the trip had been postponed.

Never one to stand on propriety, Aunt Antonia rose and poured us both another dram of whisky.

"What is to be done since the chief inspector is not forthcoming?" she commented.

I had given that a great deal of thought.

"Linnie would not simply take herself off somewhere without telling someone," I acknowledged. I knew my sister better than anyone and was quite certain about that, no matter how difficult the circumstances might have been. Unless something dreadful had happened that she *couldn't* tell anyone.

"I quite agree," Aunt Antonia replied.

I tossed back the whisky.

"I want to make inquiries of my own," I announced, having thought the matter through quite thoroughly.

It was something I had felt for the past several days, niggling at the back of my brain. I simply refused to accept that there was no trace of my sister, no word among their acquaintances, no message received from her. And now poor Mary had been brutally murdered.

"I quite agree," Aunt Antonia replied.

Mr. Munro had returned. A look passed between him and my aunt.

A slight nod of the head sent him from the parlor without a word. When he returned, he handed her what appeared to be a calling card.

"There is someone who may be able to assist." She handed me the card.

I read the name on the front of the card.

"Angus Brodie, Private Investigations?"

"Mr. Brodie knows... certain people, and has access to information that may not be available to others," she explained.

"He can be somewhat difficult at times," she went on to describe the person in question in some detail.

"However, he is most thorough and always several steps ahead, even as he keeps his thoughts to himself. Most clever, though somewhat obstinate." There was a faint smile.

"He is, after all, a Scot. But the man is most resourceful," she continued. "He'll not stop until the job is done. But most important, he gets results, and he can be trusted."

That raised the obvious question: exactly how she had come by those observations?

"He was with the Metropolitan Police for some time," she continued somewhat vaguely.

"But no longer?" I asked.

My aunt made a dismissive gesture. "Some ridiculous matter about something questionable during an investigation. He may have been intoxicated while on duty." This, with her typical laugh.

"The address on the Strand where he may be contacted is on the reverse of the card."

#204 at the Strand, was written in a hasty scrawl, and barely legible in the way of someone who was either impatient or suddenly distracted. Or possibly intoxicated?

~

"Beg pardon, Miss Mikaela?"

I looked up from the list of questions I'd made for the following morning, and my meeting with Mr. Brodie.

My aunt's housekeeper, Agatha, had returned with me to my town house in Mayfair.

She had been with my aunt for several years and had assisted with the furnishing of the town house in the simpler, less cluttered style that I preferred. She was well familiar with my routine, often working late into the night on my latest novel. However, tonight that was the farthest thing from my thoughts.

"I did a bit of laundry," she explained. "Should Alice want the clothes you brought back with you."

I thanked her. "I appreciate your taking care of it."

Still, she hesitated.

"Is there something else?"

"I found this sewn into the hem of Mary's gown."

She handed me a key.

It was quite large, made of brass with the number 436 stamped into the metal at the curved bow at one end.

It was not unusual for one to sew valuables into the hem of one's gown. I had done that very thing before crossing the Sahara, when informed it might be prudent to conceal valuables against thieves we might encounter.

But what reason would Mary have to sew a key into the hem of her dress? To keep it safe? From whom? Equally important, what was it a key *to*?

Three

#204, THE STRAND

THE NUMBER WAS BARELY visible over the entrance to the alley that led to the stairs. It was covered with the accumulation of grime, soot from the smoke of coal fires that lay over the city, and the ever-present dampness from the river.

The street in front was clogged with the congestion of horse-drawn trams, cabs, and omnibuses. Along the sidewalk, a fishmonger had set up his stall.

The smell of fresh cod was thick in the morning air, as more daring souls ventured across the thoroughfare afoot. They ran and dodged out of the way of traffic and shouting vendors.

"Are yer certain this is the place, miss?" the driver called down from his perch at the rear of the cab.

The address on the back of the card matched the one over the entrance. An arrow indicated the stairs just beyond the entrance to the alley, set back from the street.

"If this be the place, miss, I got ter move me rig or get runned over," the driver reminded me as a horse-drawn tram filled with passengers bore down on us.

I paid the two pence fare and stepped down from the cab.

"Right yer are, miss," he said, tipping the brim of his hat.

The cab lurched away from the sidewalk in front of the establishment of C.W. Butler at the ground floor—importer of foreign cigars, tobacco, and Taddy's snuffs, according to the sign over the bow windows that faced onto the street.

A man sat at the side of the arched entrance to the stairway that led to the upper floors of the building. He was perched on a platform with wheels, both legs missing above the knee. Each pant leg had been rolled then tucked under what remained of his legs.

His cap was pulled down over a tangled mat of brown hair. He wore a much-worn coat with patches, buttoned up to his neck against the morning cold. Watchful brown eyes narrowed on me.

I had encountered many such scenes in my travels. The usual recommendation from companions or guides was to simply ignore those found with their hand out. Such encounters could be dangerous, the beggar often working in tandem with another person hiding nearby. They then overtook the unsuspecting traveler and robbed them.

The man grabbed at the hem of my skirt as I would have passed by.

"A penny if you please, miss," he said. "Possibly tuppence to purchase some food on a cold morning?"

That, in spite of the fact that he appeared quite healthy in spite of his handicap. He spun round on the platform that was approximately the size of a daily paper, his hand tightening at my skirt.

"Ye'll not deny the Mudger some food, now would yer, pretty lady? No? How about a coin then? Jus' trying to survive, I am!"

"Payment denotes a service provided in exchange for compensation," I pointed out.

"Aye," he replied hesitantly.

"I will gladly pay you for information."

"Wot might that be?"

"Regarding the gentleman at Number Two Hundred Four. Do you know if he is in this morning?"

He glanced over his shoulder to the stairs at the alley.

"He's there, all right. He's been there all the while, except when he went over to the Old Bell last night. "

"The Old Bell?" It was safe to assume that he was not referring to the local church.

"Over in Holborn," he explained. "The Old Bell Tavern. Went to see someone. Asked me ter keep me eye on things 'ere, he did."

A tavern. Of course, considering the information Aunt Antonia had shared with me.

I gave the Mudger two coins, and wondered just what I might find at the top of those stairs.

He smiled, several teeth missing, and winked.

"Right yer are, miss, and thank ye kindly. Mr. Brodie, Number Two Hundred Four. Yer can't miss it. And if I can be of further service to ye...?"

"I will be certain to let you know," I assured him. "And you may tell your companion hiding there in the shadows, that I will not hesitate to use this on him."

I showed him the slender knife Mr. Munro had given me when I first set off on my travels some years before.

He laid a hand across his heart as if I had sorely insulted him.

"I've no idea what yer speaking of, Miss. But if I did," he added, in a voice that seemed much louder than before, "be assured there'll be no trouble."

I walked toward those stairs and was immediately aware of movement. A slender form melted back into the shadows along the alleyway, then disappeared completely, as there was a loud slamming of a door. It was followed by rapid footsteps attached to a woman who came running down the stairs toward me.

Her hair was brilliant red, of the sort that is rarely natural, with bright red color at her lips. Her gown was a glaring shade of chartreuse, with black lace at the bodice that she was in the process of tucking something into. The swell of pale flesh above was amply displayed by the low-cut gown, and looked as if it might fall out at any moment.

She looked up, obviously surprised to find me in her path by the expression on her face, red lips curved in a frown as she glared at me.

"Now I sees where he's been keepin' hisself," she commented. "A bit up-market this time. But he'll be off with someone different next week, mind yer, dearie. Best collect what he owes ye now." Then she was off, passing a comment to the Mudger on her way to the street.

There was only one doorway at the second floor. That could only mean that the woman had come from the office of Angus Brodie, Private Investigator. It was not exactly the beginning I had hoped for.

There was no signage at the door. I considered the possibility that the Mudger might have deliberately provided the wrong information as I knocked lightly. When there was no answer, I knocked a second time.

When there was still no answer, I tried the knob. The door was unlocked and opened freely.

Smoke filled the room. It stung my eyes and sent me into a coughing fit with the immediate concern that the building might be on fire.

Through the haze, I could tell that it was the usual

sort of establishment to be found in the working-class district, including scarred wood floors and badly smudged windows that appeared to overlook an alley along the back of the building.

A coal stove sat at the opposite wall with a mantel over which hung a poor landscape painting. A desk sat at the adjacent wall with a scattering of papers, and there was a wood file cabinet.

I called out from the doorway.

There was a muffled response followed by what could only be described as a curse in Scots Gaelic. Then a large mass lunged across the room.

However, instead of Angus Brodie, a great lumbering beast charged through the cloud of smoke toward me.

The animal was mostly brown, with a white patch across the back, a long tail, and a brown patch at each eye, with a flattened nose. It slid to a stop, tongue lolling out the side of its mouth.

That raised the question if the beast intended to attack, or lick me to death. Then it abruptly thrust its flattened nose into the folds of my skirt on a level that was decidedly private.

I had been raised around hounds as a small child, but never one so ill-mannered.

A well-landed punch to the snout and the beast flattened itself to the floor. It stared up at me with what could only be described as a wounded expression in large brown eyes.

More smoke billowed from the doorway of an adjacent room as another body appeared amid more curses.

"Ye bloody *eijit*!"

The pungent smoke cleared enough to determine the source as a man, presumably Angus Brodie. The accent confirmed it.

He stepped into the outer office, shirt open to the waist exposing a slightly furred chest, dark disheveled hair with a day's growth of beard, a bruise below his left eye, bare feet, and trousers that were conspicuously undone.

"Yer not Maude!" he snapped, a bloodshot gaze glaring at me.

"Quite obviously not," I replied.

"What the bloody hell do yer want?"

It occurred to me that it was certainly no way to greet a prospective client.

I had to admit that even in his present condition, Angus Brodie cut a rather attractive figure in spite of his disarray. He was not at all what I had expected—someone gray at the temples with a row of jowls, bushy brows and side whiskers, and a paunch of belly.

"Mikaela Forsythe," I replied, quite enjoying the view and what appeared to be his obvious discomfort.

"You were recommended to me by Lady Antonia Montgomery." I handed him the card my aunt had given me.

"Lady Antonia..." The rest of his comment was lost in a round of coughing, or possibly choking with all the smoke in the room. It was a miracle that the entire place wasn't afire.

"Bloody Christ!" he swore looking over at me once more. He snarled at the hound and directed a curse at the large beast that was now sitting at the floor staring up at me.

The hound wagged its tail in what might have been a sign of peaceful co-existence as Angus Brodie disappeared back into the adjacent room.

We both stared after him. Not exactly an auspicious beginning.

When he reappeared, his appearance was decidedly

improved. Pants and shirt were both buttoned, and he'd pulled on his boots. He had also donned a coat, and smoothed his disheveled hair that was in need of a trim.

He could have been of an age with my brother-in-law, or twenty years older. Admittedly, there was a passably agreeable-looking man under that days-old beard and that sharp line of dark brows.

"Lady Antonia," he repeated.

The look he gave me then was a little disconcerting, as if he was trying to decide whether or not we might have met before.

"Lady Antonia is my aunt. I believe you may have had some business with her in the past," I suggested, with the hope of jogging his memory.

There was a faint reaction in those dark eyes that glanced briefly in my direction, then focused on the annoying creature at my feet, who was attempting to resume his own investigations.

"Leave off!" Brodie ordered the beast, which had almost no effect at all on the slobbering animal.

I thought of the amiable spaniels our mother had when my sister and I were children. They all had names and distinct personalities. But I had much preferred the animal of questionable breeding that occupied the stables. He was a smelly, wily beast named Rupert—not unlike this unruly animal.

That childhood companion was constantly dragging in some foul dead carcass it had found or captured—squirrels, rabbits, and once a hedgehog it had gone to battle with. He was constantly at my side when I went adventuring in the forest and hedgerows.

"Does it have a name?" I inquired.

Angus Brodie looked at me as if I might have taken a step away from sanity.

"A name? Christ, no! He's a beggar off the streets."

Rupert it was, I decided, and considering the disheveled company the animal kept, it was appropriate. When the slobbering mass came at me again, I scolded him firmly.

"Down!" I ordered in a firm voice, and made the gesture with my hand. "Or I will have your bollocks, you rude beast!"

Whether it was the threat or the sound of my voice, Rupert as he would be known from that day forward, returned to his prone position with a faint whimper and lay down with head resting on outstretched paws.

Angus Brodie stared at the animal that lay at my feet.

"He's never done that before. Worthless animal!"

"Perhaps he's never been told before."

Brodie rounded the desk to the opposite side, placing it between us as if he thought he might be similarly threatened.

He opened the bottom drawer of the desk and produced a bottle of amber liquid, then proceeded to pour a healthy portion into a smudged glass. That dark, penetrating gaze fixed on me.

"I received no message from her ladyship that she had need of my services."

"This is not on behalf of Lady Antonia," I explained. "I am here on my own business." I handed him my calling card.

"Some difficulty of yer own, then?" Mr. Brodie asked, in that broad Scots accent.

"It's a private matter regarding a member of the family."

"Aye, well it usually is—an errant husband, a bit of scandal ye want to keep quiet, or some other indiscretion. Possibly an affair of yer own?" he added.

Mr. Brodie certainly lived *down* to expectations, appearances aside, more particularly in the matter of drink — and it was not even noon yet. I seriously considered the wisdom of procuring his services.

The only thing that prevented my turning around and leaving was the recommendation from my aunt, who had insisted that he was the only man she would trust in the matter.

"My sister is missing... " I began again.

"Aye, the missing sister." He splashed another portion of whisky into the glass.

"How long?"

"I beg your pardon?"

"How-long-has-she-been-missing?" he repeated, enunciating each word carefully, as if he thought me to be impaired.

"She has been missing for eight days. It is not like her to take herself off without a word to anyone... " I started to explain only to be cut off.

"A quarrel with the husband? A lover perhaps?"

"No! Of course not!"

"*Of course not*," he repeated imitating my response.

"Mr. Brodie... "

"Eight days, yer say? And yer just now concerned about it?"

"Her husband insisted on taking matters into his own hands and making his own inquiries..."

"Ah, the husband. A quarrel then, and yer sister has taken herself off in a fit of temper."

"Mr. Brodie!"

We were suddenly interrupted by a commotion, the sound coming through the open doorway from the street below. The hound leapt to his feet and charged toward the door, taking me off my feet in the process. Then he was off.

I thought of the Mudger on his rolling platform and

hoped the poor man survived the encounter that was surely to take place at the bottom of the stairs.

My hat had come loose and fell over my eyes. I pushed it back and looked up to find an outstretched hand extended toward me.

All things considered, I seriously considered telling Angus Brodie what he could do with his ill-mannered dog, my request for his services, and his assistance.

However, I did not.

This was not about me—it was about finding my sister. Truth was, I had no confidence in my brother-in-law's weak assurances, and knew of no one else who might help in finding her. Furthermore, Angus Brodie had been recommended by my aunt, although God knows what her need of his services in the past might have been.

"Are ye going to remain on the floor, Miss Forsythe?"

I reluctantly accepted his assistance. It was a strong hand, his grip firm on mine. He hesitated and I was aware of the direction of his gaze, on the design at the inside of my wrist. It was a tattoo I had acquired on one of my adventures, of a rather lovely lotus blossom.

I saw the surprise and something else in that dark gaze as he hauled me to my feet.

Amusement? Disapproval? I did not know him well enough yet to be certain, and had no time for either.

"Shall we get on with it then, Mr. Brodie?" I said, once more on my feet.

"Ye say, there's been no word in all this time? And it's not like her to go off on her own?

"To visit a relative perhaps, or possibly because of an affair she was afraid the husband might discover? Or some other indiscretion?" he added, while pouring himself another portion of whisky.

"Mr. Brodie," I began again, struggling for patience since he appeared to be somewhat lacking in memory, or possibly *in his cups,* as the saying went.

"My sister is missing," I began again. "She is not the sort who would become involved in an affair! No one has been able to provide any information as to her whereabouts, or the reason for her disappearance.

"I am her only family relation other than Lady Antonia. And yesterday her maid, who disappeared with her, was found dead in Whitechapel." I laid the key that had been found on his desk.

"This was sewn into the hem of her gown.

"If you cannot, or are not willing to help me, then please say so, and I will be on my way!"

He picked up the key with the numbers stamped into the bow at one end, and examined it.

"What is the key for?"

"That is precisely the question, Mr. Brodie. I have never seen it before, nor do I know what it might be for. Nor do I know how my sister's maid came by it."

Still holding the key, he tossed back the contents of the glass.

"Lady Antonia sent ye..." he repeated.

I was seriously beginning to doubt my aunt's recommendation of the man.

"She did say that you were the only one who might be able to help."

He stared at the key.

"I can make inquiries, speak with the constables who were on the watch when the girl was found, see what information they have about the girl's murder, and inquire about yer sister. For certain, a lady would not go unnoticed in that part of London."

"Do we have an agreement then, Mr. Brodie?"

He nodded. "I will need a description of yer sister."

I provided a photograph taken on our last holiday together in Brighton two years before.

It was the usual sort of staged photograph, both of us in our bathing costumes in the photographer's studio. We had struck a pose, Linnie in a striped beach chair with an animated expression of surprise as I stood just behind her. I had taken a section of my hair and held the end of it curled over my upper lip, much like a mustache.

The photographer, quite unaccustomed to such antics, had insisted on taking a second photograph, at which Linnie had crossed her eyes. They were the last photographs of the two of us.

Brodie studied the photograph with a somewhat bemused expression.

"Yer sister, Lady Litton? She's quite fair."

"She favors our mother."

"And ye favor yer father."

I ignored the obvious.

"The photograph was taken two years ago," I explained, steering the conversation away from the subject of our father.

There was something in Mr. Brodie's expression that I was not yet familiar with, a faint smile as if he found something amusing. Then it was gone. He tucked the photograph into his coat pocket.

"Once I've spoken with the police regarding the maid's murder, I'll send round my report."

Send round a report? While I sat on my heels waiting? Not bloody likely!

"You misunderstand, Mr. Brodie. I intend to accompany you in your investigations. When do we begin?"

His eyes narrowed. "I work alone, Miss Forsythe, and occasionally with an associate. I move about more easily unencumbered. The people I need to see and the places I go are often no place for a lady."

By *unencumbered*, he obviously referred to me. I retrieved the key.

I had traversed the Alps on wooden skis, navigated the Nile, witnessed an ancient Maori haka on my South Seas voyage. I had encountered more than a few unsavory characters on my travels, present company included, and I was not about to be set aside in this.

"As I will be paying your fee, Mr. Brodie, I *will* accompany you, and I assure you that I will not be a burden."

"What of someone else who might object to ye endangering yerself, Miss Forsythe?" he asked. "I've no desire to find a disagreeable husband at my door over the matter."

"I assure you there is no one who will object, Mr. Brodie,"

"Ah, spinster," he replied in an irritating tone.

I had heard the word often enough and chose to ignore it.

"I should think you would welcome my involvement, Mr. Brodie. There are things only I would know about my sister that might be helpful. And there is no time to make your reports, send them round to me, then carry on with the next step in your investigation," I continued.

"I could have had that from the Metropolitan Police. Therefore, we will continue in this together."

"Ye've already spoken with the police?" he asked.

"Inspector Abberline was politely indifferent."

He tossed back another swallow of whisky, and I considered the very likely possibility that he might show me the door.

It was there in his expression, and I was struck by

the oddest sensation that I had seen that same expression glaring back at me before.

He set the empty glass on the desk.

"I will need funds to begin the investigation. People are often more likely to part with information if there is coin involved."

"I pay for *results*, Mr. Brodie. I will reimburse you for any expense incurred in the investigation, as well as your fee.

"Do we have an agreement?"

Four

THE BOW STREET police station was a cinder block affair at the end of the street, with an attempt at ornate decoration along the roofline, the spire of St. Mary Le Strand church shrouded in clouds of mist in the distance.

I had not been aware of so many other people about when we were last here, with my concern for Alice and the sad, gruesome task ahead of her.

There was now a uniformed constable at the desk, along with several individuals, including one in a black frock coat who might have been an undertaker, presumably there to collect a body.

In addition, there were clerks who came and went as if they were in the business of selling cabbage heads instead of attending to the business of crime. And poor Mary was inside awaiting the man my aunt had contacted who would see to her burial.

"Mr. Brodie." The greeting by the uniformed constable at the front desk of the police station was barely civil. His curious gaze slid past Brodie to me.

"What brings yer here?" he asked.

"The matter of a young woman who was found

murdered and brought here, Jenkins, by the name of Mary Ryan," Brodie informed him.

"Now, Brodie, you know very well that I can't be letting just anyone through here for a look—official personnel and family only. Them's the rules."

"Ye have permission," Brodie replied. "This is the young woman's *sister*."

Sister?

I wasn't certain who was more surprised, myself at the deception, or Officer Jenkins.

Aunt Antonia had mentioned that Mr. Brodie had departed the MP over some difficulty. It seemed that he was still not on the best of relations with his former employer.

I raised a handkerchief to my face as though to stem the tide of tears at *the loss,* and played the part of the grieving relative, uncertain that Brodie would be successful.

"Sister, you say?" Jenkins' gaze narrowed, first on me, then on Brodie.

I nodded, and kept to my handkerchief.

"Aye, well, I suppose that's acceptable," he replied. "Sign the book and then go on through. Room number two, if the body hasn't been removed yet."

Brodie signed the register and then escorted me through the same door I had entered the day before.

"Sister?" I whispered.

"It seemed the most efficient thing to tell him in the moment," Mr. Brodie replied.

The smell hit me first, thick and sharp, overlaid with something else that could only be the smell of death.

I hadn't noticed it the day before, but now it choked at the back of my throat. When we reached the door to the appropriate room, Brodie hesitated.

"Yer certain ye don't want to wait out here? Most people are not up to the sight of a dead body."

I stepped past him into the room. It was as it had been the day before, plain stone walls and floor, a long counter at one side of the room with electric lights overhead. Except now there were three additional tables lined up like cots in a common sleeping room. They all had sheets draped across and placards at the end of each table with information written on them.

"Always a busy night when the workhouses pay the workers," Brodie commented.

"They find their way to the nearest tavern instead of going to their room or flat, most likely a woman and children waitin' for them. It's a sad fact of life in the East End, Miss Forsythe."

He found the table and the card with Mary's name. He stepped to the side of the table and pulled back the sheet that covered her body.

In spite of the fact that I had seen it the day before, I experienced that same instinctive reaction. It was a combination of horror and sadness at seeing her body there, a young life cruelly ended.

Of course, Mary was not actually there any longer, according to beliefs I had encountered in my travels. Many believed that the soul moved on after death leaving only the shell of the body. But it was difficult, nevertheless, having known the girl when she was alive.

"Are ye all right, Miss Forsythe?"

I looked up to find Brodie watching me with that dark gaze.

"Quite all right," I assured him. I still had no idea what he hoped to learn from this.

"Please continue."

He picked up one of Mary's hands, then the other, both now quite stiff, and proceeded to examine them. Then he examined the wound at her throat, gently moving her head from one side to the other, bending over to look more closely.

"Aye, a good amount of bruising there," he commented.

An understatement in the least, I thought. But as to what that might mean, I did not know.

He continued in silence with his inspection of the body, with only an occasional nod or comment to himself.

"I would appreciate you sharing your thoughts, Mr. Brodie."

He looked up briefly, then continued. "Hmmm. Interesting. Most certainly one or the other would have been sufficient to see the deed done."

"One or the other?" I asked.

"The laceration at the throat," he explained. "Or the broken neck."

He took a pen from inside his coat and proceeded to inspect the wound, pushing back the skin to expose the tissue underneath, and it occurred to me that he might very well be attempting to frighten me with his examination of the wound.

I refused to be intimidated, or turn away, gruesome as it was. All the more so because it was poor Mary, someone I had known.

"I quite see your point, Mr. Brodie. What would be the reason for both injuries if Mary was already dead from one or the other?"

He looked up. "Very good, Miss Forsythe." There was something in his expression.

"Now, let us see what else Mary Ryan can tell us."

I considered the possibility that the man was either intoxicated, or quite mad with that comment.

"Mr. Brodie, I don't see..."

"The cut at the throat was made from right to left," he continued.

I ventured a guess. "Her attacker was left-handed?"

"Aye." Brodie nodded. "Not a common trait."

"What else, Mr. Brodie?"

"This mark at her left wrist," he pointed out. "It might be from a rope or some other binding, but there is no indication at the other wrist that she was bound."

"Could it possibly be from something she was carrying? A reticule or carpetbag?" I suggested.

"Perhaps," Brodie replied, again taking hold of one of Mary's hands once more. He proceeded to examine each finger closely.

"There is some sort of residue under the fingernails."

He pulled a small pocketknife from his coat pocket and proceeded to scrape beneath the fingernail. He took out an envelope and deposited the residue inside.

"It may possibly be tissue from her struggle with her attacker," he explained.

He tucked the envelope into his coat pocket, then pulled the sheet down further.

"There are bruises about the legs and ankle." He pointed out, as I recovered sufficiently from the sight of poor Mary completely naked, nothing more now than an object to be probed and prodded.

"She fought back, not that it did her any good." He turned Mary part of the way onto her side.

"The police surgeon has already made his examination..." I protested as I saw no reason for this part of his examination. I jumped, startled, as Mary seemed to emit a sound, almost as if she had groaned.

"Air trapped in the lungs," Brodie commented as if it was the most natural thing in the world for a dead body to make noises.

"But no sign of water," he continued matter-of-fact.

"Mr. Brodie, I don't see the purpose..."

"There are things that are often missed by the casual eye, Miss Forsythe. That might provide valuable clues. It has been my experience that the smallest detail that might provide the most important clue, is often overlooked."

He gently eased Mary's body back down onto the examination table, then picked up the placard that hung at the end of the table with the police physician's handwriting scrawled across it.

"No indication of sexual assault," he commented.

I remembered that much had been written about that sort of thing in the dailies the past year with the Whitechapel murders.

"What might that mean, that there is no indication of it?"

He looked over at me. If he was trying to shock me with his blunt observations that might have seemed cold or possibly crude to others, I was far beyond that with what had happened the past twenty-four hours.

"It means, Miss Forsythe, the attack wasn't for that purpose, even though it may have been made to look like the other murders." He replaced the card.

"It's difficult enough to survive in the East End," he continued to explain. "Many women are on their own with children to feed and no man to help pay the rent or put food on the table. They're often forced to survive by other means."

I saw his meaning. "Mary was gainfully employed and lived with my sister. She had no reason..."

He held up a hand. "I'm not sayin' the girl was the victim of such an arrangement, only what others are forced to do in order to survive."

"Is that important, Mr. Brodie?"

"It could be. It's often what *isn't* found that provides a valuable clue, Miss Forsythe.

"The girl's death *appears* to be the same as the others that have been murdered in Whitechapel."

"But you think that it's not." I frowned. "Someone wanted it to seem as if it were the same?"

"Very good, Miss Forsythe."

"But to what purpose?"

"Deception." He pulled the sheet back over Mary's body, then turned on his heel and headed for the door of the examination room.

We stepped out on the street into the congestion of soot-filled air, and street vendors amid the tangle of coaches and trams.

People went about their business, completely unaware of a poor young girl lying on a table inside that building.

"Mr. Brodie..."

"Strangulation and a cut to the throat from the right to the left side of the throat," he commented, lost in thought.

"Bruising to indicate that she was come upon, then dragged down from behind and strangled," he continued. "Her throat was cut, body found in the water, but no water in the lungs, and no sign of sexual assault..."

"What does it mean that there was no water in Mary's lungs?"

He looked up as if only just aware that I was there. He frowned.

"It means, Miss Forsythe, that she was most likely dead before she was put in the water. That rules out any possibility of drowning. Ye are obviously familiar with the dangers of swimming."

"Yes, of course..." I wasn't certain what that had to do with anything.

"What about the substance you scraped from under her nails?"

That dark gaze fastened on me once again.

"There is someone who might be able to tell us something about that. Ye might want to make notes in the matter if it can be arranged. Contrary to most women of yer position, ye seem to possess the ability to think for yerself."

I wasn't at all certain that was a compliment.

"What is to be done now, Mr. Brodie?"

"A visit with Inspector Abberline," he announced, and assisted me into a cab.

"The driver will see ye to yer residence. I will send word round of my conversation with the chief inspector."

He seemed to have a convenient loss of memory regarding our previous conversation on the matter.

"You will need someone to make notes," I told him. "It will be useful later, if you should forget anything." I then gave the driver instructions to take *us* to Scotland Yard.

Five

SCOTLAND YARD, LONDON

"MR. ABBERLINE IS PRESENTLY OCCUPIED," Officer Endicott, according to the name plate at the front desk, repeated, without looking up. I found his attitude to be extremely rude and quite unacceptable.

"It's in the matter of the body found at St. Katherine's dock in Whitechapel two nights ago," Brodie informed him.

"As I said, the chief inspector is not available." The constable finally looked up.

"And you'd do well to remember you no longer have any authority here, Mr. Brodie."

He seemed to have quite a reputation that had preceded us, not to mention those somewhat vague reasons Aunt Antonia had mentioned regarding his former employment.

While I wasn't in the habit of using influence, I was quite done with formalities and politeness. I reached around Brodie and gave the officer my calling card.

"Please inform Chief Inspector Abberline that we wish to speak with him on behalf of Sir Charles Litton."

It had the usual effect.

"Sir Charles Litton?" Officer Endicott replied, his manner now quite different. "The Home Secretary?"

I smiled in response. "The same."

"Wait here. I'll let Chief Inspector Abberline know that you wish to see him."

He left another officer in charge as he went to inform Abberline.

"Ye have a devious nature, Miss Forsythe," Brodie commented.

I smiled.

Officer Endicott quickly returned.

"Mr. Abberline will see you, Miss Forsythe. And you as well, Brodie." He added in a decidedly different tone.

"Thank you," I replied with a smile. "You have been most helpful."

Brodie shook his head as we were escorted to Abberline's office.

"Pitiful. Downright pitiful," he said. "A bold-faced lie, and then poor Endicott groveling like a youth still wet behind the ears."

"Most effective though, you must agree," I pointed out.

Abberline rose from behind his desk as we entered his private office.

"Good afternoon, Miss Forsythe." He read the card Endicott had given him, but merely nodded at Brodie.

It was obvious there was no love lost between the two men, as Abberline turned to me.

"Endicott mentioned you are here on behalf of Sir Charles Litton."

I caught that flicker of amusement on Brodie's face at the lie I had told, as if to say, *"What now, Miss Forsythe?"*

I chose to ignore him.

"It's in the matter of the death of Mary Ryan, a maid in the household of Sir Litton." I explained.

"Ah yes, most unfortunate. I believe we met briefly yesterday, Miss Forsythe."

I was aware of Brodie's look of surprise at a detail that I had failed to mention.

"Dreadful business," the chief inspector acknowledged. "How may I assist Sir Charles?"

My impression of the chief inspector the day before was not misplaced. Behind the hooded gaze was a keen mind. I needed to be as keen if I hoped to get any information from him about Mary's murder.

"The young woman was the personal maid to my sister, Lady Litton," I explained. "Naturally, our family is most anxious to learn what information you might have about who may be responsible."

"I quite understand," Abberline replied. "However, I would expect Sir Charles to send his own representative to make inquiries into the investigation of the girl's death."

His reaction only confirmed my suspicion that the chief inspector was not aware that Linnie was also missing.

"The girl's mother has been in the employ of Lady Antonia Montgomery for many years," I continued. "And I have been sent to inquire if anyone has been apprehended."

Brodie made a sound as if something had suddenly caught in his throat at the mention of my aunt. I refused to look at him and plunged on ahead.

"Any information you might be able to provide would be greatly appreciated by Sir Charles, and Lady Montgomery as well." While I was not usually given to using influence, difficult times required different measures.

The change in the chief inspector's demeanor was

quite noticeable. While Aunt Antonia would have scoffed at the notion that her name and position held any power, it was a known fact that she had a long-standing acquaintance with the royal family, the Queen in particular.

"Lady Montgomery has insisted upon Mr. Brodie's services in this matter," I continued. It was not exactly a lie.

"Whatever you have learned you may share with him, and it would be enormously helpful and a comfort to our family. It would be looked upon most favorably."

"Of course, I quite understand." Abberline replied, his manner once more that of the polite official.

"Naturally, we will follow up with the officers who were on the watch that night. They may be able to provide information about the incident."

"Have ye spoken with witnesses at the dock where the body was found?" Brodie asked. "Or anyone on the street who may have seen the murderer?"

"We will continue to make our inquiries in the matter," the Chief Inspector replied.

Which told us precisely nothing. I thought of mentioning the key that was found in the hem of Mary's dress, then decided against it, considering Abberline's banal responses.

Whatever the chief inspector's reasons—past issues, personal dislike, or arrogance—I sensed that he would make the same response to every question, that being that he would *continue to make inquiries.*

"I assure you that I do understand the urgency of this most delicate matter, Miss Forsythe," Abberline repeated. "And we hope to find the person responsible. I will most certainly send word on any information we may be able to provide."

And with that, it appeared that we were dismissed.

I had heard it said that some experiences left one with the feeling that they needed to wash themselves afterward. Our meeting with Abberline was certainly one of those.

"Arrogant ass!" I fumed, as we left his office. "Bumbling fool! He told us nothing."

"Make no mistake about it," Brodie replied. "Abberline is no fool. He has one priority at all times—his aspirations to be the next Police Commissioner. He needs to solve the Whitechapel murders, and Mary Ryan and yer sister are now right in the middle of it," he continued.

"Which means that he needs be careful. But there are other ways to find out what Mr. Abberline and the MP have learned about the girl's murder."

Brodie greeted the sergeant as we returned to the front desk.

"Mr. Abberline has asked for ye to provide the names of the constables who were on the watch regarding the Mary Ryan case," he informed the constable, much to my surprise.

"Aye," Endicott replied. "You just can't leave well enough alone, eh, Mr. Brodie? I'd think you've had enough of police matters."

"The chief inspector said ye were the man to ask in the matter."

It was, of course, a lie. *Other ways*, indeed!

I angled a glance to the hallway should the chief inspector have followed us.

"I have it 'ere," Endicott found his report. "Dooley and Thomas were called in from their rounds when the call came in about a body that was found. They both served under you, as I recall."

"And the name of the person who found the body?"

Endicott checked the report. "A dockworker by the name of Spivey."

"Yer a good man. My thanks for the information. We'll trouble ye no further."

Brodie's hand closed around my elbow as Abberline suddenly appeared and headed in our direction.

"You're quite good at that," I commented as we quickly left before Abberline learned that we'd acquired substantially more information from Endicott than he had been willing to provide.

"What did you mean about information on the street?"

Brodie waved down a driver. "There are times information can be found among those reluctant to trust the police."

"And you have your *sources*?"

"In a manner of speaking."

"And that is?"

"There are those who would just as soon cut Abberline's throat as provide any information to him, particularly when it comes to those they work with or have other business dealings with."

By *other business*, I assumed he meant illegal activities, the sort that filled the crime reports in the dailies.

Mary had been murdered in a part of London I was not familiar with. It was a dangerous part of London, where people might be reluctant to speak with me. It was apparently a different matter with Brodie.

"The Old Bell, Holborn," he called up to the driver.

The Mudger had mentioned the name of the pub.

"Mr. Brodie, you may visit whichever establishment you wish on your own time," I protested. "However when you are working for me..."

"We have not yet determined that I am working for ye, Miss Forsythe. As for the Old Bell, it is near St. Katherine's dock. Workers frequent the pub at the end of the day. They may be able to provide information about the night the girl was murdered.

"However," he continued. "If the notion of entering a tavern offends ye, Miss Forsythe, then the driver may take ye back to Mayfair."

"Not at all, Mr. Brodie," I assured him. "I see your purpose."

He signaled the driver. "Quick time, if ye please, and there's extra coin in it."

I was pressed back into the seat as the cab lurched away from the curb.

"I take it that you've had some disagreement with Mr. Abberline in the past," I commented, as I recovered and braced myself against the inside of the cab at the next corner.

"We had a difference of opinion in the matter of an investigation that might very well have meant his position."

A difference of opinion? I thought of my aunt's explanation, and presumed there was more to it than that. A difference of opinion didn't seem the sort of thing to end one's career over. It must have been something far more serious than that.

"And you chose not to speak of it to higher authorities," I deduced.

He looked over at me, then finally replied, "Ye have to pick yer battles, Miss Forsythe."

Whatever the case was, he had obviously chosen to depart Scotland Yard rather than fight that particular battle.

The driver cut through side streets and back alleys, no doubt eager for the promise of extra coin. We arrived at the Old Bell in short time, the fetid smell of the nearby docks and the river washing over me as I stepped out of the cab.

St. Katherine's dock was nearby, according to Brodie, and I thought of poor Mary Ryan found dead in the water, that ghastly cut at her throat. The image of her on that examination table, the wound at her throat gaping open, wasn't an image I would forget.

The tavern was at the street level of the four-story building in the middle of a row of other buildings. Various signage overhead advertised a bootmaker's shop, physician's office, and an enormous sign at the uppermost floor advertised rooms to let for the night in the same building.

"A hotel?" I remarked with some surprise.

"For the crews that come in on the ships, and others that need to spend the night," Brodie explained.

By that, I presumed he meant an evening of drink and whatever else was provided at the tavern.

The gallery that opened onto the street led back to the main entrance of the tavern. On one side of the gallery was a row of a half dozen handbells over an entrance.

"For summoning the staff," Brodie explained at my curious glance.

Staff? Which raised obvious questions.

"Chambermaids for the rooms, a man for the horses, and... others," he explained

By others, I assumed that meant *companions* for the evening.

My travels had exposed me to many interesting characters. There had been a certain gentleman in Paris who offered to put me up in his *house*. As he spoke, I realized precisely the sort of *house* he was suggesting. It was both insulting and flattering at the same time.

"There is much demand for beautiful young ladies," he had said with a charming smile.

I had laughed so hard I couldn't catch my breath. I

thanked him, and declined his offer. He had smiled and then turned his attention to another young woman as we toured the Louvre.

Whatever might have transpired from their conversation I could not be certain, however they had left together.

"It's not the usual sort of establishment yer most likely accustomed to," Brodie added.

I was not about to be put off, as I recalled what the Mudger had shared about the previous evening.

"I appreciate your concern, Mr. Brodie, but I *will* accompany you. So that I may make notes later regarding any information we learn, of course," I added.

"Brodie!" a call went up from behind the bar as he followed me into the Old Bell.

"Isn't it a wee bit early for ya, and with a woman!" the tavern keeper remarked. "Lizzie won't take kindly ter that. Step up and I'll pour ya a pint."

Brodie escorted me to a nearby table.

"There must be a great deal to talk about since last evening," I commented.

"Ye have a sharp tongue, Miss Forsythe," he said as he pulled a chair out for me then turned to the bar.

"I've a powerful thirst this afternoon, Mr. Abernathy," he called out to the man behind the bar. "Ale if ye please."

There were only a handful of people there that time of day, two men leaning into the bar while two older men sat at a nearby table, a game board between them.

"Yer here with Brodie, are you?"

A woman who obviously worked at the tavern approached my table. She was as round as she was tall, cheeks bright with color, hair piled on top of her head. An apron circled her ample girth, while on one hip she balanced a serving tray bearing two mugs of ale, apparently intended for the men at the game board.

"Yer not his usual sort," she added.

By *usual sort*, I assumed she referred to the company Brodie kept, and thought of the woman I had encountered coming out of his office that morning.

"I'm a business associate of Mr. Brodie's."

That seemed the easiest way to describe our relationship, and possibly to ask questions, since my '*associate*' was presently occupied at the bar.

She snorted with laughter. "I ain't heard that one before, but I'll take yer word for it. The name's Bettie," she introduced herself. "What can I get ya? A pint? Maybe something to eat? I've a pot on the cook stove," she continued. "And the meat and vegetables is fresh today."

With a hand on that ample hip, she gave me a wink. "And a healthy portion of ale in the broth."

I ordered a bowl.

"And some information," I added, as another round of ale was set before Brodie at the bar.

Bettie delivered the ale to the two gentlemen I watched with interest, then disappeared behind the bar. She returned a few minutes later with a steaming bowl of pottage, then sat down across from me.

"I got to rest me feet while I can. There won't be room to stand in this place when the men come in from the docks wanting food and the drink."

The stew was hot and surprisingly good. I had to admit that the ale added to the overall taste, and didn't question the source of the meat.

"What sort of information might you be wantin'?" Bettie asked.

"A young woman was found dead at St. Katherine's dock two nights ago."

"I heard 'bout that." She shook her head. "Them other women all cut up, it stirred everyone up again, thinkin' that madman struck again.

"I told Abernathy I wanted someone to walk me home when I get off at night. Gettin's so's it's not safe for a woman to be out and about."

Five women had been found murdered in a part of London known as Spitalfields, not far from where we were now. The gruesome details had been in all the newspapers.

All five of the women had been brutally slain, their throats slashed and internal organs removed, then set out beside them in some sort of macabre ritual. Terror had gripped the city ever since.

Women were warned not to go out alone at night. Then the murders stopped as suddenly as they began. There was speculation that the killer had either moved on or had possibly been caught for some other crime. Until now.

"We were told a man by the name of Spivey was the one who found her."

"I know him," she replied. "He's been workin' the *Polly* the past several days, unloading cargo with some of the other men."

I made a mental note of the name of the ship.

"Is it possible he might come in later?" I asked.

She shrugged. "Maybe, maybe not. There's other places they go, and sometimes they just take themselves home, if the missus is waiting for them to bring home their pay."

"When do they usually arrive?"

"About this time of day. They can't work when they lose the light. Next hour or so, the place will fill up. You might be able to catch Spivey then."

More customers had started to come in, including

several who appeared to be from the docks. Two of the men argued between themselves as they stepped up to the bar.

"Time to get back to work," Bettie announced, clearing the table. "Spivey ain't with them, he might be in later. There's no mistakin' him once you see him.

"He's tall, built like a bull, and dark as sin, with black hair and beard, and the look about him that you wouldn't want to cross him.

"He sometimes keeps company with that one." She aimed a look in the direction of a young woman who had followed the men in and joined Brodie at the bar. It appeared they knew one another.

"That would be Maggie. Like a cat, she is, with a different man each night. Not that I begrudge a workin' girl, but she might jus' find herself floating in the river, wot with that madman still out there.

"I gots ter watch her," she added. "She has a habit of pinching the customers. It's not good for business, if yer know what I mean."

Brodie seemed to be handling the situation quite well as Maggie stroked a hand across the front of his coat.

Sources indeed!

It would soon be dark, the heat from the warmth inside the pub fogging the edges of the windows. The sensible thing to do would be to wait for Brodie.

Yes, that would most definitely be the sensible thing, I thought, glancing at the bar where he was in deep conversation with Maggie. Another pint of ale sat in front of him.

"How might I find the Polly?" I asked Bettie when she returned.

"Just up a ways at the docks, pier number six I heard

one of the men say wot came in last night. But yer ain't goin' there yerself?" she added.

"It's quite all right," I assured her, as an argument had broken out between the two new arrivals at the bar.

I paid for the stew, and wrote a quick message on a corner of the note I had made earlier, informing Brodie where I had gone. I tore it off and gave it to Bettie.

"Please see that Mr. Brodie gets this."

The argument now included fists as one of the men landed a blow that sent the other backwards into the chess game that was in progress.

"Not again!" she exclaimed. "We just got the place set right from the night before."

That explained Brodie's bruised cheek.

Bettie moved with surprising speed for someone her size as she sailed off like a ship into battle, waving her serving tray like a weapon. I slipped past the conflagration and out into the night.

Six

LONDON WAS A FAR different place by night.

I had heard the stories with countless warnings from Aunt Antonia, and read about the crime in the East End.

With the recent murders, I had taken the extra precaution of slipping the knife I carried on my travels into the pocket of my walking skirt before I left the town house.

Only once had I been forced to pull it out on an enterprising youth in Paris who thought to relieve Linnie and me of our reticules in our last year of school.

Linnie had been terrified when the young man stepped out of the shadows and brandished what turned out to be a common dining knife no doubt stolen from someone's table.

He had demanded that she hand over everything of value, as I had just stepped out of the patisserie on the Rue Montorgueil with friends and a package of French pastry.

I am often reminded that I can be impetuous, going off on my adventures, as Aunt Antonia calls them.

All I remember was the anger that some idiot had

frightened Linnie and thought he could force her to turn over everything of value.

Without another thought I had thrust the box of pastry at a companion and launched myself at my sister's assailant much to the shock of our companions, and others on the street.

Mr. Munro's instructions were quite valuable that day as I pushed between Linnie and the man, and thrust the knife at him. To say her assailant was surprised was an understatement. He had quickly fled amid a string of French curses.

Now, my hand tightened around the handle as I followed the directions Bettie had provided. I took the short walk on Little Tower Hill until it ended, then turned onto the street that ran along the docks. As fog rolled in, shadows along the street deepened, sliding down the sides of warehouses.

Light from lanterns on the ships glowed back at me like the eyes of strangers. Mooring ropes creaked and chains rattled as the hulk of a ship loomed up out of the misty darkness, then disappeared once more.

The next ship was dark with no sign of crew aboard or dockworkers. Its name appeared briefly in the glow of a lantern at a dockside hut. I continued on, my hand firm about the handle of the knife in my pocket.

The fog and cold wrapped around everything, giving my surroundings a ghostly appearance, along with different sounds, the smell of things, and the fog hiding its secrets. Just as it hid the brutal murder of a young woman, then gave her up with even more secrets for those left behind.

I was neither naive nor foolish, in spite of the fact that I had taken myself off, leaving Mr. Brodie behind. I knew very well that it could be dangerous to be in an unfamiliar place. Especially after what happened to Mary. And the docks had a certain reputation.

But if there was the possibility that I could find the man, Spivey, I might be able to learn something about what happened that night, and it might very well help me find my sister.

There were suddenly voices, muffled at first then nearer, as a handful of men appeared up out of the fog. I cautiously approached them.

"I'm looking for a man by the name of Spivey. I was told that he's working on the *Polly*."

"Spivey?"

One of the men stepped from the group and slowly approached. "That's me name... if yer want it to be," he said with a leering grin.

I was neither frightened nor intimidated even though the man before me obviously outweighed me by several stone, with well-developed muscles from hard physical labor.

"If you could please tell me where the *Polly* is moored," I repeated.

A younger man stepped from the group. He was slender and wiry. A knit cap was pulled low over sandy blond hair, a wool jacket loose over his shoulders, as if it might have once belonged to someone else.

"I worked the *Polly* today, just down the way. Yer might still find him there."

"You think she prefers 'em young, eh, Tommy?" One of the men laughed as the others moved on down the pier. The one called Tommy held back.

"You shouldn't be here alone, miss," he warned. "There was a young woman wot was found dead two nights ago. Be careful."

I thanked him. He nodded, almost shyly, then continued on his way.

I passed two more ships. Then, an illuminated sign at the side of a dockside hut appeared at Dock 6. Like a ghost ship, the *Polly* loomed up out of the darkness.

According to the young dock worker, Spivey was still aboard, but there was no sign of him.

Was it possible that he had already left the ship and then continued on in another direction?

A large shadow appeared out of the fog.

I instinctively took a step back as a man well over six feet tall appeared at the edge of the pool of light from the lantern at the hut. By the description Bettie had provided, I knew that I had found Spivey.

I saw surprise, then another expression as his eyes narrowed. I had seen that sort of expression before.

A member of the crew on a ship I once sailed on had come topside, and had suddenly loomed up out of the darkness as I took a turn about the deck with my young travel companion.

She was no more than twelve or thirteen years old, traveling with her parents back to England, and without any instinct about others in the world. The crewman made an indecent comment toward her.

I had immediately stepped between them. There was a moment, the same as now, when I was certain he would come at us, and I had been genuinely afraid for her. The situation had resolved itself as other guests joined us and we departed.

It was a reminder of the lessons I had learned in my travels, and that it was best to simply walk away if at all possible. However, tonight I was not of a mind to simply walk away.

It was very possible Spivey had information that might provide a clue as to what happened two nights before when he found Mary's body.

"I would like to ask you some questions, Mr. Spivey—"

He cut me off before I could say more. He laughed, a humorless sound that sent a warning across my skin.

"Mister? Ain't yer got airs tho'." He slowly walked toward me.

"I'd like to speak with you about the young woman that was found here two nights ago," I explained, my fingers closing around the handle of the knife in my pocket.

"And yer out here all alone?"

He took several steps closer, the light from that single lantern falling across sullen features.

Dark as sin, Bettie had described him, and I was inclined to agree as I remembered the young dockworker's warning.

A smile spread across Spivey's face.

"There ye are."

That broad Scots accent reached through the dark and fog. Brodie.

"I see ye've found Mr. Spivey," he commented quite good naturedly.

I had to admit that I was glad to see him.

"I was held up a bit speaking with Mr. Spivey's companions," he explained as he drew closer, his expression unreadable.

"Now, a few questions about the girl ye found night before last."

The two men were of an even height, although Spivey outweighed him, and with much the look of a bulldog, where Brodie more resembled a lean hound, ready to pounce. The look in his eyes was cold and deliberate.

"What are you, the bloody peelers?" Spivey demanded. "I already told them everythin' I know." His gaze slid past Brodie. "And wot's the woman got to do with it?"

"It's a private matter, regarding the disappearance of her sister."

"I wouldn't know nothin' about that."

"But ye might know something about the young woman found with her throat cut."

Spivey's eyes narrowed.

"There's coin in it." Brodie continued. "If ye provide something useful."

"Coin, you say?"

Brodie nodded, his hand at the edge of his waistcoat, and in the light from the lantern at that dockside hut, I glimpsed a pistol tucked inside. By the change of expression at Spivey's face, he had seen it as well.

Spivey gave a jerk of his head. "I'll not be standin' out here in the cold. There's a pub on the High Street, the Rusty Anchor."

He flicked a glance at me. "Not exactly the place for the likes o' her."

"That is not yer concern," Brodie informed him.

"Aye," Spivey snapped. "As long as there's coin in it."

Brodie took hold of my arm as we followed him.

"You have a pistol." I whispered.

"I have found it to be most persuasive on more than one occasion."

"I never seen nothin' like that before," Spivey said over his third tankard of ale at a table at the Rusty Anchor.

"Pretty thing she was, even with that cut across her throat, just floatin' in the water with her arms spread out, starin' at me."

"Did ye see anyone else about before the constables arrived?"

Spivey shook his head. "It was like tonight, the fog rolling in as soon as the sun went down. The rest of the lads had finished for the day. I saw her as I was leavin'. She'd been in the water a while." Spivey continued."

I looked at Brodie in surprise, but he gave no indication that Spivey's comment meant anything to him.

"What about a weapon that might have been used? Did you see anything?"

Spivey shook his head. "There weren't nothin."

"Was there anyone else about?"

"I told you, I was alone when I found her."

"Were there any other injuries to the girl? "

Spivey shook his head. "Just that cut at her throat, like them others."

"Do ye remember what the girl was wearing?" Brodie asked.

Spivey shrugged. "Like most girls round 'ere—skirt, blouse," he described vaguely.

I thought of the mark at Mary's wrist, and ignored Brodie's obvious warning not to say anything.

"Did she have a lady's bag with her?" I asked.

Spivey shook his head. "Like I told ya, there weren't nothin' else."

"And that's when ye put the call out for the constables?" Brodie continued.

"That's right." Spivey downed his ale. "They was there right quick."

I caught Brodie's look as he pushed back from the table and stood.

"Thank ye for yer time, Mr. Spivey."

I stood reluctantly. I had hoped to learn more.

"You did say there was coin in it?" Spivey reminded as we turned to leave.

Brodie tossed a couple of coins down onto the table then escorted me from the tavern.

"He didn't tell us anything we didn't already know," I said as we reached the street.

"It certainly wasn't worth what you paid him! And he lied about the other marks on Mary's body."

"A handful of coins was a small price to pay for leaving without an altercation with his friends," Brodie pointed out. "And there are times ye learn something by what *isn't* said."

His hand was tucked into the front of his coat as he took hold of my arm and quickened our pace.

"Come along, Miss Forsythe. I could handle Spivey and perhaps one of the other lads, but more than that...? Ye would be on yer own."

I glanced over my shoulder. Spivey and two other men had come out of the tavern and watched as we crossed the street.

When we reached the High Street, Brodie waived down a cab. There was some negotiation that took place, the driver on his way back to the stables at the end of the day and not particularly of a mind to take another fare.

Brodie assured him that *I* would pay extra for his time. He gave him the address of my town house in Mayfair, then assisted me into the cab.

"What did you mean that we learned something by what *wasn't* said?" I asked when we were well on our way.

"Spivey lied about what happened when he found the girl."

"Please continue, Mr. Brodie." I wanted very much to know his thoughts.

"He told us the other workers had concluded their work for the day and that is when he said that he found the girl's body. That time of day would have been at low tide," Brodie continued.

"It would have been near impossible for anyone to see a body in the water from the docks. He also lied about when he notified the Night Watch. He said that he sent word round right away. The report stated it was near midnight when they were called to the docks."

"I see your point."

"He also stated that she appeared to have been in the water for some time. However as the police surgeon noted in his report..."

Unpleasant as it was, I recalled the surgeon's exact words—that there had been no deterioration of tissue, which he had explained meant that Mary hadn't been in the water long.

"He also lied about the girl not having a bag or purse with her."

We had both seen the mark at her wrist, and while it was possible that it might have been lost in the struggle when she was attacked, it was also possible that it had not.

"If Spivey took it, what did he do with it?"

"My guess would be that he kept whatever coins he might have found, then pawned anything else of value the girl might have had with her."

"Then we have nothing."

"I wouldn't say that, Miss Forsythe. There are only a handful of pawn shops in the area, and people like Spivey are creatures of habit. He would go no further than necessary to pawn something."

There was something else that bothered me.

"What reason would he have to lie about when he found Mary?"

"That is the question, Miss Forsythe."

The driver slowed and pulled to the curb as we

reached my residence. The street was well-lit by street lamps in this part of the city.

I paid the driver, including the extra coin Brodie had promised. The driver waited as Brodie escorted me to my door.

"Ye'll not to go off on yer own again, Miss Forsythe."

"Perhaps I didn't make myself clear..."

"Ye *will not* go off by yerself again, or I will end our association," he informed me as I stood at the doorstep, caught between surprise and anger.

I saw his point and knew that he was right. There were those moments before he arrived at the docks that I realized I might very well have miscalculated going there alone.

However, I was quite prepared to handle the situation. It was apparent that he was equally prepared to end our partnership unless I agreed.

"Then you will take the case?" I inquired.

Having obviously heard our arrival, Agatha appeared at the door.

"Good night, Miss Forsythe," Brodie said with a tip of his hat.

I was left standing there as he climbed back into the cab and told the driver to drive on.

Damned, arrogant Scot!

TWO NOTES WERE WAITING for me when I arrived back at the town house.

The first note was from Aunt Antonia, delivered that afternoon by Mr. Munro while I was out. It would have been far easier for my aunt to simply call on the telephone, but she refused to use the *contraption* as she called it.

"Noisy demmed things! A bell to let me know someone is calling at any time of the day or night? How rude and obnoxious! A note sent round is far more civilized and discreet. Who knows who is listening in on one's conversation?"

To my knowledge, she still refused to use it. Instead it was used to call round the daily order to the grocer.

Her note was in her perfect handwriting, though obviously hastily written by the scrawl at the end, with a puddle of dried ink as if she had been thinking of including more, then decided against it.

'Sir Charles called on me today. He seemed most agitated, and wishes to speak with you.'

The second note was from my brother-in-law:

'Please call on me as soon as possible. It is most urgent. Charles.'

Most urgent? Had he received word from my sister?

"When was this delivered?" I asked, as Agatha accompanied me into the parlor, and inquired what I might want for supper.

"Late this afternoon," she replied. "I thought it odd so late in the day. The man who delivered it seemed quite agitated that you were not here to personally receive it."

"Did you recognize him?"

Was it possibly a messenger from the Home Office, or one of Charles's personal staff?

"No, miss. Perhaps it was someone from one of those messenger services they have now in the city. Although, the man didn't look the sort, and he had an accent. He was quite odd."

"How do you mean?"

"He had a very odd way about him. He kept looking about almost as if he thought he might find you about, even though I explained you were not here. Most unusual fellow and not the sort I would want to encounter on the street at night.

"Will you be responding to Sir Charles?" she inquired.

I frowned. If the reason he needed to see me was concerning Linnie, he most certainly could have added that to the note, and I thought of the message Aunt Antonia had sent round, that there had been no word from my sister.

I couldn't imagine that Charles would keep something as important as news about my sister from our aunt. Unless, of course, something dreadful had happened.

"I'll have a note for you to send over to the Home

Office first thing in the morning when you go for daily shopping," I replied.

After she had gone, I sat down at my desk and made my notes on the day's events.

I wasn't naive to the fact that the East End, with its workhouses, taverns, and dark streets, was far different from Mayfair. However, that had been the least of my concerns, considering Brodie had been otherwise *occupied* at the Old Bell Tavern when I learned where Spivey might be found.

Resourceful, my aunt had said of him. He was certainly that, if one considered his resources to be found in taverns and pubs!

Trustworthy, was another word my aunt had used. That was yet to be seen.

Somewhat difficult at times. That was an understatement, to be certain.

However, I grudgingly had to admit that we now had more information about what had happened the night Mary was murdered than I might have otherwise been able to obtain. And there was his professional expertise in such matters regarding speculation about other things.

I thought then of the poor girl and couldn't help a shudder at the thought of how terrified she must have been...

I stared at the key that had been found in the hem of her gown.

Did it belong to Mary, hidden there as a precaution? Or did it belong to someone else? My sister, perhaps? Hidden there for safekeeping?

What was it a key to?

~

This morning I had dressed and was on my third cup of coffee by the time Agatha returned from delivering my note. Sir Charles had replied immediately with the request to meet him at the Grosvenor Hotel at noon.

Ironically, the Grosvenor at Victoria Station, was a favorite meeting place for high tea among Linnie's circle of friends.

I declined invitations to join them after my first encounter, with one excuse or another. I would much rather have had a fingernail ripped off than listen to their gossip and endless nattering. As if any of it was of any importance.

With its location, the Grosvenor Hotel was also favored by travelers, gentlemen meeting business associates who traveled to the city for the day, or a place for guests visiting family during holiday.

A driver now waited to take me to the hotel as the noon hour approached.

Was it possible that Sir Charles had word from my sister that he had not shared with our aunt?

"Should I wait supper for you, miss?" Agatha asked, as I prepared to leave.

I shook my head. "I don't know when I'll be returning. I can always find something myself."

"Very good, miss. And what should I tell Lady Antonia, if she inquires where you've gone?"

What indeed?

That the police had no idea who the murderer might be? That I'd spoken with the man who found Mary's body? That I now had more questions than when I started? And that I found Mr. Brodie to be quite irritating?

"If she should inquire, you may tell her that I have gone to meet with Sir Charles." I paused as I started out the door.

"Do you remember the name of the locksmith who repaired several of the old locks at Sussex Square?"

"Why yes, miss. It was a man by the name of Leeds in Piccadilly. Quite reputable. He has a royal warrant, as I recall."

Locksmith to the Queen, no less. Whatever was good enough for the Queen was good enough for Aunt Antonia. I made a mental note of the name, then set off for my meeting with Charles.

The Grosvenor Hotel was an elegant multi-story building in the style of French chateaus, and was preferred by my aunt for her guests when she was entertaining friends from the Continent.

The interior of the hotel was also modeled after a French chateau, with a grand entrance, marble floors, and gold-leafed columns in the lobby. There was also a gentlemen's smoking lounge, and one of the first *'lifting rooms'* that had been installed in London.

Given Charles's responsibilities dealing with the security not only of London but the Commonwealth as well, I was surprised by his invitation. I was even more surprised now to find that he had obviously arrived quite early for our luncheon.

I had acquired the habit of watching people while on my travels—their expressions and mannerisms, reactions that often conveyed a different message than what was spoken.

It was there now, that reaction I always had with my brother-in-law, that perfect deportment, with lean features that might be considered handsome by some. He was always perfectly groomed, with perfectly groomed side-whiskers. Too perfect, I thought, not for the first time.

More than once I berated myself for my criticism. I told myself that it was nothing more than a reaction to his aloof nature. If my sister was happy in her marriage, that was all that mattered.

Yet, once again, I felt that instinctive reaction as Sir Charles rose from his private table as I entered the elegantly appointed dining room.

"Thank you for meeting me on such short notice."

There was a decided uneasiness in his manner.

"Has there been any word?" I asked, not one to have a tolerance for social pleasantries. I can be abrupt and blunt. It was a trait my aunt often reminded me of.

"Sadly, no," he replied. "I hope I'm not keeping you from an important appointment."

I removed my gloves and took the chair opposite at the table. We waited before speaking further, as plates of finger sandwiches filled with cheese and nuts, along with watercress magically appeared, even though I had no appetite.

"Your note seemed most urgent," I reminded him when we were alone once more, or as alone as one might be in an exclusive restaurant.

"I hoped you might have heard from Linnie."

He shook his head. "Sadly, no, and poor Mary, most dreadful, and in that part of the city. I can't imagine what the poor girl was doing there."

Dreadful indeed, I thought, at the memory of Mary's body beneath the stark white sheet at the mortuary.

His comment sounded somehow detached considering the horrible reality of her murder, as if he were reading a report or diplomatic dispatch. He seemed to hesitate as though uncertain how to continue.

"I know how very close you and Lenore are..."

He hesitated again as a waiter returned and poured tea, then continued when the man departed.

"I'm deeply concerned that she is perhaps... unwell,

possibly suffering from some emotional malady. I know the past months have been difficult for her... the loss of the child. I'm certain you'll agree that it's not like her to take herself off somewhere."

I very much agreed. The last time we were together, she seemed to be dealing with the loss as well as could be expected, although she seemed distracted. As if there was something else, although she had not spoken of it.

Having no experience with such matters, I could only guess how deeply the loss of the child had affected her, as the loss of our mother and father had affected the two of us differently.

Linnie had become withdrawn as a child afterward, even though she was quite young, while I had reacted quite differently, as Aunt Antonia had pointed out after one of my many childhood escapades.

"I understand that you've made inquiries of your own," Charles continued, quite surprising me.

"I've inquired among Linnie's acquaintances as anyone naturally would," I replied.

I had contacted two of her friends to simply respond to one of the many invitations we had both received. Both ladies made no mention of anything that would assuredly have been food for gossip. Nor had they questioned me. Clearly, neither one was aware of her disappearance.

"Ah, yes," he replied. "Not the most reliable of sources with their gossip."

There was something in his voice, something I had heard before and found irritating. It was a subtle but clear reference to those of Linnie's acquaintance as if they were somehow less credible because of their gender, and that included me as well.

Or was he referring to something else? That I had hired a private investigator?

How could he possibly know anything about that? And so quickly after my meeting the day before with Mr. Brodie and Inspector Abberline?

I pushed aside the plate of sandwiches. I had no patience for polite conversations, or innuendo.

It was obvious that he hadn't invited me there to tell me what he might know, but to find out what *I* knew.

Considering past conversations about our aunt's hesitation over my sister's choice of a suitor and now husband, I was certain Aunt Antonia wouldn't have said anything about hiring Mr. Brodie.

"What of your sources?" I asked, pushing back at him. "A man of your position must certainly know people who would know things others might not."

Always calm and reserved, I caught a different reaction in his manner, as if I had struck a nerve.

He smiled. "I forget how direct you can be. Thank you for reminding me." He moved the silverware around on the table with obvious irritation in spite of that smile.

"I see no reason to play games," I bluntly informed him. "My sister has disappeared. She may very well be in some difficulty."

I thought of poor Mary Ryan, who had taken her secrets with her to a violent end.

"I have every intention of helping to find her if I can." I stood abruptly, with no appetite for the food or the company.

"She *is* my wife," Charles reminded me, with an expression that seemed somehow remote, almost as if he was discussing an employee with the Home Office who had somehow failed in their duties. Or possibly some bothersome matter that needed to be straightened out?

"She was *my* sister, long before she was your wife," I reminded him.

"Quite so," he replied, then, "You must forgive me. This has been a very difficult time, and still no word." He slowly relaxed his hand and smoothed the linen napkin at the table.

"Lenore has not been well as you know."

I felt that familiar irritation. He always insisted on calling Linnie by her full name—Lenore. It was a small thing, but it was not what I would have expected between a loving husband and wife. And, as for her not being well?

I had seen her only days before she disappeared. She had seemed in perfect health, if a bit pale, and was looking forward to a trip to our aunt's estate in Sussex, a much welcome respite after the loss of the child.

"It will be good to get away, just the two of us. Like it used to be."

I hadn't thought about it at the time, but wondered now if there was something more behind her words.

"You will, of course, let me know the moment you learn something in this sad affair," Charles continued. "I am most anxious to see Lenore returned."

Returned. As if she was a parcel or a piece of baggage that had somehow gone astray.

"However, the longer this goes on..." he continued, "I am inclined to fear the worst."

Whom was I seeing now?

"*You don't know him as I know him,*" Linnie had said when I had raised questions about her engagement to him two years earlier.

"He can be very charming, and he truly does care about me."

"The way our father cared about our mother, and us?" I had bluntly replied, and immediately regretted it.

At the age of eight, I had been all too aware of our father's long absences, the gambling debt that he argued with our mother about. Then there were the strange men who came to our house and met with him behind closed doors. I later learned they were money lenders.

All the things I shielded Linnie from, even as things of value were sold off to pay his debts—the horses, paintings, the silver service that had been handed down through his family. And then our mother's illness, and that last day.

Linnie never saw what I saw in the stables, our father's final act of cowardice when he took his own life amidst the ruin our lives had become.

The fact that Sir Charles was Linnie's husband, that he would *take care of it* through his sources, mattered little to me. I had always protected Linnie. We shared a bond, tragic as it was, and I would continue to do so unless she spoke against it.

I had no appetite for further conversation, or the lunch that had been served. I made my excuses, and departed, my thoughts turning over and over, trying to understand what had just taken place.

A polite conversation? Questions that could have been asked and answered in a note or over the telephone?

I had the hotel attendant at the entrance signal for a cab, still lost in thought and no small amount of irritation.

At myself? I refused to apologize for being blunt, or protecting my sister.

At Charles? Most certainly, but as always, there was that feeling that was impossible to put my finger on. As if there were far more beneath the surface.

The rain that had threatened all morning had set in, other guests quickly arriving and departing as they hurried to and from coaches.

A cabman had arrived and a hotel attendant stepped

forward to open the door. As he assisted me into the cab, I caught a glimpse of a man in workman's clothes very near the entrance, as though he was waiting for someone.

He was quite slender, with white hair tucked under a cap, and quickly ducked back into the entrance when he noticed I was looking at him.

I am not given to wild imaginings. I have found the real world to be far more strange and often more unbelievable than anything I might imagine. I was not mistaken that the man suddenly stepped back inside the hotel entrance as if he hadn't wanted to be seen.

IN THAT WAY that is so typically London, everyone went on about their day, even in the midst of a downpour that flooded the streets, adding to the congestion that made traversing them almost impossible.

Craftsmen shops, tea exporters, goldsmiths, and commodity brokers went about business as usual, with flower sellers and newspaper boys selling to those who passed by on Regent Street where it intersected the Quadrant.

The driver navigated the weather and the street traffic with a daring that only an Irishman with his firm belief in the Almighty would attempt.

He delivered me to the door of J.T. Needs, Locksmith, at number 128 Regent Street. A bell over the door announced my arrival as I lowered my umbrella and stepped into the entrance.

The shop was much like an exclusive jeweler's or art gallery, with displays under glass of a variety of medieval locks and keys.

Another cabinet held a collection of intricately carved boxes and traveling cases all with locks, and an iron box with a peculiar-looking clock-like device set into the front of it.

I gave my calling card to the clerk, explaining that I was there on an errand for Lady Antonia Montgomery. Much as I loathe name-dropping, I had found long ago that it was often the surest way to cut directly to the business at hand. And it opened doors. Unashamedly, that connection to an influential name had led to a rather memorable experience with a very handsome travel guide.

The reaction was much the same now, as the clerk nodded and excused himself. In a matter of moments Mr. Needs, the now quite middle-aged son of the original owner, appeared and introduced himself.

"How may we help you today?"

I took the key from my pocket and laid it on top of the glass case.

"What can you tell me about this key?"

He picked it up and turned it over in his fingers, examining it quite thoroughly, then frowned.

"Hmmm," he said thoughtfully. "Yes, yes, most certainly." He looked up.

"I am happy to assist Lady Antonia in any way that I can, of course. If you will accompany me to our work room, I am certain that I will be able to assist in identifying this for her."

I followed him behind the main counter to the back of the establishment. The work room, as he described it, contained a long wood counter against one wall where two craftsmen sat working.

One of them worked with tools at a metal box that might have been a privacy box, while the other worked a lock set into a vise attached to the counter.

Mr. Needs proceeded to a separate work space at the end of the counter. He laid the key on the wood counter, then took out an assortment of tools that included a magnifying glass from one of the drawers. He laid the key on the sheet of paper.

"The better to see all of the key's features," he explained.

The shop had electric lights, and Mr. Needs pressed the button to a light overhead, then took out a pair of spectacles that gave him a somewhat myopic appearance, much like an enormous bug. He passed the magnifying glass slowly over the key, inspecting it from different angles.

"Excellent workmanship," he spoke as if to himself, then turned the key over, all the while adjusting the magnifying glass for the best angle under the light.

"Yes, of course, most certainly," he commented.

He eventually looked up, with a vaguely absent stare, as if only just remembering that I was standing there. He smiled.

"It is as I thought." Then like an archeologist who had just discovered buried treasure, "I don't see many of these. Most people keep them safely secured, under lock and key." He chuckled at the joke he'd made.

"What can you tell me about it?"

"Well you see, this is a very finely made key. " He then set about giving me a thorough explanation on what that meant.

"This is the bow," he indicated the round shape at one end of the key. "This is the shank which slides into the lock, then the collar, and pin. This," he held the key so that I could see, "is the box of wards. And this is the bit."

None of which explained what it was a key *to*.

"Please, Mr. Needs. I need to know what it might be a key for."

"This is the fascinating part," he continued, much like a child opening a package on Christmas morning.

"The key is made of iron but very finely made, case-hardened—very fine indeed."

"Have you seen this type of key before?" I attempted to intervene; however he was well into opening his *Christmas package*, figuratively speaking of course, and I was after all a captive audience.

"This is the part that takes a genuine craftsman." he continued. "The key ward and the bits."

Bits again. All I could think of was horses, but assumed that had little to do with it.

"These slots are cut into the box, and along with the projections create a very complicated feature that will only work in one particular mechanism."

"One mechanism?"

"For security purposes, Miss Forsythe. And for Lady Antonia that would be a most important feature, to secure things of value—documents, perhaps coins, or jewelry. No two keys are alike." He smiled as he continued.

"The Queen has several such vaults and security boxes, but this key was made for a security box in one of the city's banks. Needs and Company has provided many keys for security boxes for the Bank of England over the years. Of course, there is also Westchester."

"Then you must have a record of the keys and locks you provided the bank," I assumed with growing excitement.

"The bank is provided the boxes and their corresponding keys. The boxes are then assigned to clients by the bank. We are not given that information. Most assuredly Lady Antonia is well aware of the security box she has with the bank."

"Yes, of course." I didn't bother to clarify that the key did not belong to my aunt.

The obvious question was... whom did it belong to?

Since it had been in Mary's possession, the only other possibility was that it belonged to my sister. At least I now knew what the key was for.

"If Lady Montgomery has need of our service, I can send round one of my people," he commented.

I thanked him and dropped the key into the pocket of my skirt.

"I will be certain to let her know."

It was a bank security box key. The number embossed on it, corresponding to a particular box. But which bank? Bank of London? Westchester?

It had been quite some time since I had been in that part of London with its import-export offices, trade merchants, sidewalk vendors, and theaters with their glaring advertisement boards street-side, showcasing the latest play.

Point of fact, the last time I had been with my sister was just before she and Sir Charles were married.

I had finally persuaded her to accompany me to the Adelphi to see a play by Oscar Wilde. The famed author and playwright had been scheduled to present his one-act play *Salome* at the St. James Theatre, with Theodora Templeton in the title role.

However, the play was banned by the Lord Chamberlain's office, which had deemed it '*unsuitable.*' Supposedly it was due to scenes that bordered on *risqué,* as the French would say. Unsuitable indeed!

It had been printed in the Times that the London Examiner of Plays, Albert Edward Smith Pigott, had expressed his revulsion at the portrayal of Salome's *desires* and had described the play as "*half Biblical, half pornographic.*" That had only heightened the public's fascination.

The restriction on the use of biblical characters on the London stage was the '*official*' reason given for the decision to ban the play. Never one to be outdone, Mr. Wilde sought to have his play shown '*underground.*'

Lady Antonia, of all people, learned through one of her acquaintances that the play was to have a one-night exclusive showing at the Adelphi, for men only.

I smiled as I remembered the three of us—Aunt Antonia, Linnie, and me—dressed as men as we arrived at the back entrance of the theater and attended the one-act play.

Afterward my aunt had exclaimed, "*I never knew women did that! How very marvelous!*"

Linnie and I had exchanged looks and then laughed until tears rolled down our cheeks on the ride back across London to Sussex Square.

I purchased a paper now as I left the locksmith's shop from a lad who shouted out the titles of the latest plays at local theaters—most of them Shakespearean, with the exception of one that was hailed as a comedy. But it was the headlines on the front page that caught my interest.

There was continued conflict in the Middle East that came out of the latest meetings between the Prime Minister of England and the new minister of Persia. Sadly, it appeared that both sides were near the breaking point, and travelers had been advised to return to England with the threat of looming conflict.

I had traveled across the Persian empire, sleeping in a tent with other travelers as the warm winds moved through tent walls—stark contrast to cold, wet English winters.

But my favorite memory was of the city of Esfahan, with its hand-painted tiles and magnificent public square, and the mosque with its multi-colored gold-and-blue dome and blue tile walls.

I had abandoned my travel group. Having been

warned early on that it was not safe for an English woman to go about alone, I had donned traditional robes and face covering, and wandered the bazaars in the district. Upon hearing of it months later after I returned, my aunt had been shocked.

"What did you wear beneath the robes and veil? It must have been devilishly warm and uncomfortable."

"I didn't wear anything at all under the robes."

"Good heavens! What would have happened if the wind had come up?"

"I suppose the vendors in the bazaar would have had a very fine view," I had replied.

"I should like to have been there," Aunt Antonia said at the time. *"To see the mosque and temples, of course, and to experience the food, and the people."*

Of course.

Those were the adventures that filled the pages of Emma Fortescue's travel tales when I returned, that the very proper Victorian ladies of London waited for each month with voracious anticipation.

It was a part of the world with such a rich ancient history, and I had been following the on-going reports from the region and hoped that a peaceful solution might be found.

Now, I stopped at a nearby shop to look at porcelain vases imported from China that were displayed in the window case. I thought of Linnie's birthday the following month.

I had brought her small mementos from each of my adventures, but the trip to Hong Kong had ended abruptly when several fellow travelers were taken ill. It was the one piece missing so far from my sister's collection that she had taken with her after her marriage, and then displayed in her private sitting room at Litton Hall.

"So that I can remember all the stories you've told, almost as if I traveled there myself," she once said.

Perhaps a vase from China to add to her collection, I thought, when Linnie returned.

If she returned...

Those last three words pulled me back to reality. After all my adventures, in places where some people would not dare go, I had safely returned. Yet, here in London, apparently nothing was safe.

As I tucked the daily under my arm then turned, I caught a reflection from across the street at the glass. It was a man who much resembled the man at the Grosvenor, and he was staring in my direction. He was quite lean and wore the same workman's clothes, with his cap pulled low over his head. When I turned, he had ducked into the tobacconist shop.

The same man seen twice in the span of only a few hours? It might be nothing, I told myself. A coincidence, or...?

I crossed the street, dodging a carriage and an omnibus. The shopkeeper looked up as I entered the shop.

"A man just came in." I looked about the shop, empty except for the owner.

I caught his look, one I was more than familiar with, that blend of curiosity at finding a woman in his shop, with that undertone of disapproval.

What might the man have thought if he knew that I had been known to smoke a cigarette on occasion?

"Can you tell me where he went?"

"As you see, miss. There's no one else here."

No one else, as I spotted the trail of wet boot prints that led to the back of the shop. I followed them to the door at the back of the shop.

The door opened onto an alley. I looked both directions, but it was empty. Whoever had been in the shop was now gone.

"You've been most helpful," I told him returning to the front of the shop. "I will be certain to recommend your establishment."

My sarcasm was undoubtedly lost on him; however, I felt better for it as I left the shop.

I wasn't imagining things—I was certain the man who had been watching me was the same man I had seen at the Grosvenor. But who was he? And what reason did he have to be following me?

Along with my meeting with Charles, I was quite frustrated by the day's events that had produced no new information.

Brodie indicated the evening before that he would make inquiries at the pawn shops in the area of London where Mary's body was found. Perhaps he had some news from his inquiries.

I hailed a cab and gave the driver the address on the Strand; however, Brodie was gone on some matter when I arrived, the door to the office locked. Rupert lay in front of the door dozing. He raised his head, tail thumping in greeting.

I left my card tucked in at the edge of the door, then bent down and scratched the hound behind the ears. He continued to wag his tail as he rolled over onto his back.

"Late night, was it?" I commented as the dog groaned, then proceeded to go back to sleep, sprawled on his back with all four legs in the air. At least the day was most agreeable for someone.

I returned to the street and signaled for a driver.

Nine

MAYFAIR, THE THIRD DAY 5:00 A.M.

"I'VE BROUGHT MORE COFFEE."

I looked up from my desk as Agatha crossed the room with a pot in hand.

"Working through the night again. " She shook her head. "You should at least try to eat something.

"Coffee will be fine," I replied, skimming back over the notes I had made since rising at a little after two in the morning, according to the downstairs clock, unable to sleep.

"Your new book?" she asked, as she set the pot at the edge of the desk and retrieved the empty carafe.

I shook my head, my next book was the farthest from my mind.

"Some notes I made..."

She hesitated. "When I think of Mary, that poor girl. And Miss Lenore..." Her voice caught, and she dabbed at her eyes with a handkerchief.

I rounded the desk and wrapped an arm about her shoulders. It was a reminder that we were very much like a family—impossible for Agatha and the rest of the staff not to know what had happened, especially with Alice's return to Sussex Square.

"I beg your pardon, miss, I didn't mean to speak of unpleasant things."

"It's alright," I replied. "It's difficult for everyone right now."

She nodded, returning a handkerchief to her pocket. "I'll set things aright in the kitchen, then do a bit of shopping. Will you be home for supper?"

That was impossible to know under the circumstances. Everything had been turned upside down with my sister's disappearance.

"I can manage quite well, no need to go to all that trouble. And perhaps you should return to Sussex Square," I suggested. "There's not a lot for you to do here."

She nodded. "I'll make certain there's food in the pantry before I leave," she said with a knowing look.

"Thank you. I do appreciate it."

In the past, Alice had seen to the laundry, shopping, and housekeeping. She had also prepared meals.

However, I was quite adept at taking care of things for myself, although admittedly my skills in the kitchen left a great deal to be desired.

A roast fowl I had once experimented with had been reduced to cinders, smoke billowing out of the kitchen when I became deeply immersed in my latest novel and forgot to check on it.

That adventure precipitated Alice's arrival when my aunt suggested it might be better than burning the place down. She had cleaned the kitchen rather than declare it a disaster area, and announced that she was staying at my aunt's insistence.

I now retreated to my notes over that next pot of coffee, reading through to make certain that I had remembered everything. Mr. Brodie would provide me his report! Indeed!

I would provide him with mine!

I had learned the purpose of the key found in the hem of Mary's gown, and intended to investigate that further. However, there were pieces of information that contradicted others, or made no sense at all with my limited knowledge of such things.

I again read my notes regarding Mr. Spivey's account of finding Mary's body in the water at St. Katherine's docks. I then made note of Mr. Brodie's comments that according to the examination by the police surgeon there wasn't any water in Mary's lungs... I had more questions.

I rose from the desk and collected my notes.

"I will be going out," I informed Agatha, as I ran up the stairs to change my clothes into something more suitable.

~

It was well past one o'clock in the afternoon when I reached Teddington Lock in Richmond, that is part of the Thames river system.

In my adventures I had acquired a bit of knowledge about the Nile river from the man who had piloted the boat my party had sailed on. In his broken English he had explained how the currents pushed the craft to various locations along the river, often requiring no sail at all, then in the opposite direction in other places along the way.

He had continued to tell us that things accidently lost over the side—a crate or barrel—might well be found far downriver because of the current that rose and fell during different times of the day and night.

The time of day when work had ended on the *Polly*, the tide on the river would have been out as Brodie explained it. I wanted to know more about the tides at St. Katherine's docks, and there was a man who might be able to provide that information.

The Teddington Lock was actually the location where three locks in the river system converged. Skiffs were available for a fee to take passengers from the city to the countryside in mild weather.

They then often carried cargo on the return trip—fresh fruits and vegetables, eggs, chickens, from farms along the way. The produce from farmer's fields and orchards beyond the city provided food for many London tables.

Linnie and I had traveled to the country aboard one of the skiffs owned by Captain Turner.

He had retired from the large merchantmen after losing a leg in an accident and owned a half dozen of the small vessels that traversed the locks back and forth. With my usual curiosity, I had asked questions about the system of waterways, and he had been more than accommodating.

I found him this morning shouting at one of his crewmen apparently over damage to one of the skiffs on a return trip from the countryside.

"If you can't navigate the water without damaging me boat, then you can settle up your wages at the office!" he bellowed.

"Mick!" he shouted to an older man, bent and stooped, wearing a typical stocking cap against the damp and cold.

"Keep an eye on 'im!"

The Captain stumped along the landing on that artificial leg, much like a bear with a wounded paw, growling and snapping at everyone.

"A long voyage on a merchantman would do the lad some good," he snarled. "If he lived through it."

He hobbled his way to the steps, then finally looked up.

"Good morning, Captain," I called out.

The snarl turned to a frown.

"Wot the devil do yer want?" He glared up from the wood landing with that usual gruffness that I was more than familiar with, but not the least intimidated by.

"A bit of your time. In exchange for a carton of biscuits." I held the baker's box aloft.

They were made with an exorbitant amount of butter, laced with cinnamon and hazelnuts. It was a favorite that we'd shared on my prior trips on the canal.

"And you come all the way across London just to deliver them biscuits?"

"All the more difficult for you to ignore me."

"I never ignore a pretty girl." He stumped his way up the steps. "Come ter the office, and bring the bloody carton."

He was a bear of a man, near sixty odd years, with an unruly shock of red hair just beginning to streak with gray. He sat before a coal stove in the office at Richmond landing, the peg that was now his left leg propped on a wood crate.

"Wot else brings yer here, missy? Surely not a trip to the countryside with the bloody weather," he commented between mouthfuls of biscuits.

"What can you tell me about the currents on the Thames River, specifically at St. Katherine's dock?"

His bushy eyebrows disappeared under the bill of his cap. "Now, wot would a young woman such as yourself be wantin' to know that for?"

I explained as little as necessary, avoiding any mention of my sister's disappearance.

"Aye, bodies in the river, nasty business," he replied. "For one of your books I s'pose."

I had consulted with him previously regarding my character, Emma Fortescue's adventures on the Nile, and he had provided valuable information.

"St. Katherine's dock, you say." He seized another biscuit. "Nasty currents there, constant churning and back-washing." He gave me a thoughtful look, as he continued munching.

"A body wouldn't likely stay there long but get swept back out, if you get my meanin'."

"How long *might* a body remain there?" I asked over the cup of strong coffee that tasted as if it might have been made the day before.

"No more than the time it would take for the next swell to roll in, then it would be gone. Most likely never to be seen again. That's the way of the river."

I made a mental note of that.

There had been no water in Mary's lungs according to the police surgeon's report, information that had obviously been important to Brodie at the time.

"What would it mean if there was no water in the victim's lungs?" I asked.

Another biscuit found its way into the Captain's fingers.

"It's been my experience that the person was most likely dead before they ended up in the water. One trip out of Shanghai, one of the crew got into a fight with another crew member. Hit on the head, he was, and knocked over the side. He was dead before he hit the water. When we pulled him out, there was no water in him.

"That's the way of it. If the person was alive, they might have struggled, tryin' to save themself. If you get my meaning."

I did indeed.

Dead before Mary was put into the river! And

highly unlikely that her body had simply washed up with the incoming tide, given the turbulent water surrounding St. Katherine's dock!

That, of course, cast considerable doubt on Mr. Spivey's account of finding Mary's body floating in the water near the Polly. And that raised even more questions about what Mr. Spivey knew that he hadn't shared with us.

"What might the overall condition of the body be under those circumstances?" I asked.

It was something that had bothered me after the shock at the sight of Mary's body had worn off.

"Well, that's a different matter. The Thames is cold year-round, particularly so in winter right off the channel and that bein' out of the Atlantic. There wouldn't be noticeable wasting of the body for several days. But here's the thing..." He leaned closer, his hand snaking out and grabbing another biscuit.

"With them currents at St. Katherine's, a body would be tossed about fer certain. And with them pilings, there would be damage so to speak, and after a time, what's left will sink to the bottom."

He munched thoughtfully. "Beggin' yer pardon, but it would be like crushing a walnut under yer boot heel. It would be smacked around then broke to pieces. You wouldn't recognize the poor soul."

It appeared there was a great deal more that Spivey hadn't told us. But for what reason? Robbery as Brodie had suggested? Or some other reason?

That brought me back to the reason Mary was in that part of London in the first place. What was she doing there? And what had happened to my sister?

"Wot might your interest in such things be, missy?" Captain Tom asked.

"Curiosity," I answered vaguely. There was nothing

to be gained in going through everything, particularly since I didn't know what *everything* was.

We spoke further as the biscuits disappeared, and I realized that I should have brought more.

After winter had set in, trips from the city were limited to the occasional day travelers, with less cargo on the return trip, as the last of the summer crops had been harvested.

I listened as he spoke of his time at sea, crossing to the Continent, then on to the Mediterranean, or rounding the horn of Africa on the longer voyages to those far places.

His adventures were filled with long weeks at sea, the occasional encounter with pirates, and somewhat off-color adventures in exotic foreign ports—Lisbon, then Calcutta and places beyond.

"Do you miss it?" I asked of his adventures to those far places in exchange for the obviously far tamer ventures on inland waterways.

"Aye, well, there are times when I think I would like to feel the roll of the big deck beneath me feet again—or foot, as it be. And there's nothing like the snap of the sails overhead on a clear day. But it's not a life for an old man, and it's changed. More ships go by steam now than sail. There will be a time when all the big sailing ships are gone."

"How is that?" I asked.

"It about profit, there's no getting away from that. The steamships are faster and not delayed when there's no wind." He made a gesture over his shoulder in the direction of the three skiffs moored beneath a sky where clouds lowered once more.

"I understand. I need to make a profit like any man. But there's nothing like the roll of the deck under sail."

His eyes crinkled with humor. "It's for young men, aye. And I don't run as fast as I use to."

He rose and went to the window, and shouted another order to Mick, then returned.

"Weather coming in and one last boat to be unloaded. The boy will have most of it in the water if I don't watch him like his mother."

A sharp gust of wind buffeted my umbrella as I left, the water of the canal almost as dark as the sky.

I watched Captain Tom as he stumped his way down the landing, that rolling gait still there, shouting orders, and thought about what he had told me.

Ten

THE STRAND, DAY FOUR

"GOOD DAY, MISS," the Mudger greeted me from his platform. "Be warned, Mr. Brodie is in a right foul temper. And mind yer step on them stairs. It's treacherous this mornin' with the ice."

I didn't know the man well enough from our previous encounter to know whether or not he was playing some prank with that comment about the stairs. However most important, Brodie was in his office.

I entered the passage, took the first step at the stairs, and was greeted by what could only be described as a volley of Scottish curses from the top landing.

There was a brief pause then another explosion of curses, accompanied by an object that looked decidedly like the leg of a chair that shot through the air and landed in the alleyway.

Treacherous indeed!

I was not up on my Gaelic curses, but from the tone and volume, I needed no explanation. It was apparent that Brodie was extremely displeased about something. I picked up the broken chair leg and proceeded with caution.

The door to the office was open as I reached the

landing. A glance inside revealed the destruction, including a chair laying on its side, one leg missing.

Another curse filled the air.

Brodie stood in the middle of it all, disheveled—however, fully clothed this time—the broken chair overturned, papers scattered everywhere from open file drawers.

His expression much resembled Captain Tom bellowing to his crewman, although he was somewhat more agreeable-looking than Captain Tom.

In point of fact, I supposed some women might find Brodie quite handsome when he wasn't snarling like some wild-eyed beast.

"Difficulties with your cleaning lady?" I inquired. "Or possibly a *female acquaintance*?" I suggested, considering our first meeting and the half-dressed woman I had encountered.

"It has been my experience that a chair functions far better on four legs." I added and laid the broken chair leg at the desk.

That dark gaze fastened on me.

"Yer have a vast knowledge of such things," he fired back. "Impressive, for a woman."

I let that pass. But certainly not my observation of his office in its present condition, much deteriorated from our first meeting.

"I've brought you *my* report," I replied.

"Yer report?"

His expression darkened as he eventually understood my meaning.

"If ye have nothin' to contribute to the situation, Miss Forsythe, then ye may leave."

I looked around the office. "What precisely *is* the situation, Mr. Brodie?"

"The situation is that someone has taken it upon himself to turn out the place!"

I could well see that. But the question was *who*, and to what purpose.

It was obvious there was little of value to be stolen other than the few odd pieces of furniture that looked as if they might be better purposed for the fire box, which at present was smoldering. I crossed over to the stove and shut the door against suffocating from the smoke.

"Do ye always go about as if ye own the place?" Brodie snapped.

"When necessary," I replied. "I have no interest in fleeing a burning building because someone is careless."

I didn't bother to explain my past attempts at cooking. Instead, I began gathering papers from the floor. Perhaps his *report* was among those scattered about.

"What reason would someone have to break into your office?" I hardly thought robbery was the motive.

"That would be *the* question, Miss Forsythe."

"You must have some thought on the matter," I replied.

"Aye," he grumbled as he propped the three-legged chair against the desk, then began picking up the pieces of a broken picture frame that held a certificate with a gold seal that was somewhat crumpled. It appeared to be some sort of award or commendation. It joined the growing pile of trash.

I ignored his surly manner, and looked around for Rupert but there was no sign of the hound.

"I came round yesterday, and left my card in the door. Everything was quite in order then."

"Is there somethin' ye wish to discuss?" Brodie asked as he righted a chair, upholstered in a garish shade of purple that looked as if it had been appropriated from someone's front parlor.

I continued picking up pieces of paper, what appeared to be notes in an almost indecipherable scrawl. There were also several outdated newspapers, a list of some sort, and a reminder that his rent was due on the first of the month.

"You're quite correct that Mr. Spivey was not completely forthcoming," I commented matter-of-factly.

"And how exactly did ye arrive at that conclusion?"

"I've spoken with someone who has considerable knowledge of the waterfront, specifically the area at St. Katherine's dock."

His head came up, those dark eyes narrowed. But whether it was interest in what I'd learned or aggravation was difficult to discern by the expression at his face.

"It seems that the currents are quite treacherous in the area of St. Katherine's dock." I explained what Captain Tom had shared with me.

"Nothing in the water would remain for more than a few minutes before being swept back out into the main channel of the river and never seen again."

"Who is this expert in matters of the river?" he snapped.

"A man with many years' experience. And he's most familiar with the currents at St. Katherine's dock."

Brodie straightened, eyes narrowed as I found a broom and was presently sweeping scattered paper and rubbish into a neat pile.

"Who might this gentleman be?"

"I suppose that one would hardly consider Captain Turner to be a gentleman," I allowed, however most certainly he was a connoisseur of buttered biscuits.

"However, he's always been forthright in his dealings with me."

"Have ye considered that you might have put yerself in danger going about London on yer own asking questions?"

I paused my sweeping. "I assure you there was no

danger from Mr. Turner, and I am quite accustomed to going about by myself. I have found it most productive when others cannot be relied upon." I received a dark glare at that one.

I thought of telling him that I was quite capable of physically defending myself. However, given present circumstances and Brodie's surly temper, it was probably not the time to explain that I could easily have dumped Captain Turner, on his backside.

And him as well for that matter. Something I would have enjoyed, given his ill-humor. But the truth was, I needed his expertise, and it was probably best not to go about *poking the bear*, as it were.

"What other piece of highly valuable information might ye have learned in the time since we parted?" he asked, picking up an umbrella from the floor and tossing it into the stand by the door, then proceeding to put overturned drawers back into the file cabinet.

In spite of the sarcasm, I told him of my meeting with Charles. I made no effort to disguise my annoyance or frustration.

"Has he learned anything of yer sister's whereabouts?"

"He wanted to know if I had heard from her. He was most agitated about it."

Brodie disappeared into the adjacent room.

"How long have yer sister and Sir Charles been married?" he called from the room.

"Two years this April."

"And no children?"

I didn't see what that had to do with anything and didn't mention the loss of the child Linnie had hoped for.

"No."

"Has yer sister ever mentioned clubs that her husband might belong to? Most men of his position belong to a private club."

I heard the unspoken. I knew well the reputation of certain *'gentlemen's'* clubs in London.

Our father had belonged to one of those clubs, with its gambling tables and betting on the most ridiculous of things—horse racing, the conquest of a certain lady in a specific amount of time, how high a rat could jump, and other ridiculous things that relieved those in attendance of their money. Never mind those left at home.

I had always believed the seemingly endless evenings that our father was away until late into the night might have contributed to our mother's *'illness.'* Not to mention his gambling debts. After her death, he had gone out most every night, drinking and gambling, and then he, too, was gone.

"What about some difficulty in the marriage? An affair she might have been having?" Brodie asked amid sounds of drawers being opened then closed, and another round of curses from the adjacent room.

"No! And I don't see..." I protested.

"I ask it, because a great deal of my work is finding out about such situations, the unhappy wife keeping company with another man."

"What about the man who might be keeping company with another woman?" I asked pointedly.

Brodie came out of the adjacent room. He'd donned a clean shirt and pants, and looked far more presentable.

"It's a necessary question, Miss Forsythe. There's a considerable amount of that sort of thing among those of Sir Charles's class."

"You don't understand. Linnie would not become involved in an affair. I can say without a doubt that she would *not* do such a thing."

Even as I said it, though, I wondered if that was true,

if there might not be something that precipitated Linnie's disappearance, something she chose not to tell me?

"Tell me about Sir Charles," Brodie continued.

"He comes from a very old family. He was educated at Eton and Oxford," I recalled what Linnie had shared with me.

"He was appointed Home Secretary eight years ago," I added, and realized that other than these things, I knew very little about him. I had no idea what other interests he had, if he had traveled, or anything about his family other than their names.

His position as Home Secretary hadn't been as important to my sister as the fact that there wasn't a breath of scandal in the family through many generations.

"Home Secretary—an important position to be sure," Brodie commented. "But yer not impressed by such things."

"I have found that titles have little to do with the character of a person." I discovered the rubbish bin, overturned by the chair when it met its demise, and dumped the contents of the dust pan.

"And he pursued a relationship with yer sister?"

Brodie had touched upon something I had thought at the time when Charles had courted my sister, that they did not seem well suited. Granted, our aunt was from one of the oldest families in England and was quite wealthy, though no titles came to either Linnie or me.

Charles was ambitious, well-placed in government office, with important responsibilities, while my sister was somewhat shy and insecure in such things. She was far happier when she was in the country and at her painting, whereas Charles...?

She seemed to have adjusted quite well with guidance and assistance from our aunt. Who was I to question the attraction between a man and woman, when I chose to remain unmarried—a *spinster,* quite simply because I hadn't met a man who could carry on an intelligent conversation.

I continued to scoop up papers and was about to deposit them into the rubbish bin, then suddenly stopped. Among the crumpled papers was a broken picture frame that contained the certificate with an embossed gold seal.

I smoothed the badly wrinkled certificate. It was a commendation for exemplary service awarded to Inspector Angus Brodie, C.I.D., and it was signed by Chief Inspector Henry Moore of Scotland Yard. I looked over at Brodie.

"Criminal Investigation Department with Scotland Yard, for meritorious conduct?"

Aunt Antonia had made a vague comment that Brodie had abruptly left the service over some difficulty, something that greatly contradicted the commendation I now held in my hand. Had the disagreement happened afterward, over a case involving Inspector Abberline?

That might well explain the animosity between the two men. It was an interesting insight.

"Worthless as the paper it's printed on," he replied, and disappeared into the next room once more.

Instead of tossing it in the rubbish bin, I set it atop the file cabinet.

When he returned, he'd donned a black waistcoat, his shirt tucked into the waist of his pants, with a black tie that hung loose about the collar. He fidgeted and fussed with it, cursed, then would have simply removed it.

I crossed the room and pushed his hands aside, then proceeded to cross one end of the tie over the other, then under, around and through.

"Ye've some experience with this," he commented.

"Men usually don't have the patience to tie them," I replied.

"And damned uncomfortable, if ye ask me."

"Very much like a lady's corset, I would imagine." I smiled to myself at the sudden angle Brodie's brows had taken.

He made one of those typically Scottish sounds that might have meant anything. I was becoming quite familiar with them as I tied off the knot and wondered the reason men had to wear ties. I looked up to find him studying me.

"Something about the meeting with Sir Charles bothered ye," he commented.

It wasn't the first time Brodie seemed to know my thoughts. It was a little disconcerting as I was not in the habit of sharing them with anyone. That a man might sense such things was new to me. Perhaps merely the skill of a competent detective.

"It was afterward, as I was leaving the hotel. I saw someone; he seemed to be watching me."

He frowned. "What did the person look like?"

"I didn't see his face as he turned away. His hair was white, and he wore the clothes of a workman with a red scarf about his neck."

I looked up to find Brodie studying me as I finished tying his tie.

"Ye have an excellent eye for detail."

"For a woman?" I suggested.

I ignored the glare and proceeded to tell him what I'd learned about the key found in the hem of Mary's gown.

"I saw the same man again as I left the locksmith's shop." I left out the part about following him, since he had in fact disappeared.

"Ye seem to be attracting attention," Brodie commented, something different in his voice.

"What do you mean?"

"The same man, seen twice in the space of a few hours?"

I had thought the same, and there was more to the thought. I could see it in the expression on his face, but he chose not to share it. He glanced at the clock that hung askew on the wall but had managed to survive the chaos in the office.

"Do ye know which bank yer sister might have business with?"

"We both had accounts with the Bank of England. I assume she still has hers."

"That could be useful."

He stopped at the door and frowned at the damage that had been done to the latch, then headed for the stairs. I was forced to run after him or be left behind. At least we weren't still arguing about my involvement in the investigation.

The Mudger was in his usual place at the sidewalk. He nodded as Brodie asked him to see about having the lock repaired.

The hound had finally put in an appearance. The poor beast looked much the worse for wear and limped as he came up to me, tail slowly wagging in greeting. He also had a gash over one eye. I knelt down and stroked his head.

"The bastard—beg pardon, Miss—wot broke into Mr. Brodie's office put the boot to him more than once.

"But he gave as good as he got. Took a piece out of the man's leg." He held up a bit of woolen cloth with a dark stain that looked very much like blood.

I gave Rupert a gentle scratch about the ears and made a mental note to bring him some biscuits.

"I'll be looking for a man wot has a limp," the

Mudger added, brandishing a blade. "There be a score to settle."

I gave the hound a pat on the head then quickly joined Brodie. He had waved down a cab.

"Where are we going?" I asked as the driver pulled to the curb. I ignored Brodie's look of disapproval or the opportunity to discuss the matter, and quickly climbed into the cab ahead of him.

"Ye have a most stubborn nature, Miss Forsythe."

Wasn't that a bit like the pot calling the kettle black? I thought.

"Are you going to just stand there getting wet?" I inquired as rain thickened.

He muttered something and climbed into the cab, then called up to the driver.

"You haven't spoken of your inquiries yesterday," I reminded him as the driver swung the rig about and set off.

Brodie reached inside the front of his coat and pulled out a parcel wrapped in brown paper and handed it to me.

Inside was a woman's reticule. It was made of satin brocade in a shade of deep burgundy with black draw-string ties. It was not the usual sort that a servant might have, but what a lady might carry, and it was badly stained and wrinkled...

As if it had been in the water?

"Do ye recognize it?"

I nodded. "It was a gift to my sister on her last birthday."

"There are papers inside, along with some other things."

I took out the contents—a lady's watch, papers that had been neatly folded, now water stained but remarkably intact.

The watch no longer worked. It had stopped at 7:45, the glass cover cracked and fogged over. I turned it over, but already knew what I would find. The initials A.E.F. were inscribed across the back.

"It belonged to our mother. Aunt Antonia gave it to Linnie on her eighteenth birthday, something to remember our mother by."

God knows I had no use for something so fine. It would only have been misplaced or lost on my travels.

Brodie had been staring out the cab, his expression unreadable. "Ye might want to take a look at the papers."

I carefully unfolded the pages that were stuck together, the ink badly smeared. One note was about a commission Linnie was owed for one of her paintings.

She had first taken up painting when we were at private school in Paris, and had studied under Monsieur Chabot. He considered her to be quite talented, as our mother had been, and she had continued to paint until her marriage. Then she had no time for it, with her new social responsibilities as Lady Litton.

There were other odd papers, including two rail tickets, and a note—*To whom it may concern...*

The note was written authorization for the person bearing the letter to have access to Linnie's personal security box at the bank!

Was that the reason Mary had the key? To access my sister's security box at the bank instead of going there herself? But for what reason? What was she afraid of?

Eleven

THE FACADE of the Bank of England with its gigantic columns and arches loomed up out of the wintry gray morning at Threadneedle Street. Businessmen in their long coats and hats huddled against the cold and damp as they entered the financial establishment.

The driver pulled to the curb some distance from the entrance, the way through blocked by coaches and other cabs because of the weather.

My aunt had done business with the Bank of England for as long as I could remember. She was one of their preferred clients, meeting with her personal banker, the vice president Aldous Trumble, each month regarding her finances.

I had met Mr. Trumble previously for my own far more limited banking needs. He had arranged foreign currency prior to my setting off on my trips to the Continent. Now that we knew what the key that Mary had been carrying was for, I wanted to find out what was in the security box it went to.

Brodie accompanied me into the bank with its overstuffed chairs in private alcoves where clients met with representatives of the bank.

We were initially informed that Mr. Trumble was not available. Undaunted, I gave the appearance of being quite distressed.

"Oh, dear," I told the young clerk at the desk, putting on an act that would have rivaled that of my good friend, actress Theodora Templeton.

"I do hope you might be able to assist," I told the clerk, who appeared not at all certain what to do with a client on the verge of a hysterical episode.

I abhorred the affectation, but found it quite useful in certain circumstances. This was one of them.

Brodie looked away.

"I need to retrieve a security box," I explained. "Perhaps you could assist me?" I added the appropriate smile that had enabled me to slip away from the London Police in the Ascot affair, when I had appropriated one of the horses and proceeded to participate in the race. It was most exciting.

Then there were the Greek authorities who were called in to assist a certain young *Englishwoman* who had been seen bathing nude in the Aegean on one of my other adventures. One did what one had to.

"Of course, Miss Forsythe," the clerk replied, between blushing and tripping over his words.

"You have the key I presume?"

I smiled again. "Yes, and an authorization letter from the owner."

I retrieved the letter that had been inside Linnie's reticule, water-stained as it was.

"And you are?"

"Lady Litton's sister," I replied. "She is indisposed and unable to call on the bank herself, but most anxious to retrieve the contents."

"Yes, of course. I quite understand." He blushed again beneath the sparse sprinkling of side whiskers, then opened the side gate and escorted us behind the marble counter, as Brodie seemed suddenly taken with a fit of coughing.

"Pitiful," Brodie whispered as we accompanied the clerk. "Downright pitiful. Ye should be ashamed of yer-self, teasing that poor lad, and lying to him. He'll not be right for a month."

"A slight stretch of the truth, but most effective," I pointed out.

We followed him back through a long hallway, past several closed office doors to a wrought iron lift with a sliding gate.

"If you please, Miss Forsythe..."

The clerk slid the gate shut after we had boarded, pushed a lever, and we began a slow downward descent.

The walls of the floor beneath the main bank were plain, stark contrast to the ornate gilt decor on the main floor. The lift bumped to a stop and the clerk opened the gate.

We followed him down a short hallway to a set of double doors. He produced a key, and unlocked one of the doors that opened onto a large room, the walls of the room filled with row upon row of security boxes. They were all numbered, and somewhere among them was the security box that belonged to my sister.

What would it reveal? Something? Nothing?

The clerk went to a wood file cabinet at the end of one wall. We waited as he entered the combination that opened the drawer. He pulled out a ledger.

"Ah yes, Lady Litton," he acknowledged. "Box 436. Fourth row from the bottom. The ledger is kept locked in the cabinet, to protect the privacy of the owner. I'm certain you understand," he explained, as he made an entry, then returned the ledger to the cabinet and set the lock.

His mother would be most proud, I thought, for I was certain that he undoubtedly still lived with her.

"When you're finished simply press the button," he indicated a brass panel at the wall near the entrance to the room. "I'll return to escort you back to the main floor."

"You've been most helpful." I gave him another smile.

We waited until he had gone, the faint rumble of the lift indicating that he had returned to the main floor. I turned to the wall filled with security boxes.

"Ye should have been an actress," Brodie commented.

"A friend tried to persuade me," I replied, as I found the correct row. I scanned the numbers on the front of the boxes for number 436.

"However, I had an aversion to managers seducing understudies in order for them to obtain a role in a play."

I found the security box and inserted the key into the lock. It turned easily, the box sliding out from the wall. Brodie retrieved it and placed it at one of the tables in the middle of the room. I lifted the lid.

Everything I could have expected—valuables, possibly jewelry given to my sister by Charles and put there for safekeeping—most certainly did not include a slender leather-bound journal. There were also what appeared to be a couple of letters, and a substantial amount of pound notes.

I had never thought myself to be a particularly emotional person. Linnie was always the one when we were children, and had accused me more than once of hiding my feelings.

She suggested it was the reason I was always going off on my adventures, avoiding any sort of attachment. She had even so much as suggested that *Emma Fortescue*, the heroine of my novels, was the emotional other half of me.

Now Linnie had disappeared. And after the loss of both our parents, the thought of losing her as well was unacceptable. Then, what was to be done now?

What of the journal in front of me? What was in it? Something she didn't want others to see? And the pound notes? Possibly from the sale of one of her paintings?

Was that the reason Mary had the key in the hem of her skirt? Had my sister sent her to retrieve the contents including the pound notes? For what reason? To leave London?

"Our mother gave her the first journal when we were very young," I explained. "I suppose it was a way of putting her feelings down on paper. Perhaps understand them, particularly after our mother's death, and then... our father shortly after."

"A difficult thing for a child to experience. But not for ye?" Brodie suggested.

"What's done is done. No reason to keep going over it," I replied. I looked up to find him studying me.

"What else is in the box?" he eventually asked.

"A good amount of money, probably from the sale of one of her paintings. I could never draw a stick, but she is quite talented. And two letters..." I frowned.

"One is dated almost four months ago." I looked over at him. "The other one is dated less than two weeks ago."

Brodie nodded. "It might be useful to know when yer sister was last here."

"We could always ask the clerk's assistance," I suggested.

"We could," he replied. "However I suspect not even yer feminine charm could entice him to break bank policy and risk his position."

And with that he went to the file cabinet at the wall. I watched, fascinated as he slowly turned the dial first in one direction, then the other. He pressed an ear against the front of the cabinet, listening intently. Then, still listening, he slowly turned it back in the opposite direction.

"There it is," he said with satisfaction, then pulled the drawer open.

"You are a man of unusual talents!" I complimented him. "You obviously have some experience with this sort of thing." I was not at all certain Mr. Needs would appreciate one of his locks so easily tampered with.

"One picks up certain skills on the streets." He handed me the ledger.

There was a flash of a smile that quickly disappeared at a sound from the hallway as the elevator returned.

"Quickly, before the clerk returns."

I opened the ledger and scanned the entries of the past month, then suddenly stopped.

"What is it?"

"December 28. " I looked up. "Box number 436, and she signed with her maiden name."

"Perhaps the account was in her name before she married," Brodie commented.

I shook my head. She had been so proud and happy over her marriage to Charles. I was certain she had changed her name afterward. Now, to have changed it back to Forsythe?

The sound of footsteps came from the hallway.

"Bring everything from the security box," he told me. "It might be useful."

He quickly returned the ledger to the drawer and closed it, then slid the empty box back into the slot at the wall and retrieved the key.

We passed the clerk on our way to the lift. I thanked him for his assistance.

"Ye have all the makings of a first-rate thief." Brodie whispered as we left the bank.

A career option, I thought, should my writing career come to an abrupt end.

~

Instead of returning to the Strand, Brodie gave a different location to the driver.

"The establishment of a man who may have something to tell us about the residue under the maid's fingernails," he explained.

"You already inquired about it?" I replied, with more than a little surprise. "We agreed that we would proceed in this together."

"Aye. It was when ye took it upon yerself to visit the locksmith, quite on yer own," Brodie replied pointedly.

"Mr. Needs is a long-standing acquaintance who has provided service for my aunt and me in the past."

"And yer acquaintance at the Richmond canal?"

I had the distinct impression that I was losing this argument.

"I felt it was in the interest of time that it might be helpful to speak with him," I explained. "And it was."

"Precisely the point, Miss Forsythe."

Infuriating as it was, I knew that he was right. I had been soundly caught in a trap of my own making.

The apothecary shop was on Haymarket Street, with a sign overhead at the second story that advertised tooth extractions and replacements, and *other medicinal procedures*.

"Other medicinal procedures?" I asked.

"Aye, he provides services for women who canna afford a physician. They pay him what they can."

"Such as?"

Brodie held the door open as we entered the shop.

"When a woman finds herself with child and no way to care for it. It's a sad fact of life in the East End for women who are often on their own, Miss Forsythe, and have to find a way to put food on the table and pay the rent," he explained.

"Oh."

I wasn't ignorant to his meaning—prostitution was, after all, the oldest profession in the world.

Other societies had their way of dealing with unwanted pregnancies. Someone in the family might take the child and raise it as their own. A girl who found herself in such a situation might be shunned, even stoned to death for the shame she had brought upon her family.

The East End, with its workhouses that paid low wages, overcrowded housing, poverty, and crime was such a place where a woman might obviously find herself alone.

Churches, charity homes, and orphanages were filled with those who had been cast off for one reason or another. And there were those other situations that were whispered about in so-called *polite society*. It was a sad fact of life.

The apothecary shop was lined with glass-front cabinets behind a long counter. Inside the cabinets were a variety of bottles and jars filled with liquids and powders, some with leeches, others with what looked like worms and an assortment of small dead animals. Still other jars bore labels that described the contents—laudanum, quinine, digitalis, antipyrine, something called salicylic acid, and various other treatments for a variety of ailments.

A counter ran along the back wall with various instruments for measuring, beakers for mixing then warming over a burner, a pill rolling device, and a microscope.

The man who owned the shop was assisting a customer and providing instructions for a bottle of elixir the woman had just purchased.

"Linctus syrup," he explained. "It should help the boy's cough. Give it to him for three nights. It will help him sleep."

He handed her a wrapped package. When she would have handed him a coin, he waved it away.

"Purchase some bones for a fresh broth instead and feed it to the lad. It will help ease the chills."

When she had gone, he turned to us.

"Ah, Mr. Brodie. I have some news for you." He looked over at me with obvious curiosity.

"And who might the young lady be?"

Brodie frowned.

"An associate," he finally replied. "In the matter we discussed yesterday."

"Ah, yes. This way."

"*Associate*?" I whispered, as we followed him to the back of the shop.

"I thought it better than what he might assume," he explained.

Given my observations of the company Brodie usually kept, I saw his point.

"I suppose I should thank you for that."

The chemist, Mr. Brimley, was a wiry little man with thinning gray hair atop a balding head, mustache and beard, and large round spectacles that gave him an owlish appearance.

"The sample was quite small," he commented as he pulled out a stool at the counter.

"I examined it under the microscope for the usual contents—hair, fragments of skin, that sort of thing. It's definitely skin."

From the murderer? I exchanged a look with Brodie, and wondered what it might possibly tell us.

"As I said," he continued, "there was not a great deal to work with. However, I've worked with far less before, as you well know, Mr. Brodie."

"What can ye tell us?" he asked.

"Upon closer examination, the tissue was from a blister. It had a yellowish tint to it. Most likely from a chemical burn of some kind. See here, under the microscope."

Brodie stepped to the counter. He peered into the microscope at the glass slide affixed below.

"For certain it's not blood," Brodie commented.

"May I?" I asked, most curious.

He stepped back and I peered at the piece of glass that held the tissue.

"What sort of chemical is it, Mr. Brimley?" I asked, as I stared at the brownish-yellow color of the tissue.

I looked up and caught the look that passed between Brodie and the chemist. Brodie nodded.

"From the small sample, it was almost impossible to determine. I tested it with the usual substances that I have here in the shop. There was a small reaction when I added a bit of sodium hypochlorite."

"I beg your pardon?"

"Chlorine," he explained. "Mostly used for cleaning and disinfecting in hospitals against the spread of typhus. However, I've not seen a compound like this before, although I've heard of experiments that some have tried.

"A German scientist by the name of Huber conducted several experiments with disastrous results, several people were killed," he went on to explain.

"As I remember, he was forced to leave Paris over the matter. That was four or five years ago."

What would that sort of substance have to do with Mary's murder and my sister's disappearance?

Brodie was thoughtful. "I trust ye will keep this in confidence."

Mr. Brimley nodded. "As always." He shook his head when Brodie offered to pay him.

"I don't forget the favor you did for me, Mr. Brodie. It goes a long way, to my way of thinking."

"A favor?" I asked, as we left the shop with this new information. Although I did not know yet what it might mean.

"Mr. Brimley has helped a great many people in need in the past," Brodie explained. "In turn, he needed assistance in a particular matter."

I thought of the sign above the apothecary shop.

"Someone who had need of his other medical *specialty*?" I suggested. "And you helped him in return?"

"It's not what ye'd be thinking. A man thought to extort a good sum from him over a matter.

"And you provided a *favor*."

"In a manner of speaking. I persuaded the man that it was in his best interests not to make further demands."

A most interesting way of putting it. I could only imagine how he might have persuaded him.

It was late afternoon when I returned to Mayfair.

Agatha was gone, with a note left on the table by the front door. She returned to Sussex Square as I had suggested.

I fixed myself a cold supper and retired to the parlor. There I read through the entries in my sister's journal.

She wrote of her sadness at the loss of the child months earlier. There were other entries where she seemed much improved and was looking forward to our trip to Brighton. She had written about her disappointment when that was cancelled.

I suppose that was to be expected, and in those months after I had tried to be there for her in whatever way I could, and she had seemed truly much improved and was looking forward to the holidays. Then, her more recent entries took a more serious and ominous turn...

Twelve

THE MUDGER WAS at his usual place, along with Rupert, the hound, when I arrived at the Strand in the morning.

I handed the Mudger a muffin, sliced in two with a slice of ham—my breakfast that morning, rummaged from the kitchen. The hound consumed his muffin in one bite and looked at me expectantly, as I started toward the stairs.

"Mr. Brodie was up most of the night," the Mudger commented with a frown.

"Again?" I replied, recalling our first encounter days earlier.

"It's not wot yer might be thinkin'," he replied. "He's been with Mr. Dooley since late last night."

As I recalled that was the name of one of the officers who was on the watch at St. Katherine's dock the night Mary's body was found. But what reason had he been there since the middle of the night?

In the short time of our acquaintance, I had learned that the Mudger was usually well informed as to Brodie's activities. I was suddenly most anxious.

"Has something happened?"

"Best speak with Mr. Brodie. Just thought you should be warned aforehand."

Warned?

Something had happened that he chose not to speak of—most unusual, as the Mudger was quite a talkative fellow. That sense that something had indeed happened sharpened as I turned toward the stairs that led to Brodie's office.

The office door was not locked, and I let myself in.

Brodie was at his desk. A man in a police uniform sat across from him. They spoke in quiet tones when they spoke at all, the expression on Mr. Dooley's face was weary and drawn.

Brodie looked up briefly as I entered, the only indication that he was aware of my presence as he sat in the high-backed chair. His expression could only be described as grim, in a way I had not seen before. I made myself as inconspicuous as possible as the matter seemed quite serious.

"Ye know as well as I, had it been the other way around, it would be yerself, and ye with a young family," Brodie told him.

Dooley seemed to take little comfort in the words.

"I'll go round and call on his mother," Brodie added.

Dooley shook his head. "He was my partner and friend. I'll go, sir. I appreciate it though, Inspector." He rose then, with a brief glance in my direction, the only outward indication that he was aware of my presence.

"You'll find the bastard wot did this?" he asked in parting.

Brodie nodded. "I'll find him."

"I'll be on me way then. Abberline will be expecting my report."

Brodie rose and rounded the desk. He laid a hand at Dooley's shoulder and walked with him to the door.

"Take some time the next few days. Come round any time."

Dooley nodded again.

The man's deference to Brodie did not go unnoticed. He might no longer be with the MP, certainly was no longer an inspector, but it was obvious that the loyalty and respect ran deep in spite of whatever had passed between him and Abberline, and had prompted him to leave the MP.

He looked over at me when Dooley had gone.

"Spivey is dead."

It took a moment for that to sink in.

"There was an incident last night," he explained. "It appears with the same men as before, one of them with white hair." He set his pipe at a small plate at the desk.

"Officer Thomas went after them..." Brodie went to the window and stared out at the over-cast sky.

"They saw both men, briefly." That dark gaze met mine. "By Dooley's description, the one was the same man ye saw after yer meeting with Sir Charles."

The same white-haired man I had glimpsed briefly outside the hotel, then again as I left the locksmith's shop.

Who was he, and what did he have to do with my sister's disappearance?

We spent the rest of the morning going over what I'd learned from her journal. There was her obvious sadness over the loss of the child, and mention that Charles had become most distant in the months that followed. And then there was Linnie's certainty that he was having an affair, along with a letter signed by a woman by the name of Marie.

"So it would seem," Brodie replied, in that way of his that I had quickly learned meant there was far more stirring in his thoughts that he chose not to share for the time being.

"What is this?" I asked, having discovered a shiny object beneath the disorganized chaos of papers at his desk. It was approximately the size of a large coin. It appeared to be made of brass and was embossed with what appeared to be the image of a fist holding a dagger.

"Dooley found it on the dock where Spivey was killed. He thought it might be important."

And he had brought it to Brodie, rather than hand it over to the MP for their investigation. It said a great deal about Mr. Dooley's confidence in the MP, and Chief Inspector Abberline in particular.

"It appears to be a medallion of some kind," I commented as I inspected it further. "This mark is most unusual, perhaps some fraternal organization."

"Ye have some experience with that?"

I ignored the sarcasm.

"Our father belonged to one of those secret organizations." I left it at that. No point in dredging up unpleasant memories.

"I know someone who may be able to tell us what this is and the meaning of the design. My aunt has had some business dealings with him."

I had far too many questions that had no answers. At the top of the list, what did the white-haired man have to do with this? Brodie kept to his own thoughts, no doubt of the night before and the death of Officer Thomas as we shared a meal purchased from a street vendor.

It was mid-afternoon when we secured a cab and made the trip across London, to the establishment of a man who might be able to tell us something about the medallion.

At the very least, there was no argument that we

would continue together. It seemed that we had at last reached an understanding in the matter.

~

The royal warrant with gold lettering was prominently displayed at the front window that extended out over the sidewalk of R & S Garrard, Jewelers. The three-story building was built of brick, with that bow front window, and work rooms of the royal jeweler that were on the upper floors.

Inside were glass-fronted mahogany cabinets that lined both sides of the shop with elegant pieces of silver —a tea service, platters, and several trophies displayed in one. Another cabinet contained jewelry made up of what appeared to be real diamonds, sapphires and pearls.

However, the most prestigious pieces, commissioned by the royal family were kept in vaults and only removed for one of the Garrard craftsmen to work on in those upper floor work rooms under the watchful eye of the owner himself.

"Miss Forsythe, how very pleasant to see you again." We were greeted by Mr. Haversham. He hesitated ever so slightly as he looked over at Brodie.

I made the introductions, Brodie as an acquaintance of the family, rather than his profession, which would only have raised more questions.

"How may we serve you? Something perhaps for her ladyship?" Mr. Garrard asked.

"I have come across a most interesting piece and cannot identify it." I didn't bother to explain where it was found, or the circumstances.

"Something found on one of your adventures perhaps?" he politely inquired.

In the past it was not unusual for me to return with some artifact or piece of decoration that needed his expertise. It was a sad irony that this had apparently become my latest adventure.

I smiled in response. "I thought you might be able to assist in the matter."

"Of course," he replied.

He escorted us back to one of the small private rooms, much like a sitting room, where he met with clients. He stepped behind the desk as we took chairs across from him.

I handed him the medallion Officer Dooley had found. He placed it on a black velvet pad, then took out a magnifying glass and proceeded to examine it.

"Not gold, very likely brass with gold plate over," he explained. "Adequate workmanship, very much the usual sort that one sees for fraternal organizations. However, the design is quite unique." He handed me the magnifying glass.

"There is an image of a knife and with an inscription."

I looked at it through the glass, then stepped aside so that Brodie could inspect it as well.

"I'm afraid it's not of much value." He sat back at his chair. "But most... interesting."

"In what way?" Brodie asked.

"It's very much like a military medal, though not of her Majesty's military service. I would recognize that. The inscription on the reverse appears to be either German or possibly one of the other languages of the region."

Not German, I thought, but some other language. However, we knew little more than when we'd arrived.

"This sort of thing is found in a great many places

and are quite common—coins, medallions, religious ornaments, but as I said, of little value otherwise."

"There is someone who may be able to assist with finding out who may have worn this," Brodie said as we left the shop. He waived down a cab driver.

"He left the service a couple of years ago, and does some odd work for me now and then. He used to work the streets over in German Town, and knows people there who may be able to tell us what this is and what that inscription means."

The rain had set in quite heavily as we set off, and the driver closed the cab after Brodie gave him instructions.

"Tell me about yer sister," he said. "What sort of person is she? Are ye very alike?"

I thought how best to describe Linnie.

"There are those who think of her as shy, but she simply prefers to wait and figure things out for herself. She is soft-spoken. I don't believe I've ever heard her speak out in anger or raise her voice to anyone. And she would much rather be at her painting than playing hostess at some soiree. You could say that we're quite different."

"Aye."

I looked over at Brodie. He obviously found that to be quite amusing.

"What habits? Friends?" he continued. "Where would she go if she needed to leave?"

I had thought a great deal about that since she first disappeared. My first thought was that she would come to me.

Friends? There were those she called friends, but none that I could say she was particularly close with. And because of their tendency to gossip, she would not want anyone to know that there was difficulty in her marriage. That brought me back to my first thought. She should have come to me. But she hadn't.

That could only mean that, for whatever reason, she felt she couldn't come to either me or our aunt.

"She would leave London." I was certain of it. "She has never liked the city. It reminds her too much of... the past." Our father had spent a great deal of time there before our mother died.

"And perhaps not a place Sir Charles would know of." Brodie pointed out, then on a thought, "What about one of yer aunt's estates? Might she go to one of those?"

Why was I not surprised that he knew about our aunt's other properties?

Not Kent, our aunt's country home, I immediately dismissed that. Charles knew the property well, having spent time there in the early days of their marriage. He would surely send someone there to look for her, if he hadn't already.

Some other place? Perhaps one of the other countries from my own travels?

"I envy you, going off as you please," she had once said. *"You don't give a farthing what anyone thinks. And then all of London cannot wait for your latest novel to read about it."*

"You must come with me next time," I had told her then. *"We'll plan for it together."*

"Charles would be most displeased if I were to do something like that."

There hadn't been a next time.

"Possibly France," I replied now. "We went to school there, and she loved the Louvre and the museums."

She knew her way around Paris well enough, and had acquaintances there. But without funds to do so?

Was that the reason Mary had the key sewn into the hem of her dress?

Was she sent to retrieve the contents of the box, but obviously had never arrived? And I pictured Linnie without resources, alone, perhaps terrified, hiding somewhere in the city.

The cab lurched to a stop. We had arrived in Holborn, one of the working-class districts of the East End.

Brodie paid the driver, then took my arm as we crossed the street in front of a butcher shop with parts of pig and dead fowl hanging from hooks at the window.

The lodge house was half way down the street, with steps leading up to a double door entrance. The panes of glass at the door were broken out at one side.

There was a bell pull just inside the entrance. Brodie seized it, announcing our arrival.

"Wot do yer want!" a gruff voice that might have been either a man or woman called out.

"I'm here to see Mr. Conner."

"He ain't 'ere! Ain't seen him since Tuesday when he took hisself off to the pub."

A face appeared at a doorway down the hall, then a body joined it.

"Yer with the peelers?" the woman asked, approaching cautiously. "I paid me rent tax."

"Good afternoon, Miss Carrie," he greeted her. "It's a private matter."

The tip of her head barely reached Brodie's shoulder, her hair in knotted disarray. Her gown was rumpled as if she might have slept in it. And there was the distinct scent of body odor along with alcohol about her as she looked at me with obvious curiosity.

"Like I said, he ain't 'ere. But if you find him, remind him that the rent is due or he'll find hisself out in the street!"

Brodie gave her one of his cards along with a coin.

"If ye see him, tell him to come round to see me as soon as possible. I have work for him," he added.

"Hummpf," she replied.

A new sound to add to the expanding repertoire that I was accumulating in my new partnership with him.

"Will he get the message?" I asked, as we found another cab and climbed aboard.

He nodded. "He's never gone for more than a day or two... possibly with a lady friend."

And he'd been gone since Tuesday.

"The weather is closing in and there's no more to be done today," he added. "Best get ye home."

The rain had thickened and flooded the street. Another day had passed and my sister was still out there—somewhere.

We arrived in Mayfair and the cab lurched to a stop at the curb in front of the town house. Brodie asked the driver to wait as he assisted me from the cab. He quite surprised me when he opened his umbrella and held it over both of us as he walked me to the door.

"We shall begin again tomorrow," he said, and I smiled to myself. *We* most certainly would.

I retrieved my key and inserted it into the lock. It was hardly necessary as the door swung open into the looming darkness of the house.

Brodie glanced past me. "Is there anyone else about?"

I shook my head with an uneasy feeling at my stomach.

"I sent my aunt's housekeeper back to Sussex

Square. It made no sense for her to remain when I couldn't say when I might return."

Brodie nodded. "Where's the electric switch?"

"At the left of the door, above the umbrella stand."

"Wait here." He retrieved the revolver from inside his coat and pushed open the door, then stepped past me.

The lights came on and Brodie moved across the entry to the front parlor. I followed in spite of his instructions. More lights came on, illuminating the parlor and the adjacent alcove with my writing desk, chair, and shelves of books.

The shelves had been emptied, books strewn across the floor. Drawers had been pulled from the desk and upended, papers scattered everywhere. My typewriting machine lay on its side where it had been tossed, no mean feat, considering how much it weighed.

"Oh," was all I could come up with at the sight of the destruction. And it hadn't ended there.

The entire front parlor had been sacked, two sitting chairs and a small table overturned, along with the silver tea service Linnie had given me when I first moved into the town house... as if someone had been looking for something.

"What are the other rooms?" Brodie demanded.

"The dining room and kitchen just beyond, and the servants' room."

"Stay here until I return!" he ordered.

When I would have objected, he gave me the same look I'd seen before when we encountered Spivey.

"Stay here! I'll not say it again."

It was on the tip of my tongue to tell him exactly what he could do with his instructions when he abruptly pushed past me. More lights came on as he continued his inspection of the downstairs, then returned.

"What about upstairs?"

"Two bedrooms, a bathing chamber, and my sitting room."

I was right behind him as he headed for the stairs.

He moved quickly, then returned to the landing, but I had already entered my bedroom.

It had fared no better than the parlor downstairs. Bed linens were stripped from the bed, furniture overturned including a small table where I made notes when I wasn't able to sleep. Drawers were askew or removed completely, the contents scattered about. Even the window coverings had been torn from their moorings, clothes pulled from the closet and tossed on the floor.

I made no attempt to hide my reaction at finding my home torn apart. I was furious. If I'd had Brodie's weapon and the person who had done this standing in front of me at that moment, I would have shot him.

Brodie surveyed the damage.

"What about jewelry, money? Anything else of value?"

With the mess that had been left behind it was impossible to tell. Not that I had anything of great value—mementos from my travels, photographs from my trip to Brighton with Linnie.

My manuscripts were not among the papers scattered throughout the sitting room. My finished novels were all kept at the publishers. Anything that wasn't already published was kept in the desk drawers downstairs. Fortunately I had recently turned in my latest novel.

I had never experienced this before, although I knew of others who had. On one of my travels, several fellow passengers had discovered their luggage had been tampered with, several items of value stolen. I had fared far better, as I never traveled with anything of value other than funds which I kept hidden in a pocket sewn into my corset for just that purpose. This, however, was different.

"It's as if someone was looking for something," I commented, then exchanged a look with Brodie. "The journal."

It was presently quite safe in my carpet bag, however, his expression told me that it was more than possible.

I didn't understand. "How would anyone know to look for it here?"

Was it possible someone had discovered it was missing from the lock box? If so, who else had a key?

Brodie's mouth tightened.

"Gather what ye need," he said, in a quiet voice that I'd not heard before. "And there'll be no argument in it."

It took a moment for what he was saying to sink in.

"I'm not leaving my home simply because—"

"Ye'll not stay here, and that's my final word on it."

"I'm not afraid."

He turned to me with a different look at his face.

"First Mary Ryan. Then Spivey and Officer Thomas, a good and capable man. Ye should be afraid, Mikaela Forsythe. The best place for ye is Sussex Square where Mr. Munro can protect ye."

I was now seeing a different side of Brodie—the police inspector.

"Whoever did this was looking for something," he continued. "It's safe to assume, having not found it, they'll return with the hope of finding ye here. And that little knife you carry will be no protection."

"Very well," I replied. "However, I will not endanger my aunt by going to Sussex Square."

I prided myself on being logical, and would not argue the point. He was right, of course. It was not the fact that I might be in danger if I remained that chafed. It was losing the argument. Point in his favor.

I filled the carpet bag with the clothing I could find amidst the chaos that was now my bedroom. That included a couple of my travel outfits, an extra shirtwaist, undergarments, an extra pair of walking boots that I finally located, and a handful of personal items that included my hair brush, tooth powder and brush. Brodie stopped me as I tried to set some order to the room.

"Leave it."

He turned off the electric in each room as we returned downstairs, the town house once more plunged into darkness.

As we left, I glanced across the street at the other residences along the street in this *safe* part of London and the shadows between. I wondered if someone was there even now, watching us.

"I'll make certain the watch doubles their patrol here until it's safe for ye to return," he assured me.

It was not the first time I had the impression that, although Brodie might no longer be with the Metropolitan Police, he still carried some authority with others. It was an authority I was certain Chief Inspector Abberline would have preferred didn't exist.

We climbed into the cab. There hadn't been time to discuss where I might go. I thought of the Midland Hotel, where I had stayed in the past before departing on my travels.

"Number Two Hundred Four, the Strand," Brodie called up to the driver.

I looked over at him quite surprised.

"Ye'll be safe enough there until we can make other arrangements."

I was far too exhausted, both physically and mentally, to argue the matter. It seemed most logical since I had spent most of the past few days there, and I was far from concerned what people might think.

I nodded as the cab lurched away from the curb. I hadn't realized how late it was as I watched the darkened fronts of other town houses disappear in the downpour that only seemed to add to the wretchedness of the day.

IN MY TRAVELS I have slept on board a ship, on trains and other conveyances, not to mention in a tent in the desert. I have also slept on the floor of a hut, and once on a bed with sheer silk bed hangings, often fully clothed, should the need to leave quickly arise.

This was none of those, as I slowly opened my eyes and took in my present surroundings.

The room was spartanly furnished with dark wood wainscoting at equally dark walls. A coal stove was at one wall, with a mantel above. A wash basin sat at the wall opposite.

The bed I presently occupied, that ranked somewhere between the floor of a hut and a bunk bed aboard a steamship, was questionable as far as comfort.

I sat up slowly and pushed back the thick blanket and remembered precisely how I came to occupy Angus Brodie's bed.

There had been no argument or discussion over the matter. For the time being I would be safe. No one would think to look for me here. I had the use of his room, and he would occupy the outer office at night, something he assured me that he was quite used to.

It solved the problem of logistics, a term that quite easily covered a lot of territory in our partnership. It most certainly saved time, for Brodie to *'send round his reports'*. I fully intended to remain part of the investigation, and therefore no need for a report to update me on his progress.

"Unless, of course, it offends ye at being offered my room," he had added.

It seemed Mr. Brodie had learned in a very short period of time precisely how to get under my skin.

I proceeded to tell him the places I had slept in different countries, not the least was the desert in a caravan with several Bedouin encamped nearby. Then I had slammed the door to the room in Brodie's face and crawled into bed.

"Set the chair at the door if yer concerned about the arrangement," he had informed me through the door.

I wasn't, and did not remember much beyond the few sounds from the adjacent office as he had moved about.

This morning was another matter.

I needed to speak with Brodie about a thought that had come to me in the middle of the night.

It was obvious that someone was looking for something at the town house. It seemed logical that it might be my sister's journal. The question was, what was in the journal that might be a threat to someone?

I made use of water in the pitcher at the basin, then pinned my hair into a coil on top of my head.

I had discovered on my travels, often with limited accommodations in the places I explored, that simpler was better. No ringlets or elaborately woven hairstyle that ladies in London copied from Paris or New York. It was far easier to pull my hair back, twist it up into a long roll, secure it with pins, and be done with it.

I had once considered cutting it all off as I had seen once on the stage in Paris, until Linnie pointed out that the actress obviously wore a short wig for the role of Joan of Arc. I was not of a mind to go about in a wig that looked much like a skinned rat or possum. End of conversation.

I straightened my clothes and laced up my boots, then left the room and discovered that I was quite alone, except for a hastily scrawled note at the desk: *Gone to make inquiries regarding "S".*

That very likely meant that he had gone to make inquiries about Spivey from among his sources, and perhaps the MP regarding the disturbance at the town house.

The smell of coffee, strong almost to the point of a danger for human consumption, drew me to the coal stove.

According to the wall clock, it was half past ten in the morning, and by the view out that smudged window of Brodie's office, it was still raining.

It was the sort of rain London was famous for—cold, drizzling with intermittent downpours, then more drizzle and more downpours.

Undeterred, and determined to assist in finding what information I might, I returned to the adjacent room. I donned my coat and hat, and seized the carpetbag and umbrella.

I opened the office door to find Rupert sprawled across the entrance—protective hound on duty. A scratch behind both ears had him waiting expectantly at my feet while I navigated the workings of the new lock at the door. I hadn't a key but I was determined to take no chances on another *unannounced visitor* by leaving the door unlocked.

I pulled the door closed behind me and ignored that

nagging little voice that said Brodie would not be pleased with my going off on my own. I justified my decision with the philosophy that two working the case was far better than one, potentially resolving the issue in half the time. Or something very near that.

At the very least there were places where he obviously had a far better chance of obtaining information, while the London Library was the sort of place where I might be able to obtain other valuable information.

I encountered my second *guard* at the bottom of the stairs, under the overhang, protected against the rain. The Mudger grinned up at me with that lopsided, gap-toothed smile that I found I was becoming quite fond of.

"Mornin', miss. Right fine day we're havin'."

That is, if one considered the present downpour to be a fine day.

I frowned at the Mudger's threadbare jacket. Considering his disability and short stature, the tail of the full-length coat had been tucked under.

I had the thought that he was much like a gatekeeper. He kept track of the comings and goings on the street at the same time he guarded the lower stairs, while Rupert guarded the upstairs landing.

"Where might you be off to, when Mr. Brodie said you was to be stayin' upstairs?"

"Something to eat," I replied, not entirely a lie as my stomach grumbled at not having eaten since the previous afternoon, and with only that strong coffee this morning.

I had discovered a long time ago that saying less was far better than going on and on with some elaborate explanation, particularly when striking out on my own. It always led to more questions, then more explanations. Simpler was far easier.

"I can get that for you," he announced.

He had obviously been well informed as to his duties regarding me.

"And I need to purchase some personal lady items," I added, and saw the immediate reaction to that in what could only be described as a grimace on his face at the thought of accompanying me while I purchased *feminine items*.

"What should I tell Mr. Brodie when he returns?" he asked.

"That his coffee is dreadful," I called back over my shoulder as I stepped off the curb and navigated the river of water and traffic at the street.

I was mindful of the night before at my apartment, and kept a careful eye on the street and on the people I passed, as more questions ran through my thoughts.

Who had broken into my apartment? What were they looking for? The journal?

Under the circumstances, that seemed a likely possibility. That then raised the question—what was in it that was of importance? And what did that have to do with my sister's disappearance?

At the other side of the street, and out of sight of the entrance to the office, I waved down a cab and gave the driver the address for the London Library.

It was just before noon when I arrived at St. James Square.

The library was a familiar place, a quiet haven for my curiosity as a child that smelled of old wood, documents, and leather-bound volumes.

Shelves reached from floor to ceiling, and there was the familiar scratch of a pen from the writer's room, along with a whispered question for the clerk, and the faint hum of the lift as it slowly rose from the ground floor. Quite deliciously, this haven of books was rumored to have concealed more than one amorous pair in the shadows at the back of the Issue Hall, where books were signed out.

It was here that I had nurtured an avid curiosity of people and places after consuming the volumes in my aunt's private library at Sussex Square. And it was here that I had planned my first adventure after returning from school in Paris, having read several accounts about the history of Constantinople.

That first adventure was intended to quench my curiosity of such places. It had only whetted my appetite for more. And at least one volume of each of *Emma Fortescue's* adventures now resided in the library.

"Good morning, Miss Forsythe," Mr. Reginald Soames, Chief Librarian, greeted me from behind the main desk in the main room.

"It has been some time since your last visit. It is a pleasure to have you with us again. How may we serve you this morning?"

"I am looking for newspaper articles on a particular subject that would have appeared in the dailies and other newspapers a few years ago."

"Ah, the newspaper archive."

He motioned to a clerk behind the counter who was industriously cataloguing new books. He was a gangly young man with a bowl haircut and the faint appearance of side whiskers that struggled to make an appearance.

"William is most familiar with the archives." He turned to the young clerk.

"Please escort Miss Forsythe to the archive room and assist in whatever she may need. " He turned to me.

"We now have electric in the basement archives to make your reading much easier, and if I may inquire...

perhaps a new installment from *Miss Emma Fortescue* is forthcoming?"

The question hung in the air with curiosity as to my purpose that I was not of a mind to share. I was aware of his thinly disguised criticism of my writing endeavors and the adventures of Miss Emma Fortescue.

Or perhaps more accurately, the misadventures were more accurate due to the people *she* encountered, as well as the flaunting of the usual conventions of society.

It was not the usual literature Mr. Soames prided himself on for the library that ran more to the classics. He had even been most critical of Jane Austen. However, it appeared that demand from patrons had overwhelmed his opinions.

"Thank you," I replied. "As always, I appreciate your assistance." And with that I followed William.

We passed the writing room with its long tables and the reading room with its alcoves and nooks where I had spent many hours. We then descended the stairs to the basement, where the lift did not reach. It was here that newspaper, magazine, and monthly archives were kept on rolls of film and contained in metal canisters to protect them from the damp and light.

Film archives were relatively new, the technique introduced at the Exhibition some years before. In the past decade, more and more newspapers and magazines had their publications archived on film. It was an ingenious solution, rather than thousands of actual copies that took up an incredible amount of space, and were painstaking to search through when it came to finding a particular article.

The basement of the library was a labyrinthine warren of rooms where one might easily become lost if they didn't know their way about. William gave a brief nod as he escorted me to a table with the microfilm reading machine.

It was a marvelous invention with a viewing panel and twin spools where the film was threaded. A light below illuminated the images at the turn of the handle. When one was finished, the roll of film was rewound and then returned to the storage canister that protected it.

Each canister was labeled with the name of the newspaper and the date range of the issues on that particular role of film. It was most marvelous!

I'd brought the notes I'd made, including the information Mr. Brimley had provided. I requested the newspaper archive beginning six years earlier that included the time frame Mr. Brimley had mentioned.

William returned with a canister the size of a biscuit tin that contained a roll of film. He set it on the spindle at the reading machine and threaded it beneath the plate with the viewer, and I began my search for any information about the incident Mr. Brimley had spoken of.

Major news events were usually found on the first or second page of the dailies. It made the process somewhat easier than scrolling through every page of each issue of the newspaper.

I was considerably well into the fourth roll of film, when I found what I was looking for. The headline was in bold letters on the front page of the 06 June 1884 edition of the London Times:

PARIS, FRANCE.

TWENTY PEOPLE DIE IN FAILED EXPERIMENT!

A scientific experiment resulted in the deaths of nineteen persons, and another person later succumbed to in-

juries in Paris, after a failed experiment conducted by Dr. Friedrich Huber.

The scientist, once a student of chemistry at the University of Berlin, was also taken to hospital with severe injuries.

The Université de Paris where Dr. Huber is a professor, had previously banned the experiment due to its dangerous substances.

I made detailed notes of the article. Then, according to later editions of the newspaper, Dr. Huber's teaching position was terminated at the University of Paris as a result of that disastrous experiment. He was forced to leave France after recovering from his own injuries amid rumors that he was associated with a dissident group known as the Black Hand.

I continued to scroll through the rest of the film archive for something that might tell me what had happened to Huber after he left France. I discovered another entry from three years earlier about an incident at the railway station in Budapest.

A group of anarchists had gathered to march on the imperial palace—the date was the same as my arrival there on one of my trips! The name of the group—the Black Hand! Several more incidents that occurred across Europe were attributed to them amid growing political unrest.

Their methods included demonstrations, attacks on local newspaper publishers, and suspected attacks on members of aristocracy, meant to cause unrest and suspicion. For his part, it appeared that Dr. Huber had quite successfully disappeared.

What did it mean? And how was it connected to the deaths of three people, and my sister's disappearance?

"I'll be taking these books upstairs, miss," William informed me. "I can retrieve additional film for you when I return."

"I only have one more roll to view, then I'll be ready to leave," I assured him, with a glance at the clock behind the desk. I wanted to get back to the office on the Strand and inform Brodie about what I'd learned.

William's footsteps echoed in the hallway, then faded at the stairs as I continued to scan the last roll of film.

There were recent articles about political unrest in Madrid, demonstrations by workers in Vienna, and an explosion that had derailed a train carrying the Ambassador of Hungary. At the time, the incident was blamed on Serbian anarchists amid rumors of a secret society they belonged to. The *Black Hand* was rumored to be responsible for the explosion.

I sat back at the chair, my thoughts racing—growing political unrest, violence in the capitols of Europe, and a scientist who had experimented with chemicals that killed several people before he disappeared. That same name was in my sister's journal.

I made additional notes then put my notebook in the carpet bag. A sound at the stairway reminded me that I needed to return the last roll of film.

"I've finished now," I called out. "I'll leave the film at the desk."

There was only silence. Then, that sound came again from the direction of the stairs.

"Is someone there?"

Again there was no response.

My instincts have always served me well, and I had learned to rely on them. Now, a warning tingled at my skin.

I gathered the carpet bag and stepped away from the

table into the surrounding darkness with only the light from a single overhead fixture over the nearby stacks that contained books to be rebound.

I knew the library well enough, including the basement. It was a quiet place where sound was muffled by stone walls and rows of shelves.

It was a private place where I had searched information about foreign countries, often left alone as the library staff went about their work of cataloging books by Dickens, Jane Austen, or the American author Mark Twain.

But it was different now, the surrounding darkness permeated only by the faint overhead glow of that single light at the beginning of each row along with the musty smell of books, the usual dampness of old buildings, and something else that tightened at the back of my neck.

Someone else *was* there, someone who chose not to reveal himself.

I turned and headed for the row of shelves filled with newspapers and magazines yet to be archived, with the purpose of coming around behind whoever was there.

The aisle between the rows was dim, with deep shadows down the length of each one. Seeing no one there, I continued onto the next row, my hand wrapped around the handle of my umbrella.

Row after row, and I still saw no one. But that certainty of someone else in the basement wouldn't go away, and then a distinct sound of someone moving as I moved, then stopping when I stopped.

It would have been easy to convince myself that it was just my imagination. The mind often conjures things from our fears, only to be proven wrong.

Then a new sound came, very close now. It was the tread of footsteps, slowly moving closer. Along with something else that mingled with the musty smell of the archives.

I turned down the next row, determined to confront whoever was there.

I quickened my steps, then rounded the next corner, the umbrella clutched in both hands like a weapon.

Mr. Soames suddenly loomed before me. "Miss Forsythe?"

His face was quite ashen, blending with the gray of side whiskers and mustache, his expression one of alarm, as if confronted by some wild-eyed person.

"I apologize, Miss Forsythe. I didn't mean to frighten you."

I lowered my umbrella. "I thought someone else might be there," I explained.

"Someone else?"

He had removed a handkerchief from the breast pocket of his coat and wiped his forehead.

"I came to assist as young William was given another task. I saw no one else. There are few in the library this time of day," he continued. "Only the ladies who belong to a reading group and meet regularly upstairs. I do apologize."

He was repeating himself, and in spite of his assurances I was not convinced there hadn't been someone else in the archives. I was not given to hysterics or an overactive imagination.

I thanked him.

"You've been most helpful."

Fourteen

THE STRAND WAS CROWDED with the usual congestion of carts, other conveyances, and people —workmen, housekeepers, going about their shopping in spite of the weather, in that way that those who lived in London were quite used to and simply carried on.

I stepped down from the cab and paid the driver.

The Mudger had retreated under the overhang at the entrance that led to the stairs. He wore a tattered woolen scarf wrapped around his neck as smoke from a cigarette encircled his head. He squinted at me through a smoke haze.

"Mr. Brodie's been askin' for you."

I had hoped to return before Brodie discovered I had gone out on my own, and thereby avoid what I could only assume would be a confrontation regarding the rules of our association. However that was not to be.

"He has an old acquaintance from the MP with him. You might be mindful. Mr. Conner can be a bit of a rough sort."

Whatever that might mean. However, I had learned in our brief acquaintance that the Mudger's observations were often spot-on.

I handed Rupert a meat pastry with two for the Mudger, and thanked him for the information.

He grinned. "I thank you kindly, miss. And Rupert does as well."

It seemed the name for the hound had caught on. I approached the stairway.

A man from the MP?

Was it possible there was some word about my sister?

It was what I had hoped for; however it forced me to confront the possibility— given Mary Ryan's murder as well as two other murders—that the news might be the worst possible outcome.

I preferred to be optimistic and told myself that there was the possibility that the news might just as easily be positive, that perhaps my sister had been found safe.

Brodie was at his desk as I arrived; the man known as Mr. Conner was seated across from him. A bottle of my aunt's whisky sat between them with two half-empty glasses. There was a pause in their conversation. Both men looked up as I entered the office.

"Miss Forsythe." Brodie's expression was unreadable, I thought, as I acknowledged his guest, a fellow Scot, I surmised by the name. It was confirmed by the accent, much like Brodie's.

Mr. Conner stood and took my hand. "Pleased to make yer acquaintance, Miss Forsythe. Brodie has spoken of ye."

I could only imagine what he might have told him.

Mr. Conner was as tall as Brodie, though somewhat older with close-cropped graying hair and beard. He did not wear the uniform of the MP, but was dressed much like a common worker on the street. Crisp blue eyes twinkled with what could only be amusement. Or perhaps flirtation?

It appeared, from their relaxed manner, not to mention the half-empty glasses at the desk, that their meeting was congenial, and the tight knot at my stomach began to slowly ease.

"Ye failed to tell me how pretty Miss Forsythe is," Mr. Conner commented, using that smile to full effect as he offered me his chair.

"We were discussing that Mrs. Brown seemed quite put out over something when I left word for ye," Brodie reminded him. "She mentioned that she wasn't willing to take yer rent out in trade."

"Ah, yes, Mrs. Brown," Mr. Conner replied. He shrugged and pulled up an overstuffed chair, then retrieved his whisky with a smile in my direction.

"She's not married," he explained with that twinkle in his eyes. "But she thinks the title gives her respectability. The truth of the matter is, that *I* was the one who was not willing to take the rent out in trade." He winked at me.

"The woman has certain... appetites," he went onto explain. "And I was not of a mind to accommodate her. There was some peculiar notion about something involving fruit as I recall. She said she read about it in a book by some woman named Emma... " He held out his glass for more whisky, which Brodie accommodated.

"I didn't even know she could read beyond her numbers for the rent," he continued.

Good heavens! A book by a woman named *Emm*a? Was it possible he was referring to my erstwhile heroine, Emma Fortescue?

At the reference to fruit, it seemed most likely. The room was suddenly quite warm. I caught Brodie's sideways glance and chose to ignore him.

"It's a verra fine whisky." Conner raised his glass. "Never let it be said James Conner passed up a good single malt."

His gaze fastened on me over the rim of the tumbler with interest.

"Not yer usual sort of client, Brodie. Wouldn't she be better served by our brothers in crime with the MP?"

"*She* would not," I replied, quite put off at being talked around as if I was a piece of furniture, or head of cabbage that someone was not at all certain what to do with.

I was more than familiar with the habit of the male of the species to brush aside or ignore the fact that a woman might have something important to contribute.

"I am working with Mr. Brodie in the matter of my sister's disappearance," I explained so that there would be no misunderstanding.

"And we've already asked for Mr. Abberline's assistance. He was most... uncooperative. I am certainly not of a mind to waste further time with him in the matter.

"However, if you have something to contribute," I suggested. "It would be greatly appreciated. Three people have been murdered, and I would understand if you were hesitant to participate, possibly concerned for your own well-being. "

Mr. Conner slammed his hand down at the desk, a new expression at his face.

"By God, this could be interesting," he replied, that twinkle in his eye. "I was with the MP for thirty years, Miss Forsythe, and retired only because of an injury. I work with Brodie from time to time, when it interests me and for a fee of course, not to mention a wee dram from time to time.

"It's only the devil I fear," he continued, with what

could only be described as a flirtatious smile. "However ye might change my mind."

I decided that I liked Mr. Conner very much. He was gruff and rough around the edges, but could be very charming.

"Have you considered that it's very possible the devil is a woman?" I pointed out.

The smile deepened. "I have often thought that in my encounters with the fairer sex. At least yer no weak sister. But that can get ye into trouble."

"You have no need to be concerned on my behalf, Mr. Conner. I am quite capable of taking care of myself."

"Oh, I like her very much," he announced, with a smile that no doubt had persuaded several women along the way regarding the rent, with or without the fruit.

"She'll do. But best keep an eye on her." He sat back at the chair. "Now tell me what this is about."

Over the next hour, Brodie explained everything that we knew.

"Nasty business, the disappearance of a woman, and her maid murdered. And now two more? Thomas and this man Spivey? It's not unusual for a..." Conner hesitated with a glance over at Brodie, then back at me.

"For a lady to take herself off over a disagreement, or an affair?" I suggested, then added, "That is quite impossible. There are reasons she wouldn't." I didn't go into details. The reasons didn't matter.

He looked over at Brodie. "It's been known to happen, especially among the upper class. A disagreement, or possibly some mental fit. A woman from the lower classes would settle matters in another way. Do ye remember the Adams case?

"First it was a toe that hobbled the poor man," Mr. Conner explained. "Then it was the woman's initials carved on his chest—she was a rather forceful sort. But the worst of it was the other appendage found in an alley. It was the initials that clinched the case however, otherwise we would have been sore put with just a toe and the..."

I interrupted his somewhat colorful account of that previous case that no doubt was for my benefit.

There seemed no better time than the present to inform Brodie what I'd learned at the library.

"I found newspaper articles regarding the information Mr. Brimley provided us."

"Brimley? The pharmacist?" Conner replied.

Brodie nodded. "He examined some potential evidence."

"Something ye just happened to come across that the police surgeon missed," Conner assumed with that flinty smile.

"Aye, skin tissue found under the girl's fingernails. There was a certain chemical, not commonly found, in the tissue."

"No doubt from her attacker as she put up a struggle. Common enough when someone is attacked. I wonder how her attacker might have obtained the chemical?" Conner added with a bemused expression.

"What did our esteemed colleague in science have to say in the matter?" he asked.

I went over everything from my notes, beginning with the newspaper headline about the explosion as a result of Huber's experiment five years earlier. I then explained that it was rumored that Huber was developing some sort of poisonous gas, and his association with a group called the Black Hand.

"And ye believe this information about the scientist may have a part in yer sister's disappearance," Conner concluded.

Brodie nodded. "There were traces of a sulphur dichloride and ethylene in the tissue samples."

Conner's gaze sharpened. "Not the usual sort of thing a maid or a common worker in the East End might have upon herself."

He set the empty glass at the desk and pushed back his chair.

"My compliments to Lady Antonia," he told me. "A verra fine whisky." He pulled on his coat and cap.

Why, I thought, was I surprised that he knew where the whisky had come from? I made a mental note to ask my aunt about that when next I saw her.

Brodie retrieved the medallion and handed it to him. "This was found on the street where Officer Thomas was killed."

"From the murderer?"

"Possibly," Brodie replied. "It doesn't appear to be a common piece."

Conner nodded. "Dagger and some words on the reverse; could be some sort of brotherhood, rights of initiation, that sort of thing."

"Possibly," Brodie replied.

"Aye. There are new faces in the East End with every ship that comes in," Conner said, with a thoughtful expression.

"I'll make inquiries among people I know and see if there's been any word about this group called the Black Hand. I'll send word round when I have something."

He touched the bill of his cap. "A genuine pleasure, Miss Forsythe." He looked back over his shoulder at Brodie.

"I'll take my fee for this in a bottle of whisky."

When he had gone, Brodie rose from the desk, downed the last of the whisky in his glass, then seized his coat. He was already out the door and halfway down the stairs.

He had crossed the street when I reached the bottom of the stairs. Not a good sign, I thought. So much for thinking he might have decided to overlook the fact that I had taken myself off alone to the library.

"Where are we going?" I asked, as I caught up with him. Still no response.

The farther we went, the more run-down the terraced buildings that were stacked cheek-by-jowl with run-down store fronts.

Stares followed as we passed by, from those who waited under overhangs for the weather to let up, and a woman who swept out the front of a shop. Coal smoke trapped the smell of decay, poverty, and squalor.

"Since I am paying for your services, Mr. Brodie, I must insist that you tell me where we are going..."

"*Lady items*?" he replied.

"I beg your pardon?"

"Ye told the Mudger that ye were going off to purchase *'lady items,'* so as to put him off following ye, when I had specifically told him that he was to do so."

To say that I was not prepared for that particular response was an understatement.

Brodie continued on without breaking stride, forcing me to quicken mine.

"I am familiar with the library, and it seemed the logical place to make inquiries about the information Mr. Brimley gave us." I was quite out of breath attempting to keep up with him.

"You were off and about as well," I pointed out.

He stopped in front of a building at Number One Hundred Six, Ludgate. It was like every other one on the street, brick walls with crumbling mortar, a single entrance with a small angled roof over the entrance that leaked far more rain than it kept out. A red lantern glowed in the window at the ground floor.

"Ye lied about where ye were going. Mr. Cavendish went looking for ye. Not an easy task with his limitations."

"Cavendish?" By his description, I realized that he could only mean the Mudger.

"Few people know his real name, and he prefers it that way," Brodie continued, his words sharp in the cold afternoon air. "And for some reason, which I canna fathom, he has taken a liking to ye.

"Ye'll not treat him that way again. Is that clear, Miss Forsythe?" He was most adamant.

I was rapidly discovering that anger was a far different emotion with Angus Brodie. It could be quiet, softly spoken, and uncompromising, far more effective than shouting at the walls. Or at me, as the case might be.

It was on the tip of my tongue to inform him exactly what I thought of his manner as well as taking himself off without me. I did not.

His words cut sharply, a reminder of something that I loathed in other people—deception for one's own gain. To say the shoe did not fit particularly well on the other foot was an understatement.

"You're quite right, I should not have lied." However, I wasn't about to apologize for taking myself off to the library. I had found valuable information that we would not have had otherwise.

"I will apologize to the Mudger... Mr. Cavendish, when we return."

Having said that, I realized by the expression at his face that Brodie had been prepared for an argument in the least, a pitched battle over the matter at the most.

The truth was, and I was not prepared to admit this now, I needed Brodie.

He had managed in a short amount of time, with my help of course, to learn more about Mary's murder and my sister's disappearance than the Metropolitan Police, or my brother-in-law. And that was most important to me.

A woman had emerged at the ground floor entrance to Number One Hundred Six ending our conversation over the matter for the time being.

She was dressed much the same as the woman I had seen coming out of Brodie's office that first day. That is, to say that she was dressed was an overstatement.

She smiled, exposing a gap of missing teeth, and walked up to Brodie.

"Now, what might you be looking for, luv?" she asked, sliding her hand into the front of Brodie's overcoat.

"Sixpence for a toss, double for the night, yer money well spent." Her hand wandered lower.

I watched with growing interest as Brodie disentangled himself from her.

"Not today, Lizzie. However there's a coin in it for information." He handed her one.

"Is Annie Flynn about?"

She took the coin. "Wot might she be able to do fer ya that I can't?"

Then, as if she just noticed that I stood in the foyer, listening to their fascinating exchange, suddenly it was as if a light bulb lit up, a rather dim bulb to be certain.

"Wot's *she* got to do with this?" she demanded then exclaimed. "A threesome? If that's wot yer be lookin' for, Brodie, I can accommodate ye fer sure. Might be fun, but it will cost you more."

"Annie Flynn," Brodie reminded her, less than cordial this time.

"Right," Lizzie finally agreed. "Second floor, first on the left with a bell over the door. But she's already got a customer. Let me know, if you reconsider." She indicated the door across the way with that gap-toothed smile.

"I guarantee you'll get yer money's worth."

The door snapped shut behind her, and the colorful exchange ended.

"A threesome?" I inquired. "And who is Annie Flynn?"

Brodie's expression was somewhat less than amused. "An acquaintance of Spivey's, according to information that Conner provided.

"Wait here," he told me. However, I was already moving up the stairs. I wasn't about to miss this.

"Second floor, first door on the left," I repeated over my shoulder.

And with a bell over the door, as I discovered. Much like a shopkeeper to announce customers. How ingenious. Obviously, Annie Flynn was a most enterprising sort.

Brodie quickly stepped around me.

"These situations can be dangerous, particularly if she has someone with her. Yer to stay back. Do ye understand?"

"Of course." I nodded agreeably. I decided that under the circumstances it was possibly best that I didn't argue the point.

"Are you going to ring the bell?" I inquired.

He glared at me as he approached the door and knocked. He was about to pull the bell cord when the door was jerked opened just enough to reveal the face of a woman.

"Annie Flynn?" he asked.

"Might be. Wot you want? The landlord send you? I'll have the rent money in a couple of hours."

"I'm here about Mr. Spivey. I'd like to ask ye some questions."

She looked him over. "You with the bloody peelers?"

"No, it's a private matter. It will be worth yer time."

"If he owes you money, you'll have to look elsewhere," she snapped.

"Wot's the trouble, Annie?" a man's voice came through that narrow opening at the door. It was followed by the sound of someone moving about the room. The door was suddenly jerked open, and a very large, very naked man filled the opening.

"What the bloody devil do you want?" he demanded.

"I'm here to speak with Miss Flynn. My business is with her," Brodie replied.

I listened to their exchange from a half dozen feet away.

The change in Brodie was subtle, but I'd seen it before. That mask that came down over his features, his hand slipping inside the front of his overcoat where I knew he kept his pistol.

"Go off," the man replied. "She's busy."

He started to close the door. Brodie blocked it with his boot.

"Ye have a choice," he told the man. "Step aside, or ye'll find yerself at the bottom of the stairs."

Brodie had him in height, but Annie Flynn's 'friend' was well-muscled, even quite naked, which was most interesting, I thought, and amusing.

"Is that right?" the man demanded, and in the next instant everything suddenly changed.

He lunged at Brodie, throwing him back against the rail at the landing and for a split second I was afraid they might both go over and end up at the bottom of the stairs. The man then landed a blow to Brodie's face and drew a knife that apparently was in his hand all along, considering he had no pockets.

I could offer the excuse later that I lost all sense of self control. However that was not the case as I swept the man's feet out from under him with a perfectly executed move, then aimed the end of my umbrella at the indentation of flesh just above the collar bone.

Where, I thought in the heat of the moment, was master Tanaka when I had executed such a perfect maneuver?

In my sensei's stoic manner, he would have simply nodded, then continued the lesson.

As for now, with the tip of my umbrella pressed at his throat, it was enough that Annie Flynn's friend was on his back at the floor. The knife had been jarred from his hand when he fell. And by the expression at his face, he was uncertain what I might do next.

He shouted at Brodie, a perfect example of Master Tanaka's teachings that most persons were usually quite stunned by such a move. And another would not be necessary.

"Get 'er off!" he screamed. "Get 'er off me afore she rams the bloody thing down me throat."

Mission accomplished, as Brodie kicked the knife well beyond reach, hauled the man to his feet, then slammed him against the wall beside the door. My umbrella had been replaced by the pistol, aimed at the man's eye.

"Get yer clothes, and leave," Brodie ordered. "Now!"

There was no argument this time. The man merely glared at both of us and returned to the room. He emerged, dressed in his trousers and made a dash for the stairs.

Brodie picked up the knife and pocketed it, but not before giving me a look quite different from his usual disapproval. Either terrified or in a high temper over the loss of a customer, Annie Flynn slammed the door. He kicked it open.

I was quite impressed.

"I didn't do nothin'!" Annie shouted. "Stay away from me!"

My exposure to the culture of London's East End didn't end with a naked man or rumpled bedcovers as I entered the room behind Brodie.

There was a small table with the left-overs of dried food, along with an assortment of odd implements that could only be described as most curious. There was a pair of pincers, a coiled whip, and a leather object that much looked like a...

"Leave me alone! First Spivey, now I lose a good-paying customer!" Annie Flynn screeched.

I'd quite had enough of her tirade as other assorted lodgers poked their heads from their rooms to see what the matter might be. Shouts echoed up the stairwell while the sound of running feet were heard followed by the slamming of a door. Another departing customer perhaps?

"Do shut up!" I told her.

Quite unexpected, it had the effect of getting her attention. She stared at me as if I had invoked a curse on her, which I had considered. I took advantage of the moment, shoved her into a chair at the table, and raised my umbrella.

"If you move from that chair, I will put out your eye!"

Not that I would have actually carried out the threat. It was only necessary that she believed that I would.

For her part, Annie Flynn remained seated and glared at me.

For his part, with that cut at his face from the blow he'd taken, Brodie looked over at me with more than a little surprise.

"I believe we can get on with this now," he said, and took the chair opposite Annie Flynn.

"It will be worth yer time," he explained to her, and laid out several coins that he deliberately kept in front of him at the table.

"Wot about her?" she asked, angling an evil look at me that made it difficult to understand how a man would find her appealing. But then, what did I know about such commerce. She pulled the front of her gown closed over her breasts. Not that it was much of an improvement.

"No harm will come to ye," Brodie replied, with a look over at me.

"Who are you?" Annie asked. "And wot's it to do with poor Spivey?"

"Mr. Spivey found a friend of mine murdered at the docks," I explained. "A young woman by the name of Mary Ryan."

"That poor girl wot got her throat cut?"

I nodded. "We would like to find the person responsible."

"I s'pose there ain't no harm in a few questions," she replied, far more agreeable now. "If there's coin in it."

"There will be if ye cooperate," Brodie replied.

"Right," she replied, more proof that money could purchase almost anything, including love.

"How well did ye know Spivey?" Brodie asked, which I thought somewhat ridiculous under the circumstances, but said nothing.

"Spivey was good ter me, as long as there was enough of the drink. If you get my meanin'. And he was regular, which is more than I can say for others. With him, I always knew I could pay the rent on time, but then he come up with a good deal more than he made at the docks."

"How much more?"

"He scored twenty pounds! Twenty pounds!" she repeated. "I ain't never seen that much money in me life. And he said there was more to come on account 'o another job the two men wanted him to do."

"What sort of job?"

"He only said it was like the first one."

"Did he tell ye anything about the men? A name or something the men might have said? What they looked like?"

"Only that the one fella was enough to scare the dead. Said he was pale as a ghost with white hair. And didn't talk much."

Brodie and I exchanged a look at the description.

"What about the other man?" he continued.

Annie shrugged. "Spivey didn't say much, only that he spoke with an accent. He was supposed to meet them again in three days, and then...

"Now Spivey's dead," she grumbled. "And I'm hard put comin' up with the rent money."

"Did ye ever meet him at the docks?"

Annie shrugged. "There was times when he was workin' late. We was together, you know," she added.

It was obvious what that meant. However considering the woman Maggie at the Old Bell, it was safe to say Spivey wasn't what could be described as *devoted*.

"We'd go over to the local pub when he was through for the day and have ourselves a pint."

And now Annie was with someone else, only days later. A testament to true love, I thought.

"What about the girl that was found in the water at

the docks?" Brodie continued. "Did he say anything about her?"

Annie shook her head. "I don't know nothin' 'bout that poor girl." But the expression at her face, the way her gaze slid away said something far different.

Brodie took out another coin and laid it on the table. Annie's gaze widened.

"I remember now, Spivey might o' said somethin' about that..." she continued.

He placed another coin on the table.

"Like I said, when I asked him about the money, he said it was for the job the men wanted.

"But it didn't make no sense ter me," she continued. "He said they wanted him to get rid of a body. Not that Spivey objected to that sort of thing. There's always a body showin' up somewhere in the East End.

"Like them poor women that was murdered the same as that girl. Strange part was, though, they had the body with them, and told Spivey to put her in the water, then let on like he found her there."

She looked over at Brodie. "Why would anyone want ter put a body in the water just to pull it out again?"

Unless, I thought, it was to make it *look* as if Mary had been killed there and in the same manner as the other women who had been brutally murdered in Whitechapel! And to possibly send the police in the wrong direction in their investigation.

But if Mary wasn't killed at St. Katherine's dock, then where was she killed and what did it mean?

"Do you remember anything else Spivey might have said about his meeting with these men?" I asked, in spite of the warning look Brodie gave me.

"It's important," I insisted, which required another coin.

"He said something about the coach they arrived in with the girl's body."

A coach? Not the usual hack or cab that was seen in this part of London. Nor a wagon or cart that might be used for that sort of thing.

Brodie placed another coin on the table. When she would have grabbed it, he laid his hand over it.

"What about the coach?"

She glared at him. "He said it was a fancy rig, one of them private coaches that the nobs ride around in. Not like wot you see 'round here. And he said the team was all lathered up, like they'd been runnin' a ways. They was high steppers, like what you see when the Queen is out and about."

A fancy coach and a team of horses that had been running. My stomach tightened at the possibility of what that might mean.

"Did he say anything about the *other* job they wanted him to do?"

"He said it was the same. I took it ter mean they had another body the wanted to get rid of. But now Spivey's dead," Annie lamented.

Another body? My sister's body?

I took a slow, steady breath to calm my thoughts. It couldn't be.

Annie Flynn wiped what appeared to be a tear with the edge of her dressing gown, in mourning no doubt.

The question was, what was she mourning for? Spivey? Or the loss of a customer?

"I was hopin' he'd take me to Brighton," she continued. "Wot with the extra money he was goin' to make. I ain't never been to Brighton."

A *job* was how Spivey had described it, something to be taken care of, like taking out the garbage or sweeping the carpet.

And then another *job* just like it. A private coach

and two men, one of them pale-haired and seen outside the Grosvenor Hotel, and two bodies to be disposed of in a part of London that already had the reputation for five unsolved murders.

Was it possible my brother-in-law was somehow involved in this?

"There is something else that might be important," Annie added, recovering from her grief with amazing speed.

"Go on," Brodie replied.

"Spivey said the one man limped, like he'd been injured or something."

I looked over at Brodie. It appeared that he had the same thought as myself. An injury, possibly from a dog bite?

"I don't know nothin' else, and now with poor Spivey gone, how am I supposed to pay me rent?"

Brodie laid another coin on the table.

"That should be enough to cover it."

"Blessings to you. And the lady." She added, giving me a grudging look.

Fifteen

THE TRAFFIC on the streets had thinned as we returned to the Strand, the pall of coal smoke that hovered over the rooftops of buildings giving way to darkness as street lamps came on.

I made my apologies to the Mudger. I had seen him navigate his way along the sidewalks in this part of London and shuddered to think of him on the streets, dodging amidst omnibuses and other traffic that might easily have run him over as he attempted to follow me.

Whatever his circumstances, he seemed to be a good man, I thought, far better than the likes of Spivey and the unknown men who had hired him.

I was afraid for my sister and determined to find her. However, it was obvious there was something else afoot that might be extremely dangerous. Yet I was determined to see this through to the end, and even willing to admit that I needed Brodie to accomplish it.

As much as it annoyed me, and while my sources had provided valuable information, his sources, including Mr. Brimley, Bettie at the Old Bell, Mr. Conner, the MP, and even Annie Flynn, had provided information I would not otherwise have obtained, without realizing that they had.

I had lived the present total of my years in a most independent fashion. The experiences of my adventures, not to mention navigating my publishing career dominated by men, had taught me to rely on myself. It was a new experience for me to find myself needing Brodie's assistance.

Granted, he had come with high recommendation from my aunt—something I was still mystified by.

I could not fathom why she had the need of a private detective when she could have engaged anyone, including the MP and other high-placed individuals, with a simple request for whatever matter with which she needed assistance.

Whatever precipitated their past arrangement, she had chosen Brodie to assist in the matter, and I trusted it had been successful. It was however, most curious.

I had to admit he had a particular expertise, along with his sources. And his ability to navigate parts of London where I would have drawn unwanted attention, as I went about asking questions, was quite useful.

There was also the fact that he kept a supply of very fine whisky, which he now poured for himself after removing his long coat and hanging it by the door as we entered the office.

I did the same, then retrieved the cup I had used that morning and held it out. He hesitated then poured a small portion and took the chair at the desk. That dark gaze watched me with a thoughtful expression that usually precluded some profound comment... or criticism.

"Ye'll be wanting to find more appropriate accommodations, no doubt," he commented, pouring another portion of Aunt Antonia's very fine whisky.

Not a suggestion, I suspected. But I was not of the same thought as I approached the board at the wall where I had made notes on the progress of our investigation with cup in hand.

I picked up a piece of chalk and added more notes from what we had learned the past several hours.

"It would be more... appropriate," he added.

"I would like to remain here," I replied, adding Officer Thomas's name to the notes and connecting it with a line to Spivey's name.

I had given the matter of my accommodation much thought. I wasn't at all concerned that our present cohabitation might cause a scandal. It seemed the logical thing to do under the circumstances. And I had other reasons.

I connected another line based on the description of the men Spivey had given Annie Flynn.

"I would of course pay my share of the rent," I assured him. "It makes it far easier for us to work together, I think you would agree. No need to send round your report," I pointed out and waited for the explosion of temper that surprisingly did not come.

"There's no need to pay a portion of the rent. It's taken care of for the next month." There was a long pause.

"However, ye might want to let her ladyship know yer whereabouts. She might have some say in the matter."

I didn't bother to point out that my various adventures had never bothered my aunt in the past. She had become quite accustomed to them.

My aunt might have been born in a different generation with far more stringent rules for women, and ladies in particular. However, much like myself, she had been disregarding them most of her life.

Brodie came to stand beside me at the board, scrutinizing the notes I'd made.

"What the devil was that move ye made when we met with Annie Flynn?"

Was that what was bothering him? And had perhaps persuaded him to not argue the matter of accommodations?

As little as I knew about Angus Brodie, that still seemed highly unlikely. One thing I had learned, he was not above expressing an opinion.

Or was it something else—wounded male pride perhaps?

"It's an old discipline," I replied. "A traveling companion introduced me to it. She came by it when she lived in the Far East, although it is forbidden to women. She persuaded the instructor."

"I can well imagine how an acquaintance of yours might have done that."

I ignored the sarcasm.

"She became quite accomplished in it," I went on to explain. "I was most fascinated by it and attended several of her lessons."

Lady Elizabeth, my erstwhile fellow traveler and a Scotswoman, no less, had pointed out that men found it difficult to accept that a mere woman might be capable of physically overpowering a man.

"If you would like a demonstration..." I suggested.

Brodie eyed me with could only be described as amusement.

"By all means, Miss Forsythe."

I set the cup aside and took my position in the center of the room with my back turned to him. I was going to enjoy this very much.

"Come at me as if you intend to overpower me," I told him.

He laughed. I ignored it, closed my eyes, and let my senses expand as I had learned.

I was aware of each sound—the creak of floorboards underfoot, the sound of rain at the window, and that hint of cinnamon about him that I'd noticed before, and not at all unpleasant.

Momentarily distracted, I was abruptly caught off guard. An arm clamped around my shoulder and a hand reached around to seize me by the wrist. He no doubt meant to force me into submission.

I reacted instinctively and drove my right elbow hard into the area just below the breastbone. He made a sound, the air knocked out of him. Before he could recover, I turned and swept him off his feet, very much the same as I had with Annie's friend.

Brodie dropped to the floor like a sack of rocks. I was over him in an instant, my elbow pressed against his throat for what my esteemed sensei would have called the killing blow. Brodie glared up at me.

"Oh, my," I exclaimed, not the least put off by the look in his eye.

"The wound at your cheek is bleeding. I do hope that I haven't caused you further injury."

"I can see the reason yer not married," he snapped at me from his position at the floor. "No man in his right mind would risk life and limb."

I was accustomed to those presumptions. I stood and held out a hand.

"Would you care for assistance, Mr. Brodie?"

It was a mistake, as he suddenly came to his feet, grabbed my wrist and twisted my arm sharply behind my back; at the same time he seized my other arm and pulled me against him.

"Ye were saying, Miss Forsythe?" he asked, his voice low, with a half-smile that in spite of the trickle of blood and his hold on me, I found quite charming.

"Do ye yield then?" he asked.

"Never!"

He threw back his head and roared with laughter.

"Ye've a rare spirit, Mikaela Forsythe. God help the man who falls under yer charms."

Charms? That had never been used to describe me.

"If you will unhand me now, I will see to your wound before you bleed all over the place." I didn't want to hurt him—however, if forced, there were other moves I had learned.

He released me, steadying me with a far gentler hand.

"The very proper Miss Forsythe has returned," he commented. "Who would have thought that she hides such surprising talents?

He brushed a hand across his cheek.

"Forget about the wound, it's only a wee scratch. Not the first, nor the last."

"Oh, for heaven's sake," I replied. "Sit," I ordered.

It was just like a man, as if going about with dried blood on his face was some sort of badge of honor, never mind the risk of infection.

I retrieved the washbasin from the adjacent room that I now officially occupied as his partner in crime, and returned with towel in hand.

"I said, it's no bother," he replied with that familiar grumble in his voice that I chose to ignore.

I waited.

"Oh, verra well, if yer going to stand there with that look on yer face."

He sat at the edge of the desk and I proceeded to clean the blood from his cheek and beard.

"Do ye always go about giving orders like some sort of field commander?" he asked, that dark gaze slanted in my direction.

I rinsed the towel and continued.

"When necessary."

"By God, ye can be obstinate."

Not the first time I'd been accused of that.

"Where does that headstrong nature come from?" he asked.

"Survival," I replied. "I learned at a very early age that you either become a victim of circumstances, or rise above them." Not unlike himself, perhaps, I thought.

We were from different places in life, but similar circumstances that didn't much care what one's station in life was.

When I had cleaned most of the blood off his cheek, I dipped the towel into my cup at the desk.

"Not what one finds in most ladies," he commented.

"I'm not concerned with what one expects from a lady. I find it all quite boring."

He reared back in the chair as I applied the towel, and seized me by the wrist.

"Jesus! Mary! Joseph!" he cursed. "What are ye doing, woman? Whisky?"

"It's an excellent medicinal," I replied. "I've used it in the past and I'm certain Mr. Brimley would agree. Although I do dislike wasting it."

He came off the edge of the desk. "Put away yer '*weapons*' and tell me what else ye learned today when ye went off on yer own."

It appeared that I had used the last of the whisky in my cup on his wound and by the expression at his face —handsome as it was—Brodie had quite finished his as well.

I poured myself more of Aunt Antonia's most excellent single malt, then went to the board at the wall and methodically went back over everything I had discovered that day.

I say methodically, as it gave me time to collect myself after that ridiculous demonstration. Not that I felt that I was in danger at any time. I could have flattened him to the floor a second time. I didn't bother to examine the reason that I had not.

We passed the next couple of hours going back over everything we had learned about my sister's disappearance and Mary's murder. We now added Spivey and Officer Thomas to the list of victims, along with the information we'd learned about another *'job'* the murderer apparently had for Spivey. And there was the information I'd learned at the library about Friedrich Huber.

I looked up from across the desk some time later, aware that somewhere between my third and fourth share of whisky, I had nodded off.

"Aye, that's enough for tonight." I vaguely remembered Brodie saying, and the sound of him poking about the firebox in that adjacent room.

When next I opened my eyes, light slipped around the edges of the shade at the window in the room attached to Brodie's office. The remnants of a fire smoldered in the coal stove, and my boots and stockings had been removed. I was still otherwise fully clothed beneath the thick blankets. It was an interesting insight to Mr. Angus Brodie. Honorable indeed. I didn't examine the reason I was disappointed.

I rose and splashed cold water on my face. Then pinned my hair up and followed the aroma of coffee into the outer office.

Coffee was on the stove bubbling away. I poured myself a cup. Biscuits and sausage sat at the desk along with an object wrapped in plain brown paper.

Upon closer inspection, I discovered that it was a knife. It had a long blade much like a hunting knife, and it was covered with what appeared to be dried blood!

"A SOUVENIR," Brodie said, looking up. "From Mr. Conner. He left it with the Mudger late last night. He thought it might be of interest, along with information that might be useful."

I sat down across from him at the desk. It was impossible not to look at the knife, and realize that it had possibly killed three people. I took a long drink of coffee.

"However did he come by it?"

"Someone *'found it'* on the street where Officer Thomas was killed. He persuaded the individual to hand it over."

I could imagine how he had accomplished that.

I set down my coffee and examined the knife closer.

The blade was approximately eight inches long, the shorter handle made of wood with an elaborate carving.

"It's the same as the pin Mr. Dooley found."

"Aye, the question is, who does it belong to, and what does it have to do with yer sister's disappearance?" He pushed the piece of paper across the desk.

"From Mr. Conner?" I asked. Brodie nodded.

The hand-scrawled message—obviously that of a man quite accustomed to hasty messages and perhaps even hastier reports in his former work with the MP—was brief along with information: *Ernst Schmidt at the German gymnasium.*

Was it possible this man might know something about the murderer? Perhaps had contact with him? I was out of the chair.

"We need to speak with him."

Brodie wrapped the knife in that brown paper and put it into a desk drawer, another piece of information we had with no idea how it was connected to my sister's disappearance.

"It's not the sort of place for a woman," he cautioned.

I grabbed my coat and umbrella, and was already out the door. I could have sworn I heard a curse. They were becoming quite familiar. I ignored him and wrapped the woolen scarf around my neck against the morning cold and took to the stairs.

I arrived at the sidewalk where the Mudger greeted me with that toothy grin, with Rupert beside him gnawing on a bone. I didn't care to know what creature the bone might have been attached to. I waved down a cab.

"Do come along, Brodie," I told him, as he reached the bottom landing along with another curse, something along the lines of *'damned fool woman.'*

I ignored the rest of it as I climbed into the cab and gave the driver instructions.

~

The German Gymnasium occupied the entire corner at Kings Cross Road, the four-story brick and mortar building wrapped in gray overcast.

"Schmidt is a rough sort," Brodie commented. "Let me do the talking."

Inside the gymnasium, the domed ceiling soared well over the main floor that included a boxing platform, an area roped off where two men competed against one another with swords, and another area where several men competed in Indian club swinging that I had once seen on my travels.

A young man, quite lean and fit, greeted us at the main desk. A variety of classes were announced on a wall board behind him, including— and I smiled to myself— women's exercise classes. Not the sort of place, indeed!

"Please let Mr. Schmidt know that I wish to speak with him," Brodie announced.

The attendant looked at Brodie with a faintly bored expression, followed by a comment. It was something I loosely translated as *'filthy, arrogant police swine.'*

Or something very near that, obviously a reference to Brodie's former position with the MP.

I smiled, and in spite of Brodie's previous instruction to let him handle the situation, thought it quite necessary to insert myself, or we might possibly find ourselves on the sidewalk. The young man looked very much as if he would do it.

"*Herr Schmidt, bitte.*" I smiled at the look of surprise on the young man's face, and included a little flirtation along with the man's own language.

"*Dein Namen*?" he asked, somewhat taken aback.

"*Herr Brodie, Fraulein Forsythe, würdest du bitte,*" I replied. *"Wir möchten mit sprechen Herr Schmidt."*

I smiled again as he hesitated, then replied with a nod.

"Bitte warte einen moment."

"Ye speak German?" Brodie snapped

"A pastime before traveling to Germany during Oktoberfest one year," I explained.

"You should go. It's a marvelous experience, an entire week of festivities and the most remarkable selection of beer and food."

Brodie had gone quite white around the mouth, even with that dark beard. He really was quite handsome when he was in a temper.

"Translation?" he demanded.

It was difficult not to feel smug. He really *did* need my assistance.

"He asked us to wait a moment, while he goes to locate Herr Schmidt."

"Pitiful," he commented. "He won't be right for a week."

That seemed to be a favorite comment.

"Perhaps," I agreed. "However it got results. Honey is often far better than vinegar, wouldn't you agree?"

I had managed to poke a hole in his male superiority. I was becoming quite good at it.

"Most people are usually more forthcoming when you speak their language," I explained. "And, when they realize that you understand everything *they* say."

"I suppose that applies to Greek as well?"

He caught me quite by surprise with that one. However there wasn't an opportunity to respond as the young man returned, followed by a thick-set man with mutton-chop whiskers, a blunt nose that had apparently been broken several times, and arms the size of tree stumps.

His hair was streaked with gray, but his blue eyes were sharp, with an expression that was both curious and cautious at the same time.

"A rough sort," Brodie whispered.

"You've had some encounters with him?"

"A few. Behave yerself."

I let that pass for now, as we were joined by Herr Schmidt.

"Brodie," he said, in that thick German accent, obviously not at all pleased. "To what do I owe this regrettable encounter?"

Herr Schmidt rather looked as if he would just as soon pummel Brodie into the floor, and by the size of him, I had no doubt he could do it. It spoke volumes as to their past relationship.

"And who is this?" Schmidt gestured in my direction.

"An associate," Brodie replied and quite surprised me. Honey instead of vinegar?

I gave Herr Schmidt my most engaging smile. "Mikaela Forsythe," I introduced myself.

"*Ich freue mich sie zu treffen*. And I hope you can help us," I added.

Brodie's eyebrows disappeared into his hairline as I neglected to *'behave myself.'*

He eventually recovered, with a look at me that he usually reserved for Rupert when he had misbehaved and left something quite disgusting on the floor of the office.

"A bit of your time, if you please," I added.

Schmidt smiled, or at least what passed for a smile on a face that had obviously received blows from more than one fist, possibly in the sport of boxing, considering the environment.

"We do not usually have a *lady* visit our establishment," he replied, with particular emphasis. Which of course raised the question about the sort of clientele who attended the women's classes that were offered.

"I've been here before," I replied. "I was quite impressed with your establishment and expertise that was offered."

Brodie's eyebrows disappeared once more, and it occurred to me that at this rate, we might never see them again.

Schmidt grunted. "Come along. I've work to do."

He led the way through the center of the gymnasium to the boxing platform. There he watched the bout that was underway. He called out instructions to the participants who were stripped down to their waists, with fists protected by gloves as had become customary in boxing matches. They moved about much like a staged performance with glistening bodies.

I thought of my friend, Theodora Templeton. We had met in Paris when I briefly entertained the idea of becoming an actress after performing with her in a Jacques Milland play. I had quickly determined that the stage was not my calling, much to my aunt's great amusement.

"I thought of joining the London theater," she had confessed at the time. *"My father was quite appalled at the notion, not that it influenced me in the least. I wanted to play more exciting roles than the ones that were seen on stage in my youth, all of them quite boring, dreary pieces."*

And she had *'played'* more exciting roles in life, with often scandalous results. It was often pointed out that the apple hadn't fallen far from that tree when it came to my own adventures.

Templeton had gone on to great success, not to mention a long-standing *'relationship'* with Bertie, the Prince of Wales. She had only just returned from a tour of America. I'd had a brief note from her only a few weeks earlier.

"We must have afternoon tea. The stories I have to tell you!"

Of course 'tea' had a far different meaning with Templeton, which I much appreciated. We got along famously and I could only imagine the 'stories,' given her somewhat eccentric nature. Along with being a celebrated actress in America and across the Continent, she claimed to be clairvoyant. It made for interesting conversations with her and her '*contacts*' in the spirit world.

"There are new people in the community," Brodie was explaining now to Herr Schmidt. He was forced to shout to make himself heard over the instructions yelled by a nearby instructor, as well as the sound of grunts as those in the ring pummeled each other. Schmidt nodded, but said nothing

"Ye might know of them," Brodie suggested. Once again there was no reply.

Schmidt moved around to the far side of the ring, and called out in German—something about one of the men keeping his gloves up.

Brodie and I followed as he then crossed the aisle where a fencing match was in progress, something I had some experience with.

"A man who recently arrived from Europe," Brodie continued. "He may be from Hungary or possibly Serbia."

That caught Schmidt's attention.

"What are you doing here then, Herr Brodie? There is no one here from those places. It would not be allowed." The last was said with obvious contempt that I knew to be well-known among the European communities.

"Ye know things," Brodie continued, not the least put off. "From the families and others who come here. Ye know before anyone when a new face arrives."

"You come here and pay compliments when I know you better. You think I will help you?"

This was not going at all well, I thought.

In our brief association I had seen many sides to Brodie. There was his easy rapport with the Mudger and his friendship with Conner. He had a congenial manner with the tavern keeper at the Old Bell, and any number of the women who worked the streets.

I had also seen the other side that undoubtedly also came from the streets—a hardness that turned in an instant.

"I know of yer feelings for these people. I know of the blood feud."

"We are like those two, I think." Schmidt pointed to the two duelists at the floor, maneuvering around each other. "They look for the advantage, then strike."

I had been watching them as well. It was apparent that they were new to the sport by the way they moved. Both men were hesitant before thrusting awkwardly at each other, then moving around the ring like clumsy dancers.

"They should shorten their steps, plant their feet, then immediately thrust again," I said thoughtfully. "Hesitation provides an advantage to one's opponent. If this was an actual duel, one of them would already be dead."

Schmidt eyed me sharply. "One does not find such knowledge in a woman."

"I've been told that," I replied.

He shouted at the duelists in German to shorten their steps, plant their feet, then thrust.

"You must be careful of this one, Brodie, that she doesn't stab you in the middle of the night."

It was not my first encounter with such an attitude—that I might be other than a friend or associate of Brodie's.

However, I was not of a mind to be dismissed. I had several questions I wanted to ask Herr Schmidt in spite of Brodie's instructions to let him do the talking, and I was not about to be set aside.

As Herr Schmidt started to walk away, I seized a

rapier from the nearby stand, took the proper stance, and tapped him firmly on the shoulder with the tip of the sword.

When he turned, I immediately thrust the sword at his midsection where—if the tip hadn't been blunted with a piece of cork—I could have easily lacerated that overlarge belly and left him bleeding at the floor.

"A few questions, Herr Schmidt, if you please," I told him.

Several moments passed where I was uncertain if I might have to carry out the threat, then Schmidt laughed.

"My Anna is much the same with a butcher knife. I sleep here when she is in such a temper. Put down your sword, fraulein. I will tell you what I can, although I doubt it will be of much help to you. I do not allow any such as the one you are looking for in my establishment.

"Politics! Anarchists! Bah!" he exclaimed, then added, "But come, so that you do not feel compelled to return and bother me further."

We followed him to the small office at the back of the gymnasium.

He pulled a bottle from a drawer and poured two cups. He pushed one across to Brodie.

"Schnapps," he said. "The English have their malt brew, but it is pitiful. Only German Schnapps will do. "

I was more than happy to be excluded. While I was familiar with it, drink of any kind on an almost empty stomach was not a good idea. I needed my wits about me.

Schmidt sat back and took a long drink. Brodie, out of courtesy, did the same—the age-old custom of breaking bread. Or pulling a cork as the case might be.

"I have heard of this one you described with the white hair. Dangerous, it is said, not one to be taken lightly," Schmidt finally said, and took another slow drink.

"What else can ye tell us about him?" Brodie replied.

"I can tell you that he and his people have blood on their hands. It is said that they are responsible for the recent attacks in my country and other places, all in the name of the people. And yet it is the people who suffer and die." His fingers tightened around his glass.

"Does the Black Hand mean anything to ye?"

Schmidt didn't acknowledge that he knew of it, but his expression revealed a great deal more.

"What do you want with the white-haired devil?" he asked Brodie.

"He may be connected to several murders. Ye must tell me what ye know. It would serve us both well."

Once again, there was that guarded look.

"Talk can be dangerous," Schmidt replied.

"Perhaps more dangerous not to speak of it," Brodie suggested.

Schmidt was silent for several moments, then rose and closed the door to the office.

"Those of the Black Hand believe that all those in authority are responsible for the miseries of the people, and should be eliminated. They have vowed to do just that. It's well known in the community."

He seemed to consider his next words carefully. He leaned across the desk and kept his voice low in spite of the closed door.

"There is one, I have heard his name spoken here and there, but only in whispers—Resnick. It is rumored that his followers are responsible for attacks in many of the cities, rail stations, anywhere they can strike. Men, women, children—it doesn't matter who dies." He sat back then.

"He leaves his mark on a victim with a symbol. It is

his way of sending a message."

"What sort of mark?" I asked.

"It is much like a dagger, cut into the forehead of the victim for all to see, a warning."

"There have been three murders," Brodie continued. "One was a young woman.

Schmidt shrugged. "And one of your own, I hear, Herr Brodie. But I know nothing of that."

It was obvious he would tell us nothing more.

Brodie waved down a cab after we left the gymnasium. We rode in silence back to the Strand. Our list of questions had grown.

An anarchist named Resnick; a medallion left behind when Officer Thomas was murdered; the murder weapon with that same image at the handle, and the same mark carved into Resnick's victims.

And I had seen it before. But where?

IT WAS WELL into the evening when we reached the Strand. Darkness hovered over the rooftops, and fog wrapped around the street lamps as we entered a public house a few doors down from Brodie's office.

Clouds of cigarette smoke hung in the air. A game of dice was underway, the tell-tale slam of the cup down onto a table top amid conversations and laughter.

Most of the customers were workers from the local workhouses and shops. Other than two women who moved among the customers with trays of ale and food, I was conspicuously the only woman there.

Brodie's hand closed around my arm as he cut a path through sweaty, soot-covered men to a narrow table that had recently been vacated near a window. A crockery plate was still in place with the leftovers of a meal. A woman with an apron eventually made her way through the boisterous crowd to our table.

"Been a while, Mr. Brodie," she greeted him. "Where you been keepin' yerself?" she asked, with a curious glance in my direction.

"Good evening, Miss Effie. What might be the special of the day?" he replied, avoiding her question.

"There's cod, day-old and cheap until its gone," she replied, with a faint accent. Scottish, unless I missed my guess.

"I wouldn't serve it to an alley cat," she shared. "Cook's got chicken pie with vegetables jus' from the oven, but it'll cost more. Two shillings each, a pint is extra."

I had no appetite. I was still thinking over what we'd learned from Herr Schmidt, or what we *hadn't* learned.

He had been vague when Brodie questioned him further about the white-haired man who had been seen by both Officer Dooley and me. It only raised more questions.

What did any of it have to do with Linnie's disappearance.

"Chicken pie will do, if ye please. That'll be for both the lady and me," I overheard Brodie give our order. She gathered the plate left by a previous customer and made a cursory wipe of the table.

More customers came in as she left to put in our order, the cold night air cutting like a knife through the heat from the coal stove and the press of bodies.

There are a great many things to be learned if one watches and listens, I thought, as I watched those gathered in the public house. It was something I had discovered on my adventures and then later applied to the characters in my novels.

There were always two sides to most people—the person other people saw on the outside through certain mannerisms, a way of talking, what they allowed the world to see. Then there was the other side, that part they kept hidden for whatever their reasons.

I had first made that observation as a child, the airs certain classes of people put on, the secrets they hid behind a carefully constructed facade. My father came to mind, a man with secrets until they were no longer secret, with a handsome, charming facade that hid that other person on the inside.

I had adored him in the way that children often do, not understanding there were two sides to him. He could be the doting, loving father, but could not prevent his own self-destruction. Like so many, I discovered, in that privileged world who had that secret side hidden from view.

But here, among these workers, tired from their labors, gathered in the public house before seeking their beds, there was an honesty of spirit I had discovered in foreign places if one was willing to see it. They were weary, but without the need to disguise it behind a facade, with nothing to be gained beyond the moment. Their laughter at some crude comment or joke was honest and came easily.

Not that I was fooled. I knew that among those gathered, there were a few secrets. But most often it was as simple as the hope to rise above one's station in life, the desire to purchase a shawl for a wife or a doll for a child. Or possibly to leave London behind and move to the country, where the air was clean, where they could take up a trade beyond the work houses. Simple things. It was much to be admired.

"Ye've not touched yer supper."

I looked up to find Brodie watching me.

The meat pies had arrived some time before. He had finished his while my plate was still untouched.

"Herr Schmidt knows more than he told us," I shared my thoughts in the matter.

"Aye."

"Why would he not tell us everything?"

"For as long as some people have been here, many feel they are still outsiders and keep within their own community," he explained. "Take German Town, for example. For all that Herr Schmidt is a businessman and has made this his home, old loyalties die hard.

"He finds himself pulled between the two—old habits, old loyalties, old debts to those left behind. It is not an easy thing to leave the only place ye have ever known, no matter how bad, for a new place that is completely unknown." he added.

"Is he afraid?"

"Perhaps. The community is closed to most outsiders."

He spoke of Schmidt, of course; however, I couldn't help but think that he was speaking from personal experience. It was perhaps a glimpse into the boy he had been. Then a young man who came to London in order to survive.

"And yet, he was willing to speak with us," I pointed out.

"Aye, as far as it went with no risk to himself."

Miss Effie had wrapped the plate with my supper.

"Take it with you, m'dear. You could use some meat on yer bones." Then she turned to Brodie.

"Send the Mudger round with the plate later, or that one will take it out o' me pay." She cocked her head in the direction of the man behind the counter who served up ale and other drink.

"You must come here often," I said, as we stepped out onto the street and decided to walk the rest of the way to the office, as the rain had let up for the time being.

"Aye, well, it's close by and Effie is a good soul. Her husband passed last year and it's hard for her to make ends meet."

I had noticed the extra coin he gave her when he

paid for the meal—taking care of someone else who found life hard.

We crossed the Strand, the traffic almost gone now, as the last of the sidewalk vendors had closed for the day and the cabs and omnibuses made their last run from the theatre district and returned to their barns.

I had just stepped up onto the sidewalk a little way down from his office when a shadow stepped out of the darkened entrance to a shop.

The man moved quickly, his features hidden by a thick neck scarf pulled up over his face. The expression at his eyes in the gleam of a nearby streetlamp was nervous but determined.

"Yer coin! And be quick about it!" he demanded, a hand thrust toward me, a knife clenched in his fist.

Brodie pulled me back and stepped between the man and me.

"Ye don't want to do this," he told him in a low voice, the warning unmistakable.

The man glanced around nervously. Emboldened by the near empty street, he lunged at Brodie. Before I could react, Brodie had deflected his arm with a blow, the knife jarred from the man's grasp. It skittered across the sidewalk and into the gutter. Brodie's other hand clamped around the man's throat as he slammed him against the wall of the darkened shop.

His face in the light of the nearby streetlamp was cold and completely void of any emotion, eyes dark as the man choked and flailed to free himself.

"Ye don't want this!" Brodie repeated as he continued to hold him there.

He hadn't drawn his pistol. It wasn't necessary. The man nodded as best he could with Brodie's hand at his throat.

Brodie didn't immediately release him, but held him

against the wall moments longer, until I feared the man might be choked unconscious.

He nodded again, the scarf dislodged to reveal a frantic expression.

Brodie slowly loosened his grip. "Be on yer way then, and don't let me find ye here again."

I was certain it was no idle threat.

"Are ye all right, then?" Brodie asked, when the man had darted off across the street and disappeared into the shadows once more. As if to assure himself that I was indeed all right and not in some fit of hysteria, Brodie ran his hands down both of my arms and then both hands.

There had been no contact, and I was quite certain that I could have handled myself as I had observed that under the layers of grubby clothes and the scarf, the man was quite thin. I nodded.

"I'm quite all right," I insisted. However the same couldn't be said for my supper.

When I had stepped back, the wrapped plate had become dislodged and had fallen to the sidewalk.

Brodie retrieved the wrapped plate that had surprisingly survived intact. He handed it to me.

"Ye shouldn't be here," he reminded me.

"But I am," I replied.

He made that typically Scottish sound in response, and might have been criticism or something else quite colorful.

"Aye, ye are," he replied. He tucked my arm through his, his eyes watchful.

We reached the opening of the alley that led to the stairway of the office without further incident.

The Mudger was in his usual place, Rupert the hound rising to greet us with a wag of the tail, picking up the scent of the chicken pie. I no longer had any appetite and handed it to the Mudger. He grinned that gaping smile.

"Thanks be to ye, miss. And this for yerself, I lifted it off a nob earlier today. A rude bugger, he was." He handed me a somewhat wrinkled and soggy copy of the daily newspaper.

"There's word in it about yer latest book."

At my surprise, he added. "Miss Emma Fortescue," and explained, "I can read. Used to know a girl by name of Emma."

My next novel was to be released soon by my publisher, but I had quite forgotten about it due to my sister's disappearance. In the scheme of things, it simply was not important.

"I hear that one's an ornery lottie," the Mudger said referring to my erstwhile heroine.

"Like to meet a woman like that."

"Yer just as well with the hound," Brodie replied, as I tucked the daily under my arm.

We left the Mudger and Rupert to the chicken pie as we climbed the stairs to the office.

Brodie stoked the stove while I added the information we'd learned from our meeting with Herr Schmidt to my notes at·the chalkboard. I had gotten into the habit of listing questions we had to one side of the board. The list was growing.

"Schmidt trusts you, but only so far," I repeated what Brodie had said earlier. "That might mean that he's afraid," I speculated. "And that could mean that he either knows the man with the white hair, or knows of him. Or possibly he's been threatened," I thought.

"Ye have a curious mind, Miss Forsythe." Brodie dusted off his hands as he rose from the stove and closed the grate.

Contrary to most women? I thought.

Brodie was very much a man of his generation, but he did have his moments of enlightenment.

"You're surprised."

He went to the desk and retrieved the pipe he smoked. He filled the bowl with fresh tobacco, tamped it down, then looked about as if searching for something.

I set my piece of chalk in the rail at the bottom of the board.

Brodie was unlike most other men in that he had a keen mind and an unusual memory for complicated details, as I had observed in our brief time together. His mind was much like the chalkboard, everything lined up in order, a list made, details ready to be plucked out when needed. That, however, did not include the whereabouts of matches.

He stood at the desk, shuffling through papers, opening and closing drawers with growing impatience, the pipe clamped between his teeth.

It took no genius or my friend Templeton's gift of clairvoyance to know exactly where he had placed the small box with the image of a devil—pitchfork and all.

The image suited him, I thought, as I retrieved the small box from the mantel over the coal stove. I pulled out a match and struck it, the flame reflected in that dark gaze as he bent his head toward me.

The moment lingered, as if we were any two people, the simple gesture quite intimate as his hand wrapped around mine to steady it.

"Ye've done this before." He took several puffs from the pipe, the tobacco flaring in the bowl as it caught the flame, a plume of smoke encircling us both.

I liked the aroma from a good pipe, although with a partiality to cigarettes myself, the slender, dark kind with an exotic blend that I'd first discovered in Morocco. They were not usually sold to women, but I had persuaded the shopkeeper.

"I could say that I much like a good smoke now and then," I replied.

"A secret revealed, *Miss Emma Fortescue*?" he asked.

Obviously a secret no longer as to my other personality and my publishing endeavors. I laughed in spite of my frustrations of the day and the scant information Schmidt had provided.

"*She* has been known to sample forbidden pleasures from time to time," I admitted.

That dark gaze met mine. "Aye."

A single word. What more lay behind that one word, I did not know.

"Ye've a rare spirit," he finally said.

A *rare spirit* that suddenly realized the match had burned quite low. I quickly put it out, but not before it had burned my finger.

"Bloody hell!" I swore at my carelessness, and headed for the wash basin of water.

"Not water, it will make it worse," Brodie announced as he headed for the file cabinet where he retrieved a jar of honey.

"Sit," he ordered.

With pipe clenched in his teeth, he removed the lid from the jar. Then, with a spoon, also retrieved from the drawer, he scooped out a small portion of honey.

"Hold out yer hand."

I watched with fascination as he spread honey on my reddened thumb, then took out his handkerchief and wrapped it.

"Who would have thought that you have such skills?" I exclaimed, quite amazed. The honey did seem to take out the sting from the burn.

He gently tied off the makeshift bandage.

"Hazards of the job. Ye learn to take care of things yerself," he replied. I sensed he wasn't referring only to his work as a private investigator.

"Have you been injured before?"

He looked up at me then, a different expression in that dark gaze, thoughtful now.

"A nick here and there, nothing serious."

It was impossible not to think of poor Mary Ryan. She had suffered more than a nick.

"And you keep honey in the drawer just in case."

"I keep it for the occasional client who likes a spot of tea. I suppose ye prefer yer honey with yer whisky."

"That sounds marvelous... to dull the pain, of course, " I added. That brought a wicked smile.

"There are some who feel alcohol can be dangerous, taken when wounded," he commented.

"No one present, Mr. Brodie. You pour the whisky and I'll add the honey. For medicinal purposes, of course."

"Of course."

We sat in companionable silence over my aunt's very fine whisky. I say companionable as Brodie was not given to inane chatter like women of my acquaintance. I much appreciated that companionable silence while I perused the daily newspaper the Mudger had thoughtfully lifted for me.

I found the mention of my recently released novel in the *News about the city* section, and smiled to myself.

Emma Fortescue's readership was going to be scandalized at her latest adventure—pure fiction, of course, I thought to myself, turning to what was referred to as the entertainment page.

"Ye need to consider stepping away from the search for yer sister," Brodie commented, through the fragrant haze of pipe smoke. I looked up from the page I was perusing.

"I beg your pardon." I was quite taken by surprise.

As far as I was concerned, we had settled the matter, albeit after much discussion, but settled nevertheless. He didn't look at me directly, but stared past me to the chalkboard.

"Three people have been killed. The man ye've seen is known, but some—those like Schmidt—are reluctant to tell us anything about him." He stood then and walked to the board, drink in hand, studying my notes.

"This may be more than Sir Charles involved with another woman. It's become too dangerous. It's best that I continue in this alone."

I had heard it all before. I understood what he was saying, but I wasn't about to be set aside now. I returned to my paper and an article of particular interest.

"He's hosting a dinner party and entertainment for guests, including the Prince of Wales, at his private club." I read the announcement in the *News about the city* section.

"Templeton will be giving a private performance for his guests."

"What the devil are ye talking about?" he demanded, coming away from the board.

I smiled to myself as I had obviously succeeded in distracting him. I read him the brief announcement.

"*Sir Charles Litton is hosting a reception at his private club Saturday evening for the Prince of Wales and guests. There is to be a special performance by actress Theodora Templeton.*"

"Teddy might be able to assist in this,"' I mused aloud, more to myself.

"Teddy?" he asked.

"A nickname between friends, although she rarely uses it," I explained.

"Why am I not surprised that ye know the woman?"

I shrugged. "I considered becoming an actress at one time, after Aunt Antonia hosted a party and Teddy gave a performance. It was early in her career. We worked together briefly in a small production, but I became quite bored with it all."

I continued to peruse the article for any information that might be helpful, such as a list of guests. But it was a private party, and none were mentioned other than the Prince of Wales.

"It might be helpful for me to speak with her before her performance," I commented.

Then with another thought, "We could enlist her assistance in the matter. However, I doubt she would be willing to speak with you about it." I peered over the top of the paper at Brodie.

There was a long silence as he no doubt realized that I had outmaneuvered him once again.

I smiled to myself. Point, counterpoint.

I SENT word around the next morning to Drury Lane where Templeton was rehearsing for the opening of her latest play, asking to meet with her.

When she was preparing for a new production, she was known to stay at the theatre all hours of the day and night, completely immersed in her character. She often dressed the part when rehearsing with fellow actors, then continued in character as opening night approached.

It was just one of the eccentricities she was known for. There had even been the occasional foray out onto the street of whatever city she happened to be in at the time. She dressed in full character and carried on conversations with whomever she encountered. In character, of course, which could be quite disconcerting—Joan of Arc on the streets of New York City?

As she once explained it to me, it helped her deliver believable performances that had made her the toast of New York, London, Paris, and across the Continent. It seemed to work marvelously.

It was late afternoon when I received a response, and we prepared to meet with her. I had included Brodie in the invitation. I pointed out to him that she was not particularly fond of London police, private investigators, or newspaper people, for reasons I could only speculate.

He frowned, with a look over my shoulder at the response Templeton had sent round.

"What the devil is that?" he remarked about the peculiar mark at the top of the note.

"I believe that is the *'all-seeing eye."*

"The all-seeing... What the devil?" he exclaimed.

"That is what some people claim... psychics, hypnotists, and that sort," I commented.

The image at the top of the note, much like a crest on formal stationary, was of an eye. Albeit it was an eye with incredibly long eyelashes. It was an excellent piece of artistry that was rumored to decorate all of Templeton's correspondence, as well as a wall in her house in Surrey. It had also appeared in an article about her in the dailies.

"The eye is a symbol of those who 'see' into the spirit world. The ability is quite old and has experienced a resurgence the past several years. It's really quite *avant-garde* to have one's cards read. I've heard that the Queen is a devotee," I pointed out with some amusement, to which I received the Brodie frown.

"Templeton claims to be able to speak to spirits," I added.

"I've heard that she's quite eccentric, " he pointed out. "Rumors about séances and such. And something about a pet lizard?”

"It's an iguana, not a lizard. There is a difference," I corrected. "Fascinating creatures, and quite harmless for the most part. He is somewhere between four and five feet long, and has a preference for roses."

"Bloody Christ!" he swore.

"Ziggy," I corrected him. "He was a gift from one of her... gentlemen friends when she was on tour."

"The thing has a name," he replied incredulously, as we waived down a cab.

Brodie's expression was most amusing.

"Teddy is really quite brilliant," I defended my friend as we climbed into the cab for our meeting with her.

Peculiarities about her pets and men aside, I was not one to criticize another independent, liberated woman.

"We first met when she gave a performance for Aunt Antonia and her friends at Sussex Square," I explained. "It was just before she left for her first tour of Europe.

"It was a performance of Joan of Arc, and quite entertaining. She tore off her steel helm and breast plate, and proceeded to give her final speech as they say... *en flagrante.*"

My aunt had been highly amused. And just the season before, Templeton had performed as the doomed Cordelia in William Shakespeare's King Lear at the Adelphi. In the final scene she was suspended from a scaffolding at the ceiling—out of sight to the audience. It was supposed to emulate the hanging scene where her character is executed.

I had attended with Linnie and Sir Charles, and shared their box with an extraordinary view of the stage and that moving death scene.

Not considered beautiful in the classical sense, Templeton was known for her dazzling personality and compelling performances. Not to mention the exotic animal collection she kept at her country estate in Surrey. And then there was the succession of lovers that were rumored to include fellow thespians, at least one powerful member of Parliament, and the Prince of Wales.

The theatre Royal at Drury Lane, Covent Garden,

was a white colonnaded building that faced onto Bridges Street and backed onto Drury Lane. It had a notable Shakespearean history with productions that went back over the last two hundred years.

Templeton had launched her career at the Drury some years before, and then embarked on tours to Europe and America.

Her return from her latest tour was celebrated with no less fanfare than a queen returning to her kingdom. Banners were flown across the main entrance of the theater with her likeness on life-size billboards framed in elaborate gold-painted frames about the theater district.

She had asked us to meet her at the entrance to the main reception hall, and had left word with the theater manager that we were to be admitted. We waited near a rather imposing, life-size statue of William Shakespeare.

I had never been much a fan of Shakespeare until I saw one of Templeton's performances. She portrayed the character of Desdemona in *Othello* with such spirit and intelligence that she quite stole the play, to favorable criticism at the time. Her response in an interview afterward became a hallmark of her personality as an independent woman.

"In your next life, when you return as a woman," she had told a well-known male critic, *"you will perhaps have far greater insight into the emotions of a woman who is about to die at the hands of her husband, not to mention her far superior intelligence."*

She seemed little changed since the last time I had seen her as she swept toward us through a side door, wearing a skirt and shirtwaist with lace trim.

Her thick auburn hair was swept up on top of her head, with side tendrils that framed those features that had been described to be like that of a Greek goddess. There could be flashes of anger one moment, tragic tears the next, and of course, her trademark flirtations with any man she encountered. That full range of talent was now aimed at Brodie.

"A moment," she said, coming to a stop a half dozen feet from us. She cocked her head to one side as if someone had just whispered in her ear.

"You have been on some exciting adventures," she exclaimed, then moved closer. "And how is Miss Emma Fortescue? Such a remarkable woman. I do admire her so."

I had prepared myself, of course. Her claim of *'psychic ability'* was well known. She had certainly been most entertaining after the private performance at Sussex Square. Most of those in attendance that evening had dismissed it as entertainment, but there were those who became devotees, many of them proper ladies of London society. Not to mention a royal prince who was rumored to have insisted on *'private performances.'* And as they say, the rest was history...

As for myself, I had traveled to many countries and encountered far too many different beliefs to say that the ability to communicate with the spirit world did not exist.

"Emma is quite well, thank you," I replied. "And about to be off on another adventure."

"Excellent! I have so enjoyed reading about them." We might have been talking about a mutual acquaintance.

I caught Brodie's side glance.

"Oh my," Templeton exclaimed, coming forward now, that notorious reputation with men on full display as she flirted outrageously with Brodie.

I made introductions and was most amused that he seemed quite taken aback. I had never seen a grown man blush before, rendered momentarily speechless, which was quite an accomplishment in his case.

"Good afternoon, Miss Templeton," he finally managed, taking her hand and inclining his head in a surprising gentlemanly manner that I had not experienced.

Rather than grumbling some colorful comment as I had become accustomed to in our association, Brodie could act quite civilized when the situation warranted it.

"The room is suddenly quite full," Templeton said, angling her head as if to catch another comment only she heard. She smiled, that very same smile that had launched a thousand ships as Helen of Troy.

"You have a most intriguing energy, Mr. Brodie," she told him. "There are several spirits surrounding you."

She could have announced that the earth had split in two and was about to swallow us for the expression at Brodie's face.

"I see a very old spirit." She took a step back, propped her chin at her hand, and studied him.

"You were raised by your grandmother. Her spirit watches over you. *She* says, don't be such an *amadan."*

She blinked and then burst out laughing. "Good heavens, where did that come from? Next I'll be speaking Gaelic. It has happened."

She looped her arm through Brodie's. "You mustn't be put off. They're always around. It's just that most people don't stop to listen.

"I have discovered," she continued much to my amusement. "that they're not evil at all, merely sad and possibly caught up by some dreadful mischief in a previous life and now must live with regret. But most are quite harmless. Like your grandmother. She hasn't moved on yet, spiritually speaking, because there is still something she needs to see done."

Brodie was, for the moment, quite speechless. Templeton looked at me then.

"Now do come along. It is so good to see you again, and you must tell me the reason for your note. I found it most intriguing. And Lady Antonia? She is well, of course. I would have known otherwise. And Mr. Munro?" she added, a certain gleam in her eye.

"If he wasn't so loyal to Lady Antonia..." This said with a long sigh that spoke volumes, as we accompanied her through the grand gallery with that imposing life-size statue of William Shakespeare.

"Oh, dear. There it is again." Templeton commented. She leaned in as if confiding a secret. "He hates the damned thing." And at my look of curiosity, "Wills, of course," she explained.

"He has hated that statue since it was brought here, insists that he looked nothing like that and considers it to be an insult. I have to agree. He thinks it makes him look as if he is taken with a complaint of the bowel."

Brodie choked and I feared he might have an apoplectic episode. However, I did catch the look of amusement in that dark gaze.

I stifled the urge to burst out laughing myself. But now that she mentioned it, I had to admit that I might be inclined to agree with Mr. Shakespeare on that one.

"I've spoken with theater management about having it removed," Templeton continued. "But they think the thing is quite marvelous. So very sorry, Wills," she said apologetically.

Brodie and I exchanged a look.

"Do come along," she said. "The schedule they have me on, I'm afraid that I have only a short while before I must start preparing for tonight's performance. And do be careful where you step. Ziggy managed to wander off earlier, and hasn't been found yet."

The change in Brodie's expression was worth a thousand words.

"He is quite harmless, of course," she assured us both. "As long as he's well fed. But quite nearsighted. He's forced to follow his nose, so to speak, so I do hope you haven't been climbing through the hedges recently. He might pick up the scent and think you're a rhododendron or rose. He's very fond of them."

"We haven't been crawling through shrubs or bushes recently," I assured her.

And that was Brodie's introduction to William Shakespeare and Theodora Templeton, with the absent Ziggy yet to make an appearance!

We met with her in her dressing room, with costumes hanging about, as Templeton, not one to stand on formalities or put on airs, proceeded to disrobe behind a screen.

"Now, do tell me what this is about."

Contrary to Brodie's insistence that we explain as little as necessary, I saw no way to enlist Templeton's help other than to tell her everything. And of course, there was her ability, had I thought to keep anything from her.

I explained about Linnie's disappearance and Mary's death."

"Oh, dear! I do remember your sister quite well. Such a sweet, beautiful young woman, and I recall that she married well. Now, this dreadful business."

I explained briefly what we had learned since her disappearance.

"Good heavens!" Templeton emerged from behind the screen and sat back in the brocade upholstered chair in the middle of her dressing room, her chin propped on her hand.

"Poor Lenore," she said sympathetically. "I never had a sister, so I can only imagine your distress."

I exchanged a look with Brodie. In for a penny, in for a pound, as the saying goes.

"You're to give a private performance at Clarendon House next Saturday evening, " I mentioned.

That unusual green gaze met mine. There was intelligence there, along with something else—curiosity to be certain. Or a message from the other side, perhaps?

"And you would like to use my presence there to find out who will be attending, as well as the reason for such a private meeting."

It took me a moment. Perhaps there was something to her clairvoyance.

"I realize it is asking a great deal," I explained. "However, it's the only way to know if there is some connection to my sister's disappearance. "

"Oh, good heavens, don't move!" she suddenly told both of us, coming up out of her chair.

"It's Ziggy."

Ziggy, as in a four-and-a-half-foot-long iguana, had suddenly arrived in Templeton's dressing room.

"He's actually quite shy and won't hurt you," she assured us both. Brodie was not convinced, while I was most curious.

"However he startles quite easily and is quite skillful with that tail."

Skillful? As in...?

"He's hungry, poor thing," she continued. "He's been on the prowl for food."

A pair of golden yellow eyes stared at us from the open doorway.

I checked with Brodie to make certain he hadn't pulled out his revolver. It was very likely that Templeton would not be of a mind to assist us if he shot Ziggy.

"They're herbivores, they only eat plants," she added for Brodie's benefit. "I had these brought in this morning since he hasn't eaten in a while. When we're in Surrey, he has the run of the greenhouse, and I keep it well stocked."

She pointed out the wall of green plants which I had assumed were sent by devoted fans, although I had thought it quite odd that they didn't include the usual roses.

"He'll be quite content now," she announced, as Ziggy ambled across the dressing room floor, tail swishing back and forth sweeping everything out of the way as he ambled past, and proceeded to enthusiastically dismantle the plants and gorge himself.

"Now, where were we...? Ah yes, the private performance I'm to give. I've been told there will be several foreign ambassadors—Sir Charles, Bertie, of course," she smiled.

Bertie of course, being the Prince of Wales, with whom it was rumored she'd had an affair. As one newspaper writer had once said about her, the list was long and distinguished.

Brodie asked her several questions with a watchful eye toward Ziggy, who continued to satisfy himself on an array of exotic plants, and didn't appear to be interested in the humans in the room at all.

"I was contacted by Sir Charles's secretary," she explained. "I was told that the request for a private performance was made by the Prince of Wales. We are good *friends*, and of course I accepted."

She rose and went to check on Ziggy, who had disappeared among potted plants with only a rustling about of his tail to indicate where he might be.

"I don't know precisely how many others may be in attendance."

"That is precisely what we need to know," Brodie replied. "We need to know whom ye recognize, names ye may overhear, something that might tell us the reason these other people are gathered in London."

"I'm to spy on those who are there," she concluded with obvious delight, catching Brodie quite off guard. "How marvelous!"

"I suppose ye might call it that," he replied.

She clapped her hands together, like a delighted child. "I haven't done this in quite a long time—Napoleon, as I recall."

Brodie and I exchanged a look at that. Napoleon?

"Bertie will be so excited," she went on. "I had thought of doing *Salome.* He was always quite fond of my performance. However, since I am doing Cleopatra starting tonight at the theater, it makes perfect sense that I will give a performance for Sir Charles."

"No one, not even the Prince of Wales, must know what yer doing," Brodie cautioned. "It could be dangerous if others were to learn of it."

"Oh, I quite understand. Obviously all good spies must rely on secrecy. You may rely on me," she assured him.

"I can be the soul of discretion. This is so exciting!" she exclaimed, then suddenly returned to her chair.

"I'm getting something..."

Brodie and I exchanged another look. To say meeting with Templeton was an unusual experience was an understatement. She leaned forward, a thoughtful expression on her face, as she seized both my hands.

"Your sister is alive. She's in a very dark place. I cannot see precisely where that is. And this man, pale-haired man, you've seen him several times. He is definitely part of it. And there's a girl... oh, dear." She pressed her fingers against her forehead.

"She was with your sister. Is her name Mary?"

Brodie and I exchanged a look. Neither one of us

had mentioned Mary's name, nor had we provided any details about any of the deaths or the man I had seen twice, only that I had been followed after my meeting with Charles.

"This man with light hair," she continued. "He is very dangerous. There's something about him, something hidden. You must be very careful," she warned me.

"Perhaps it's too dangerous," I suggested with a look over at Brodie. I was beginning to think it was a mistake to ask for her assistance.

"Never too dangerous for *Emma Fortescue,*" Templeton countered, sitting back in her chair.

She was right, of course. However, this was not an adventure. It was deadly serious.

"Would Emma go to a private club?" she asked.

I answered without hesitation. "Of course."

"There you have it, and I shall assist." She closed her eyes and reminisced. "While on my recent tour of America, our party was set upon by bandits. Several men came to our assistance. They called themselves Texas Rangers. The matter was quickly settled. It was most exciting."

"If yer certain about this, Miss Templeton," Brodie replied.

I heard the hesitation in his voice. It matched my own.

For all her experience on the stage, she was hardly prepared for what she might encounter among those in attendance if one of them was to learn of her involvement. There would be no Texas Rangers to rescue her.

"She cannot go alone," I announced.

I immediately sensed Brodie's disapproval, and plunged on ahead presenting reasons—all quite logical —and finished by announcing, "I will go with her."

I waited for the explosion from Brodie. There was only silence.

I had encountered that same silence after I had gone off on my own, risky as it admittedly was, and had encountered Spivey at the docks.

"It makes perfect sense," I argued. "Two of us can be more efficient in acquiring information."

Templeton saved the day, and at least temporarily, rescued me from Brodie's wrath.

"A smashing good idea," she announced. "I always have several people accompany me. You may go as my dresser.

"It will leave you free to go about after I begin my performance. Oh, I do love an adventure." And she was already planning my costume and make-up.

"You must come for this evening's opening performance. I'm most excited about the death scene with the asp. You will be my guests!"

One look at Brodie, I knew he would rather have all of his teeth extracted, but considering what we had asked Templeton to do, we could hardly refuse.

"Excellent!" she said. “It's all arranged then. Curtain call is at eight o'clock. There's just enough time for you to have supper. When you return, let the assistant manager know that you're to be my guests, and he will show you to my private box."

"Bloody Christ!" Brodie muttered, as we left the theater before returning for the performance that evening.

"We are relying on someone who has a lizard for a pet, imagines that she talks to spirits, and is excited about performing with an asp?"

I saw his point. However, there was no other choice in the matter if we wanted to learn what Charles was up to with this event at his private club.

"You cannot deny that she knew things that we hadn't told her. Nor could she have learned them anywhere else, since she only just arrived back in the country. She was very perceptive."

I chose my words carefully, considering that he was obviously not a believer in someone connected with the spirit world.

"And she was most perceptive about your grandmother," I added.

"Bloody Christ!"

That was two *'Bloody Christs'* in as many minutes. I did hope for his sake, that he was in good standing with the Almighty.

He survived the performance of Cleopatra and the asp, which turned out to be a fake stage prop. However, Ziggy somehow made his way into the orchestra pit just before the final act of Templeton's performance that evening. Musicians scattered in a dozen directions, not to mention the chaos it caused among the audience.

Templeton was eventually able to coax Ziggy from the orchestra pit with an enormous bouquet of roses that had been delivered for her. She then took several bows to rounds of applause. And, in true theatrical spirit, the show went on.

'Cleopatra', with her asp, made her dying speech, and the curtain came down on a successful, if most unusual, opening night.

The plan set, I discovered during the ride back to the Strand that there was something far more maddening than a stubborn, overbearing Scot. It was Brodie's silence. Never a good thing.

"Ye will not do this!" he finally announced, as we arrived back at his office.

We'd had our disagreements before, regarding my involvement in the investigation. But over the past few days, we'd struck an agreement of sorts, and on occasion he seemed at least to accept my contributions to the investigation. And there was the undeniable fact that there was information that he simply wouldn't have had without my assistance.

"It is too dangerous," he declared.

He was angry. It was there in that broad Scots accent that came through when he was in a high temper.

"It's too dangerous for me, but not for Templeton?" I replied. "I should think far more dangerous for her, if she should stumble into something she's not prepared for."

It was difficult to argue against it, and as I was now well acquainted with his temper at this point, I didn't give him the opportunity to reply. Instead, I outlined all the reasons that it made perfect sense for me to accompany her.

Never one to be outmaneuvered, Brodie appeared to listen, which made me immediately suspicious that he was not actually listening at all.

"I'll arrange for Dooley to accompany her," he announced, as we arrived back at the Strand.

"He could be recognized," I pointed out the obvious, and with enormous self-control as I stepped down from the cab, avoided telling him to go straight to the devil and take his objections with him.

"Mr. Dooley is obviously quite competent as a member of the police. However he would easily be discovered," I pointed out. "And finding a police officer in their midst would not entice those present to freely discuss whatever matters have brought them there," I pointed out.

"I will accompany Templeton," I repeated. "It is the only solution that makes sense. And I can easily move among those present during her performance."

"Ye forget that yer brother-in-law will be there," he argued.

"I will be wearing a disguise. I have already discussed it with Templeton." I turned toward the stairs at the entrance.

"Ye are not prepared for this sort of thing," he said, as he followed. "Ye have already put yerself in considerable danger, and this scheme..."

"And I have emerged unscathed," I pointed out. "Or is it that you are more concerned about disapproval from my aunt?"

Admittedly it was a low blow. Nothing in my association with Brodie had even hinted at his concern in that regard, but I was determined to have my way in this.

"I only agreed to allow yer association in this investigation because ye appeared to have a certain level of intelligence and common sense. That, I am currently beginning to doubt. I did not agree to allow ye to put yerself in danger." He slammed the door of the office.

"Allowed?" I turned on him, dangerously close to losing my temper. "I have provided valuable information to the investigation which might have taken you weeks to obtain, if at all. And you forget, that I have agreed to pay you quite handsomely for your services."

"Of which I have not yet seen a farthing," he pointed out.

I slowly removed my hat and coat, and hung them both on the stand near the door.

"If you will accompany me in the morning, I will provide you with a bank draft for payment in full for your services, if that is all that you're concerned with."

"Bloody Christ, Mikaela! This has nothing to do with Lady Montgomery, or what ye agreed to pay for my services.

I suspect we were both surprised at the use of my given name. It was no doubt an indication of just how far I had pushed him.

"There are too many things that are unknown, and the more we learn, the more convinced I am that this is extremely dangerous," he explained. "For Christ's sake, three people are dead. And now this fellow ye've seen twice is possibly connected to this anarchist group. What if ye are discovered?"

"What is that to you?" I demanded. "I make my own decisions. I go where I please, and do as I please!"

"Not if I have any say in the matter!"

"You don't!"

We were toe-to-toe, nose-to-nose.

Well, very near nose-to-nose, as he was a bit taller than I was— something I discovered to be quite unsettling. Not that I felt threatened. Quite the opposite.

I had discovered in the past that most men were quite put off by my height. It might have had something to do with my looking down at them when they are trying to make their point. There was no looking down at Brodie, unless he was seated at the desk, which at the moment he was not.

"Ye are the most infuriating, headstrong... woman!" The way he said it was definitely not a compliment.

He shoved a hand back through his hair and was the first to break eye contact, with a curse in Gaelic somewhere in there that, in spite of the anger, I found quite amusing.

"If something were to happen, and I wasn't there..."

"You were not there for the first twenty-four years of my life," I pointed out. "And I have somehow managed to survive quite nicely, thank you."

I had been left to my own devices since I was a child, in one way or another, and I had learned to function sufficiently. Not to mention take care of myself quite handily. And as for the investigation, whatever the outcome, he would be gone afterward and I would continue to take care of myself as always.

"I will meet with Templeton tomorrow to settle on a suitable disguise," I informed him.

"You may send Dooley, or whomever you chose," I added, refusing to argue the matter further.

There was another curse as I slammed the door to the adjacent room and left him to himself.

The next morning I left early and spent most of the day at the Drury Theatre. Brodie hadn't said a word as I left the office on the Strand.

As far as Templeton's manager and her acting troupe were concerned, I had previous theatre experience—a bit of an exaggeration on her part, since my acting credits were limited to two little-known plays, and she was bringing me on to assist with the private performance that was to be given the following evening.

She provided me with a gown from among her wardrobe of costumes, along with a gray wig with hair bound back in a bun.

"What do you think?" Templeton asked after her make-up person put on the finishing touches.

"Good heavens!"

Looking in the mirror, I didn't recognize myself, with wig, over-the-top make-up, including thick eyebrows, and a few other charming touches.

"Oh, this is going to be so exciting," Templeton said again.

Not exactly the word I would have chosen. For once, I much preferred that this adventure was productive, not *exciting*.

Nineteen

FOR ALL HIS OBJECTIONS, Brodie was subdued as he accompanied me when I returned to Drury Lane the following afternoon, as final details were put into place for Templeton's private performance that evening.

All the props for the stage production had already been delivered to Clarendon House earlier, along with the crew necessary to assemble the sets she required for her performance as Cleopatra.

I was soon clothed in full costume—makeup, a plain, worsted-wool dress with a pocket for the knife I always carried, and the wig.

"Good God!" Brodie exclaimed, when I emerged from Templeton's dressing room.

"Ye look like my grandmother!"

I wasn't at all certain that was a compliment, but took it as one, since I had learned that he had been raised by that stalwart woman and had a particular fondness for her.

"And what the devil is that on yer chin?"

"It's a fake mole. Templeton thought it added quite the effect we needed for my disguise."

"Mikaela..." he began again, with a critical look as I followed Templeton from the theater to her waiting coach. There was something in his voice, something different this time.

"We have no idea who may be there..." he reminded me.

I knew all the objections, I had heard them all the day before once the plan was made. I had even threatened to walk out and continue on my own.

"Give me yer word me that ye'll be careful. It could be dangerous."

A prospect that seemed highly unlikely, since we were to attend the event at Clarendon House, not exactly out on the street chasing down villains.

I could have sworn at that moment that he was actually concerned for my well-being.

"Does this mean you have a soft spot in your heart for me?" I teased, wiggling my fake eyebrows.

He swore under his breath. "It means that I don't want to have to explain to her ladyship if something should happen to ye."

"*Dinna fash*," I assured him.

To which I received another "Bloody Christ!" as I stepped into the coach.

We were a curious ensemble as we set off for Clarendon House—Templeton in full makeup for her role as Cleopatra, including black, shoulder-length hair, with a gold circlet about her forehead, exotic makeup, accompanied by her personal maid, Elvira Finch, and me, who resembled Brodie's grandmother.

Mrs. Finch reminded me of that namesake little bird as she sat silently across from me in the coach. She was in charge of Templeton's costumes and had been with her for years. She had no doubt witnessed my friend's assorted peccadilloes and transgressions, not to mention her affairs.

We had been introduced the day before, in that way Templeton had of breezily announcing that I was to assist with her wardrobe for this special performance, with no further explanation provided.

Mrs. Finch had simply replied, "Yes, ma'am," in the small voice, that suited her appearance quite well. I wondered how she had fared in America with the Texas Rangers riding to the rescue.

She was the official keeper of the secrets, so to speak. If there was a Mr. Finch, or ever had been, he was apparently no longer in the picture.

Ziggy did not accompany us. He had been sent off to Surrey where Templeton assured me that he was quite content with a fresh delivery of exotic plants and roses in the greenhouse.

Clarendon House, where her performance was to take place, was an imposing residence, constructed of Bath stone in the Georgian style, much like my aunt's house and very near St. James Palace.

I had attended a reception there with Aunt Antonia a few years earlier. The size and opulence of the mansion was truly impressive. Apparently this was where Charles regularly attended his 'private club.'

We arrived at the *porte cochere* at the main entrance, and Templeton disembarked the coach with great fanfare, assisted by a liveried footman with Mrs. Finch and me dutifully falling in behind.

Upon entering the mansion through the portico, the hall opened up to reveal a sweeping staircase with an elaborate balustrade. It was a perfect replica of the staircase at Versailles that I had once seen when on holiday from school. Above, the skylight cast light down on the glowing gold color on the walls.

At the top of the stairs, we were escorted past the state drawing room where the performance was to be given that evening. It was resplendent with candelabra, decorated with a swarm of gold cherubs, and the ornate chimney flanked by crystal bell-pulls. A fire burned in the hearth, with windows that looked out onto St. James's Park.

It was a reminder that guests would soon be arriving, while a full company of servants moved about the chairs that had been set theatre-style and faced the portable stage that had been erected, complete with red velvet curtains drawn across.

A private room had been made available to Templeton. A member of the Clarendon House staff appeared and inquired if she needed anything, and pointed out the bell-pull that connected to the servants' quarters.

She requested a half dozen bottles of sparkling mineral water, along with a light meal of watercress sandwiches. Then she sent a message to her fellow actor who was to portray Marc Antony.

He had arrived earlier by separate coach with his own costumer and a man who was responsible for the swords used in the production. And then there was the young man responsible for the other props, including Cleopatra's asp. This time, as opposed to opening night, it was very much alive. It was a touch that Templeton was most excited about.

"Quite harmless. but you must admit authenticity adds to the drama."

Indeed. I made a note to stay away from the asp.

She requested that the staff inform her when the Prince of Wales arrived, which I thought might have been somewhat over the top, considering he was very much married. And while the performance was private, there would be many in attendance, with the very real possibility that word of any liaison would undoubtedly makes its way back to the Queen.

"It's always nice to renew old acquaintances," she added, with a mischievous smile.

For my part, I dutifully helped lay out her costumes for the three different acts she was to perform that evening, while Mrs. Finch had one of the other members of our entourage set up a steaming iron and board to press out any lingering wrinkles in her other costumes. It would not do to have the Queen of Egypt mussed and wrinkled.

It was amazing the amount of work and details that were required for a theatrical performance. People came and went, most of whom I had seen the day before at the Drury. Templeton's manager was a constant presence, directing everyone like a military general.

My disguise worked perfectly. It was quite easy for me to simply get lost in the shuffle, carrying messages back and forth with myriad last-minute changes when it was discovered that the set that had been erected in the State Room was actually the set for the death scene which was the final scene. Changes had to be made to accommodate Cleopatra's meeting with her lover, Marc Antony, just before he leaves Egypt for Rome.

As courier, it provided me the opportunity to move between the private rooms and the State Room. I was completely ignored once it was determined that I was part of her entourage. It also provided me a view through windows that looked out onto St. James's Square as the guests began to arrive.

A formal supper was to be served at nine o'clock, with Templeton's performance to begin at eleven. Other entertainments had been arranged for the evening, including an orchestra, a magician who moved through the arriving guests and made small gifts appear as if out of thin air.

I watched for my brother-in-law, not wanting to take any chance that he might recognize me. I had just passed another message to the crew working on the change of stage sets when his arrival was announced. He was accompanied by a man and woman.

I paused at the second-floor landing that overlooked the entrance hall below to get a better look at the two who had arrived with him.

The man appeared to be no more than thirty years old, medium height, with a full, closely cropped beard, his hair smoothed back from a high forehead. But it was his eyes that caught my attention even at that distance. They were dark, almost black with an intensity as his gaze swept the entrance hall and other guests as they arrived. In spite of his finery, he seemed distinctly out of place.

The woman was dressed in a high-waisted gown, with her dark hair piled on top of her head. She had high cheekbones, a generous mouth, and that same watchful demeanor as she scanned those who had already arrived, as though looking for someone in particular.

She walked between the two men, then leaned in and said something to Charles... something intimate between lovers?

For his part, Charles merely nodded and seemed oddly uncomfortable, even as the woman looped her arm through his.

Who was she? Lover? Mistress?

Linnie had written of her suspicions and a great deal more—late evening 'meetings' that took Charles away many nights, often not returning at all, along with his secrecy and remoteness. And now, a woman openly accompanying him to a private event, while my sister was still missing?

I didn't recognize her from other social encounters, although admittedly my travels often kept me away from London for extended periods of time. As for Charles, if I had not been well acquainted with my brother-in-law, I might not have recognized him.

His lean features were drawn and there was a tension in his gaze as he glanced about the entry hall at the guests who had already arrived. He seemed to have aged considerably in just the few days since our meeting, and was obviously uneasy.

Was it the appearance of a husband distraught over his wife's disappearance? Or something else?

I held my breath as he looked up and scanned the second-floor landing where I stood. He glanced briefly in my direction as he handed off his overcoat and umbrella to a waiting attendant. However, it was only a cursory glance, and he was quickly engaged in conversation with another gentleman who had arrived. I ducked out of sight and immediately returned to the private room Templeton occupied for the evening.

While she added finishing touches to her make-up, I went about straightening the room, and contemplated ways I could move among the guests to gather more information.

I heard the distant sound of the orchestra and recognized the piece that was usually played to announce the presence of a member of the royal family. It appeared that the Prince of Wales had arrived.

The final touches were put to Templeton's makeup and she rose from before the elaborate, gilt-edged Georgian dressing table, transformed. Cleopatra lived once more, complete with the plunging neckline of her Egyptian style gown. She took hold of my hand.

"This is going to be such fun."

It seemed very much like a game to her. I wasn't at all certain that's how I would have described the evening that lay ahead.

I gathered the elaborately decorated floor-length cape with gold threads woven through that she was to wear as part of her entrance, and draped it over my arm.

She gave me a sly smile as our scheme was about to be set in motion.

"Let us see what we can learn tonight."

And with that, we were off to join the evening's guests, Templeton in all her regal *Cleopatra* glory, me in my dowdy gown, wig that had begun to itch, and my mole.

For my part, my goal was to follow her like a shadow and eavesdrop on the conversations of the guests without being noticed as she engaged them. Considering my costume—not to mention my drab appearance —I was certain no one would give me a second look.

We arrived at the State Room with all the ceremony of arriving royalty. The room fell silent and I stepped back into the shadows at the entrance. I was about to witness a performance worthy of the Egyptian queen herself.

Templeton paused just inside the entrance as the silence then became an excited buzz of conversation, the attention of everyone in the room focused on her. I had to admit that at that moment, I believed she *was* Cleopatra, holding court over those gathered, including the Prince of Wales.

Whatever their past or possibly current relationship might be, in that moment he *was* Marc Antony, and it was all about power—her power of seduction.

Charles broke off his conversation with one of his guests and crossed the room in our direction. I lowered my gaze, rounded my shoulders, slumped, and made myself as inconspicuous as possible. But it was obvious that he paid no attention to me as he and Templeton exchanged pleasantries and he escorted her into the State Room.

"You must introduce me to your guests," she insisted. "So many men, so little time." *Cleopatra* smiled that enigmatic smile that had conquered two kingdoms, metaphorically speaking, of course.

I followed in her wake as her dutiful servant, picking up the odd bits and pieces of conversation that flowed back and forth between them, as well as among the guests we passed.

To say that Templeton ruled the room was an understatement. She was apparently quite accustomed to such reactions, and moved among the guests with ease, a teasing banter, and an occasional name whispered discreetly back over her shoulder in my direction.

Along the way I picked up pieces of conversation here and there as I stole glances at faces and listened to accents, among them French and German, and another accent that I could not place.

While Sir Charles was hosting the event, it was obvious that the Prince of Wales was the guest of honor.

"Bertie!" Templeton said, in a smoky voice that hinted at something far more intimate as she approached the Prince of Wales.

"Teddy, you are ravishing, as always," he replied, a common enough comment, but there was a noticeable gleam in his eyes.

I slipped behind a lifelike statue of a Roman Centurion that was one of the props for the evening as Templeton continued her parade about the State Room.

From there I became almost invisible, dwarfed by the seven-foot-tall statue complete with full Roman costume and sword. A plaster twin stood guard across the room, and I could observe those in attendance, including the man and woman who had arrived with Charles.

I had searched among the workers and Templeton's entourage earlier; however I didn't find Officer Dooley among them. Now, I scanned the staff of Clarendon House as they moved among the guests. If Dooley was among them, he was as well-disguised as I was.

Charles had joined Templeton and the Prince of Wales, along with the man who had arrived with him, while the woman stood apart, observing the room much the same as me.

I overheard Charles introduce the man as Kosta Resnick—the same name Herr Schmidt had mentioned!

Their conversation was of the usual pleasantries, but with an edge in Resnick's voice. For her part, Templeton looped her arm through his and proceeded to flirt openly with him.

"I've never been to Budapest," she said, rather more loudly than necessary, with a quick glance in my direction.

"You must tell me about it." And they were off, Resnick under full assault of *Cleopatra's* seductive charms.

"Now, what might Sir Charles be doing with guests from Serbia?"

I practically jumped out of my skin at that thick Scots accent that reached out from the shadows behind me.

"Don't turn around," Brodie cautioned.

"I thought you were going to send Dooley," I whispered.

"Mr. Dooley is here," he assured me. "Sharpening his skills as part of the wait staff."

"And yourself?" I inquired, more than a little curious how he had managed to disguise himself among the well-dressed guests in attendance.

"I'm now the assistant to the stage manager," he explained.

"Discreet, and no one will pay any attention to you," I observed. There was no response.

"Brodie?"

I turned my head slightly only to discover there was no one behind me. He had disappeared. Definitely discreet, I thought, as I scratched under the cumbersome wig.

I thought of the costumes women wore in the past with towering, powdered wigs, and had no idea how they kept them on their heads.

They could have their wigs and this one as well, I thought. Just as soon as the evening was over. I scratched again, wondering who might have inhabited the damned thing before me.

Templeton and Resnick had moved toward the adjacent doorway that led to the music room.

I edged along the wall filled with stage props, then behind the elaborate curtain that had been hung over the stage. There was no sign of Brodie, not that I expected any. No doubt his past profession, as well as his current one, often required trickery and deception when moving about unnoticed in pursuit of a criminal.

Supper was announced and the rest of the guests proceeded to the Music Room, with windows at the balcony that overlooked the Stable Yard below. The recessed alcoves were flanked by Corinthian columns filled with artwork, and the elegant black piano where Chopin had given a private concert for Queen Victoria and Prince Albert decades earlier.

For tonight, the Music Room had been transformed

into a dining room, with long tables set with the finest linen, china, and crystal, as servants assisted guests to their pre-assigned places, each with an elegantly hand-written place card.

In true Templeton style, she picked up her place-card and relocated it next to Resnick.

"So that you can tell me all about Budapest," she insisted, with all the command of Cleopatra herself, then leaned forward to include the mysterious woman who was now seated at his other side.

"And you must introduce me to your companion."

Supper was a drawn-out affair with several courses served, the sort I usually avoided. However, it provided Templeton and me time to observe her fellow guests.

Among the wait staff I finally saw Dooley, wearing the formal livery of Clarendon House, a most unlikely role for the police constable from the East End, and I prayed he didn't upend a bowl of lobster bisque in a guest's lap.

Templeton eventually excused herself to prepare for the evening's performance. I slipped out of the Music Room and joined her in the hallway.

"The woman's name is Marie Nícola," she shared, as we arrived at her private room.

Marie. The name had been on a letter I had found in my sister's security box.

Templeton frowned. "I'm usually very good at such things, and my guess would be that she is not Sir Charles's lover. He seems quite uneasy around her, and she's very..." she searched for the right word. "Cold... and there's something else."

"What is it?" I asked.

"Something, I can't quite put my finger on."

"I don't suppose you might be able to find out more about her through your other *'sources,'*" I suggested. It was worth asking, even though I knew Brodie's opinion of her *psychic abilities.* I for one, however, was not willing to dismiss anything.

"I'll see what Wills has to say about her. He's very good at reading people."

By that I assumed she meant William Shakespeare, and by reading people... Well, after all, Shakespeare had authored numerous plays about a variety of personalities...

"How does it work?" I asked out of curiosity.

She looked up at me from the mirror at the dressing table as I smoothed the wig that she wore for her portrayal of the Egyptian queen.

"I usually work with the cards—tarot," she explained. "But there are times the messages just come through, often at the most unexpected moments."

Considering my aunt's predilection for having a reading done, I was quite familiar with the cards.

"I ask questions, then lay the cards out in a spread. The answer is always right there. But often, like before, they just come barging in." She turned and leaned toward me as if sharing a secret.

"It's when they have something they consider important to tell me. Like the other day. Wills was most upset about the statue and determined to have it removed. He's constantly reminding me of it. I fully expected to arrive at the theatre one evening and find it smashed to pieces."

Her expression softened. "About your sister. I've tried, but all I get is that it's a dark place and quite near." She was thoughtful.

"I will try again."

She pressed my hand. "Messages can sometimes be very confusing, and then there are the ones... Let me just say there are those in the spirit world who like to play pranks. They can't always be relied upon."

But what if they were correct?

I shook off my concerns and helped her prepare for her performance. We had finished her preparations when one of the Clarendon staff arrived and announced that supper had concluded and the guests had returned to the State Room.

I accompanied Templeton as far as the entrance. A red-and-gold carpet had been rolled out from the entrance to the stage where she was to give her performance.

Others in our party—her personal maid, her manager, and a handful of attendants, including some of the stage staff—slipped into the back of the State Room, apparently to render assistance if it should be needed. I joined them, hiding myself from view. I looked for Brodie, but didn't see him.

All the guests seemed enthralled with the performance as the curtains were drawn back by two other members of her staff. The guest's attention focused on the woman at center stage—Cleopatra in all her regal beauty, with Marc Anthony as the first of three scenes began that she was to perform that evening.

I had to admit that I was fascinated by the transformation as the orchestra that had gathered for the evening accompanied them. It began with a slow piece that gradually built as Templeton and her fellow actor began as lovers. The accompaniment then changed, as the lovers found themselves on opposite sides of a political storm that had gathered. I wondered what Wills might think of the performance.

Their scene as lovers being torn apart amid the rising conflict between Egypt and Rome, lasted no more than twenty minutes. It then ended with Cleopatra's accusation against him that she had been betrayed. Marc Anthony exited the stage with a final word that he went to meet either victory or death.

The curtain came down as the stage was prepared for the second scene. In this scene, Cleopatra had received word that Roman legions had been sent against her. She then gave orders for her own army to prepare to meet the invaders.

The woman, Marie Níkola, leaned over and made some comment to Charles, as the sets were changed. He nodded, then spoke briefly to the Prince of Wales. Both men then rose from their chairs and walked toward the doors of the State Room. Marie Níkola and Resnick followed.

I stepped back into the shadows as they passed by and left the State Room. Charles's expression was very much like that statue of the Centurion, while the Prince of Wales chatted with Marie Níkola.

Brodie was nowhere to be found, with the set-change almost complete for Templeton's next scene. I was able to make eye contact briefly with Dooley, who had positioned himself at a nearby table set with refreshments for the guests.

I had no idea where Charles and the Prince of Wales were going, and slipped out of the State Room as the curtain rose and the scene opened. The second scene was well underway with the attention of everyone focused on Templeton's performance. I used the cover of near darkness with the lights down as I followed Charles and the Prince of Wales.

There was only one direction they could have gone, the hallway ending at my left just beyond the State Room. I entered the hallway and came upon them just as they entered the Green Room at the far end near the staircase.

I remembered the room well from a previous visit to a reception with my aunt. It was smaller than the other rooms at Clarendon House, less ostentatious, with dark green walls that had a festive atmosphere so near the holidays. The chandeliers had been aglow that night with small twinkling lights, a fire at the hearth, and tall windows that looked out to St. James's Square.

I slipped into an alcove across the hall, but not before I caught a brief glimpse inside of the room through the opened doorway.

There was the faint gleam of electric lights that had been turned on, however no lights shown from the overhead chandeliers, and there was no fire at the hearth. Then the door was abruptly closed on Charles and his guests.

I thought it quite odd for a meeting with a person of the importance of the Prince of Wales. Most curious, I slipped out of the alcove and hid behind a potted palm next to the double doors.

I had no more stepped behind the enormous plant than I heard the sound of voices from within.

"What is this about, Litton?"

I recognized the Prince of Wales' voice, as he then demanded, *"Who are these people?"*

There was some reply from Charles that I couldn't make out.

Then, *"How dare you make such demands!"* Prince Albert exclaimed, his voice rising. *"Dear God, you are mad!"*

"God has nothing to do with this." A woman's voice, that could only be Marie Níkola.

"Take him!" she ordered. *" And make certain that you're not seen."*

I had no time to contemplate the situation further as the door was suddenly thrown open.

Marie Níkola came out first, smoothing her hair and the skirt of her gown. I ceased breathing altogether as she glanced both directions of the hallway, including where I stood hidden behind the palm.

"Come," she ordered, obviously satisfied that there was no one else about.

Charles was the next to leave the room, his features drawn and tight, followed by Prince Albert.

I had only seen him once before at a reception I had attended with Charles and my sister, and had considered him quite unremarkable, perhaps even boring for one who was supposed to one day sit on the throne.

He was portly and given to nervously smoothing his mustache, his eyes wide-set in a round face that much resembled his mother, the Queen, rather than his father, also named Albert, who had been quite handsome in his youth.

Now, the Prince of Wales appeared quite shaken, his steps halting, his eyes darting about as if hoping for someone to rescue him.

The situation soon became apparent as Resnick followed close behind. He was of an even height as the Prince, with one hand reaching forward on the Prince's shoulder.

"This way," Resnick ordered, and they both turned in the opposite direction, away from the State Room and toward the stairs.

It was then that I saw the gun in Resnick's other hand, the tip of the barrel pressed against the Prince's back. It took a moment for it to register.

They were abducting the Prince of Wales!

Newspaper headlines that I'd read at the library flashed through my thoughts, along with what Herr Schmidt had told us about the anarchist group, the

Black Hand—that their goal was to eliminate all royal families.

I glanced down the hallway. There was no one about, no one was coming to the Prince's aid. My decision was really quite simple.

I hadn't liked Marie Níkola from the moment I saw her. There was something about the woman, her overbearing demeanor, the way she had kept Charles under her thumb the entire evening, never more than a few paces away, moving as he moved.

Lover? Mistress? Or something far more dangerous?

I acted quickly as Resnick pushed the Prince of Wales ahead of him into the hallway. When they were very near where I stood hidden, I shoved the potted palm over along with the enormous metal basin it was planted in. It wobbled, then fell toward the two men.

Resnick was thrown back against the wall of the hallway, while the Prince staggered forward.

Marie Níkola pushed through the tangled branches of the fallen palm, with Charles behind her.

"Get him, you fool!" she shouted at Resnick.

He lunged toward the Prince as a shout came from the entrance to the State Room. A man dressed in Clarendon staff livery appeared in the hallway, a shocked expression at his face at the sight before him. He shouted over his shoulder, then ran toward the Prince.

Several more people immediately appeared in the hallway. I had no way of knowing if Dooley or Brodie was among them as they swarmed toward us.

Their plan thwarted, Marie Níkola turned to her companion, a furious expression on her face. She swore, the words unfamiliar but needing no translation. Resnick turned and ran, Marie Níkola with him as they fled toward the staircase.

I caught Charles's startled expression as he pushed aside palm branches, the question flashing through my thoughts as to what part he had played in all of this, as the others reached the Prince.

I glanced in the direction Marie and Resnick had fled. They had a good lead on the others and would surely get away, and along with them any answers they might have what this was all about.

The hallway was blocked by the palm that had no doubt saved the Prince of Wales from whatever Marie and Resnick had intended. It would be several minutes more before others were able to push their way through while I faced no such obstacle other than a palm branch that had snagged the wig that I wore.

I yanked off the wig, hitched up my skirts, and went after Marie and Resnick, Brodie's warning about going off on my own a fleeting thought that was pushed aside.

I heard shouts behind me as the alarm went out about the attack on the Prince of Wales. Staff and his own guards were joined by other shouts as I reached the staircase and caught a fleeting glimpse of the two as they fled out the main entrance.

With Templeton's performance on-going, drivers sat atop hacks and coaches at the *porte cochere*, awaiting the conclusion of the evening.

"Two people just passed this way," I called out.

One of the driver's pointed in the direction of the square. Through the looming shadows, I caught sight of Marie Níkola and Resnick outlined briefly in the light from a streetlamp as they fled across St. James's Square.

They were headed toward Charles Street. Once there, they could easily find a cab and disappear. I quickened my pace.

They had very nearly reached Charles Street when

Resnick appeared to slow down, then stopped, and suddenly turned around.

I caught the look at Marie Níkola 's face in the light of a nearby street lamp. It was filled with contempt and something else as I saw Resnick raise his arm and the revolver in his hand.

There was a sudden flash as he fired the revolver, followed by a searing pain that tore through my shoulder.

I stumbled and fell.

As I lay at the edge of St. James's Square, I caught the look of grim satisfaction on Marie Níkola's face as she and Resnick turned toward the street and disappeared.

"Damned fool *eijit*!"

Brodie?

That comment seemed a bit inappropriate as I tried to roll to my feet and pain washed over me.

"By God, ye will not die! Do ye hear me?"

It could only be Brodie, as others ran past us toward Charles Street.

Who else would curse me for having the unfortunate luck of being shot?

Fool? Idiot?

For once, it seemed that he might be right.

A JARRING MOTION was my first indication that I might not be dead after all, perhaps only very nearly on my way.

My second indication was the pain in my shoulder, and the third was the rough Scottish accent that always wrapped around his words when Brodie was in a temper.

I was vaguely aware that I lay across his lap, lights passing in a blur at the coach window, along with the constant lurching motion.

"Brodie...?"

"Aye, lass." Gentler this time, but with some other emotion that I didn't understand, and an urgency that was not like him at all.

"The Prince of Wales?"

"Safe enough. Be still, we're almost there."

I had no idea where *there* was, unless he was taking me back to the Strand, or possibly to hospital. Or, I had another thought with visions of the police morgue.

He steadied me, one arm beneath my shoulders, the other across my waist as the coach slid around a corner. The rocking motion continued, slowing, then lunged on ahead at breakneck speed and around another corner. The glare of street lights had almost disappeared altogether. Eventually the coach lurched to a stop.

The coach door opened. Brodie gently eased me down onto the seat and stepped out. I was then eased from the seat into his arms.

I was aware that the sleeve and front of my gown was wet. It was not my imagination. Resnick had shot me!

"I *can* walk," I mumbled, not at all certain where that came from, or that I could.

"And I'm the Pope. Be still, lass."

Lass. Another order from Brodie, and not at all angry this time. At least he wasn't calling me a fool or idiot, and my last conscious thought was that I was quite content in spite of it all.

I remembered little of what passed the next few hours.

Mr. Brimley was there, his round, pleasant face swimming before me, as Brodie frowned. And he was saying something... something I needed to remember.

"She's lost a great deal of blood... I've made inquiries through a friend at All Saints..."

All Saints Hospital in the East End? Had someone been injured? The Prince of Wales? I struggled to concentrate, but my thoughts scattered.

Brodie's beard needed a trim, I thought, as his face loomed over me, although I found I quite liked that slightly disheveled appearance. It suited him.

I thought then that I might have smiled at that before drifting off again. When next I opened my eyes, I was surrounded by the familiar walls of the room adjacent to the office on the Strand, Mr. Conner leaning over me.

"Aye, the man closed the wound well enough. She'll live," he proclaimed, which was comforting to hear.

"The patient is awake," he announced, and then to me, "And ye, my dear, have caused quite a stir. Our friend,"—by that I assumed he meant Brodie—"has been set upon by the Home Office. Not to mention Mr. Abberline and representatives of the Prince of Wales himself. If one is impressed by such things."

One rather disgruntled Scot was replaced by another as Brodie appeared, cup in hand.

"I do hope that is whisky," I managed to say, trying to lever myself up on one elbow.

"Broth, compliments of the Mudger."

I groaned as he sat at the edge of the bed. I had never been fond of broth. It always seemed lacking in the very thing it was supposed to restore—strength. I would much rather have preferred a meat pie from the local vendor. And a dram.

"Ye gave the poor fellow quite a fright," Brodie continued. "I don't recall seeing him concerned so much about anything before, when I brought ye back to the office."

"It was a new experience for me as well," I admitted. "I've never been shot before."

"Aye."

There was that sound he often made. In an odd way, it was quite comforting to hear. I touched the bandage at my shoulder.

"Mr. Brimley is responsible for the bandage and a few stitches," Brodie informed me as he held the cup for me.

I eyed the broth with less than enthusiasm but made a mental note to thank the Mudger when I saw him next... grateful that I *would* see him again.

"The Prince of Wales?" I thought that I might have

already asked that question as I took another sip of broth and found it quite soothing. Not that I would have admitted it to Brodie, who seemed to be taking particular pleasure in my current circumstance.

"Quite safe, thanks to yer quick thinking. The potted palm was most resourceful."

"It seemed the thing to do at the time. I should have remembered to carry your revolver."

"I hesitate to think what the outcome to that might have been," Brodie replied. "Dueling it out at St. James Square. It would have made for interesting headlines in the newspapers."

There were other questions. But they would have to wait as my thoughts drifted in that way that the body often overrules what one wants, and effectively says, '*Enough*!', even as Brodie was saying something else...

"One day ye will have to explain the tattoo at yer wrist to me," he commented. "Most interesting."

Tattoo?

~

There is much to be said for a good night's sleep after the events of the previous evening. Or possibly a half-day's sleep by the time I finally wakened. There was also much to be said about being shot, as I struggled to dress myself.

It was past midday, by the angle of gray light that slipped around the edge of the window shade, and the fire that had been lit in the coal stove had burned low.

Which begged the question—had Brodie kept the fire going through the night? And who had undressed me, as I found myself wearing only bloomers and my chemise which was somewhat the worse for wear, stained with what could only be dried blood.

I struggled into my walking skirt—no mean feat one-handed—then attempted to pull on a clean shirtwaist I had brought from Mayfair. My other clothes had been left at the Drury as I prepared for the previous evening's adventure.

I made three attempts to pull the sleeve over my arm, then gave up, quite exhausted, as it was obvious it would not fit over the thick bandage at my shoulder. I settled for my jacket pulled round my shoulders in an attempt to cover my state of undress.

Once my costume was assembled, I gave myself a brief glance in the mirror over the wash stand. Fake eyebrows and the wig from my disguise the night before were gone, as was the fake mole. I was uncertain if it was an improvement as I was most certainly pale with dark circles under my eyes.

I pushed a hand through my tangled hair and conceded the rest. As I held the front of the jacket closed and prepared to leave the room, I caught a glimpse of the lotus blossom tattoo on my wrist and vaguely remembered something Brodie had said.

In view of the certainty that Brodie and I were now on intimate terms since he had obviously removed my clothes, modesty and his opinion about the tattoo were the least of my concerns.

Water closet first, I thought heading for the door! Then, food!

I managed the water closet most efficiently, having learned to navigate ocean steamers in rough seas and trains barreling through the Swiss Alps. No mean feat in a lurching train or rocking boat.

In the process, I discovered that one takes certain things for granted when able-bodied. When not, one has to get creative—such as leaning against a wall while struggling one-handed with the closure of my skirt. Then, forced to repeat the whole thing in reverse or emerge bare-ass naked. Far simpler, but not something I was up for at the moment.

Brodie was there as I emerged and escorted me back to the office. We had company in the form of Mr. Conner. He smiled across the top of the daily newspaper.

"Very good, Miss Forsythe. Ye survived the night."

That seemed quite obvious, but I chose not to comment.

"It seems Miss Templeton's private performance last evening was quite the success," he announced as he continued to read.

And the evening's other events?

He pushed the daily across the desk toward me. I scanned the headline, then the accompanying article. There were the usual accolades for Templeton, but no mention of the other *event* of the evening.

"There's nothing about the attempt to abduct the Prince of Wales."

"Aye," Brodie replied. "It would seem that the decision was made to keep the information private for now, on the part of the royals."

"And there's no mention of Charles." I was surprised as he obviously had some role in all of it.

But again, the question—what precisely was that role, and what had that to do with my sister's disappearance?

"My sources say that he is currently taking time away from his position as Home Secretary at an undisclosed location," Conner replied.

Undisclosed? Hmmm. I frowned.

"What about Resnick and the woman?"

"Both disappeared after yer... encounter."

I was not surprised. With their plan obviously thwarted, they had fled.

The question was, where had they gone? What had this to do with my sister's disappearance? Was she even still alive?

"They undoubtedly procured a rented hack when they left St. James's Park after their plans went awry," Conner replied.

"Is there a way to find out who might have picked up the fare?" I asked.

"A driver's route and locations are not random," he replied. "They usually stake out a certain territory."

That made sense as I usually saw the same drivers on the Strand since my association with Brodie, and from my other travels about the city.

"It might be useful to question drivers who were in the area of St. James's Park last evening, specifically at Charles Street."

Conner seemed most amused at the suggestion.

"Very good, Miss Forsythe, in yer deductions."

I took it as a compliment, very much in need of one as I saw the expression on Brodie's face. I could almost hear his objections to my inserting myself back into the investigation after all his warnings.

"I need to speak with Charles," I said aloud. I wanted very much to know what his part was in all of this.

A look passed between Brodie and Conner.

"I shall leave that part of the conversation to the two of ye," Conner announced, as he stood to leave. "And see what those in the vicinity of St. James's Square might know about our two '*friends.*'"

I nodded as I continued to think on the matter. "Charles may be able to tell us something important about what happened last night."

"Ye might find that difficult, as the palace is in charge of this now," Brodie replied after Conner had gone.

"Surely it can be arranged," I replied, not to be put off.

"If I were to tell ye '*no*,' I suppose it's safe to assume ye would apply all Lady Montgomery's considerable influence to do so anyway."

Point, counterpoint. There were times Brodie was quite perceptive.

"Precisely," I replied, and set about making my plan once he had arranged the meeting.

Having never been shot before—the most serious injury I had ever received was a broken finger when smashed between two pieces of luggage on one of my travels—I found it difficult to tolerate this temporary weakness, not to mention the temporary loss of the use of the arm and hand attached to my injured shoulder.

As for the wound itself, Brodie assured me that Mr. Brimley had performed quite brilliantly after cleaning the wound, then stitching me back together to prevent further loss of blood, after he determined that the bullet had passed through—a most fortuitous outcome, I was told.

He commandeered the Mudger to acquire food. When the bell sounded quite furiously outside the office door, Brodie returned from the landing to inform me that Templeton was on her way up, and my plan fell into place.

"Ye don't have that damned lizard with you, do ye?" Brodie inquired when she arrived, even though we'd learned the day before that he was apparently quite happily in residence at Templeton's country house.

"He couldn't be persuaded," she replied, then turned to me.

"Good heavens! You look like the devil, although I am most happy to see that you're alive and well."

And with that, Templeton swept past Brodie and

delivered herself and a small package to the desk, where she proceeded to take his chair in true Templeton fashion of dominating the room.

"I have business to attend to," Brodie announced, seizing his coat and umbrella from the stand.

And with that we were left quite alone.

"Open it," she told me, removing her hat and gloves.

Her costume was considerably more subdued than the previous evening. To the outward observer, she would have appeared to be any fashionably-dressed lady out making social calls. Having known her for some time, I was not fooled. I removed the plain paper and found a package of the dark, slender cigarettes I had discovered on one of my travels.

Upon my return from that adventure, I had gifted Templeton with a package of them, well aware of her habit. Together, as now, we had enjoyed the strong but sweet taste of those exotic cigarettes.

"However did you find them?"

She made a dismissive gesture through the air. "An acquaintance has been able to acquire them for me from time to time. I suppose you should wait until you've fully recovered," she added. "As they are quite strong and can have that euphoric effect. I wouldn't want you toppling from your chair.

"And I have no desire to incur Mr. Brodie's wrath," she continued. "Good heavens, the man seemed most irritated when I first arrived. But then I suppose that's the Scot in him," she added, with a faintly mysterious smile.

Moments later, we both sat back, fragrant smoke filling the office.

"I'm told that the Prince of Wales survived unharmed," I commented, inhaling the fragrant smoke.

"Yes, quite, although understandably he was most

upset by the affair." Templeton made a gesture with her cigarette as if punctuating her comment.

"And, I might add, he is most concerned for your well-being."

"I'm told that no information is being released to the newspapers," I commented.

Templeton nodded. "I've been asked to say nothing as well, even though I didn't actually *see* anything that happened. But it was quite like the Wild West," she added.

She had poured herself a bit of Brodie's whisky. I held out my cup, no doubt forbidden as well as the cigarette. However, Brodie was not there, and together, like two gentlemen sitting across from each other, we smoked and sipped my aunt's very fine whisky.

"I really must have some of this for myself," Templeton commented. "Do you think Mr. Munro could be persuaded to bring some to the theatre the next time he's out and about?"

A case of whisky, indeed. And what else might she persuade him to provide her with?

It had not escaped me over the years, of her—shall I call it—*interest* in Mr. Munro. She never let an occasion go by when we encountered one another to inquire as to his... health. I promised to speak with my aunt about the whisky, otherwise she was quite on her own as it concerned Mr. Munro.

"Now, let us see what is to be learned about this nasty business," Templeton announced, taking a deck of cards from her reticule and spreading them across Brodie's desk—Tarot cards to be precise.

It was not the first time I'd had the cards read.

The first time was by a Romany gypsy Linnie and I encountered in the French countryside one summer while at our aunt's country estate.

Linnie had been frightened by the woman with her dark eyes and wrinkled features, but I had been intrigued, a characteristic that I was reminded had gotten me into trouble on more than one occasion.

The woman had predicted the usual things she no doubt predicted for any young girl she encountered—a long life, a handsome young man, and great wealth.

If I were to encounter the woman again now, I would remind her that there was no *young* man in my life, although Brodie was quite handsome when he wasn't frowning or bellowing some outrage at me.

Templeton leaned over the cards, her expression intent.

"Yes! Oh, most interesting!" she exclaimed.

From my previous experience, I was quite prepared for the usual romantic encounter, and perhaps a long sea voyage. I was not prepared for the startled expression at Templeton's face.

"What is it?"

In spite of my skepticism that the cards actually held any information that one might believe, there was that old devil curiosity. I had to know what she saw in the cards.

TEMPLETON TURNED over several more cards and added them to the spread.

"Yes, of course. I see now."

"Of course *what*?" I demanded.

I had never been patient when it came to word games my sister persuaded me to play, or card games which I always won. Or waiting with great anticipation for Christmas morning celebration—our parents' death within two years of each other had well taken care of that childhood fantasy. Add to the list, having one's fortune read.

"A man, see the lover's card, and this one means something hidden." She looked up then.

"And this one—betrayal! Oh my."

That needed no translation as I thought of my brother-in-law.

"You have challenges ahead of you, my dear," she continued. "But you will see your way through them."

I wondered if being shot qualified as a challenge, but that had already happened. And what the devil was that about the lover's card?

Templeton folded the cards and was about to begin

another spread. I was not up for more card readings or séances.

"I want to see Charles." I repeated what I had told Brodie, along with his response. However, there was one person whose decision in the matter outweighed any of Brodie's objections.

"I could speak to Bertie on your behalf," Templeton replied. "He does feel that he owes you a debt that can never be repaid."

I ignored the niggling doubt at what Brodie's reaction would be. I grinned and pushed my glass toward Templeton. "More, please."

I said nothing to Brodie when he returned, shaking rain from his umbrella and coat.

Hearing his steps on the stairs outside the office, Templeton had thrown open both office windows to clear the air of cigarette smoke, though I was dubious of the results knowing Brodie's penchant for details. She also emptied the dish with ash and the remnants of the cigarettes out the window.

He said nothing as he came through the door, glanced briefly at Templeton and me, then handed me one of the other daily newspapers.

"I must be going," Templeton announced, retrieving her coat and taking up her umbrella. She leaned in close and brushed my cheek, an affectation I've always thought to be quite disingenuous, but willing to make a concession in Templeton's case.

"I'll be in contact," she whispered, then turned that smile on Brodie. "So good to see you again."

"What was that about?" he commented, as Templeton swept out the door.

"She read the cards for me." Not a lie.

"And what did the cards have to say?"

I heard the disdain at his voice. "Something about a

man, a lover if the cards are to be believed." I conveniently left out the other part of Templeton's interpretation of the cards—the part about something hidden and betrayal.

"Is that right?"

If I wasn't certain that he couldn't possibly know of our plan, I would have thought that he might have overheard Templeton's offer to speak with the Prince of Wales about my request to see Charles.

"Do I smell cigarette smoke?"

There was a saying about the spirit willing, but not the body. Or something very near that.

I discovered just how very true that was the next day, as I tried to rise from a fitful night of sleep and discovered that in addition to the wound at my shoulder, I hurt all over.

"Aye," Brodie acknowledged, as I emerged from the room, somewhat dressed as I had the day before, bare of foot, hair in a tangled mass, with the feeling that I might have been tossed from a horse, then run over by a coach.

"Not unusual," he said, taking note of my slow progress and assisting me to my usual chair at the desk. "The second day is usually the worst of it. It takes time. Mr. Brimley assured there were no broken bones."

I was not at all accustomed to being an invalid and most appreciative of his assurances. However, I did not have time to sit about with my sister still missing. Not to mention Resnick and Marie Nícola still out there. Along with the white-haired man who had now murdered three people, and my brother-in-law in the custody of the authorities...?

It was possible that I was somewhat bad-tempered with the situation, and made no attempt to conceal it.

"Here," Brodie said, handing me a cup that smelled of fresh coffee, and perhaps something else?

"I don't suppose it will cause any harm, since ye seem no worse for yesterday's drink," he commented.

There were times that Brodie was far too observant. Of course, it was possible that he was aware that the bottle was somewhat depleted after Templeton's visit.

"Not that you have ever taken a dram, for medicinal purposes, of course," I replied, unable to let the moment pass.

"On occasion. However, in my experience a lady is usually concerned with appearances of such things."

A lady? How very amusing.

Perhaps he was thinking of Templeton, although I had already heard quite a discourse about that. Something about eccentric actresses who kept lizards for pets, or something very like that. I took another sip of Brodie's coffee brew.

"Have you any word from Mr. Conner?" I was most anxious what he might be able to learn from his inquiries.

"Not yet, and I would think that yer injury would be sufficient to convince ye that this has become too dangerous for ye to continue in this."

I looked at him over the edge of the cup. There were moments, he could be quite endearing, and I was very much aware that his quick thinking had very likely saved my life, and I was grateful.

I had a vague memory of him bending over me on the green at St. James's Park, yelling at me not to die, and something else in there about his opinion of me. I was also aware that it could be against my purposes to give in to that overbearing Scot attitude.

It might work with others, it would not work with

me, however handsome I found him to be when his Scot *was up*, so to speak.

In answer to his comment, I held out my empty cup.

~

With food and sufficient drink, my mood lightened somewhat, although I was already feeling the restrictions of my so-called confinement, not to mention the discomfort at my shoulder. I did the only thing a woman in my position could do when he went out—I sat on the floor and meditated.

I had acquired the habit on a tour of India and become quite accomplished in detaching from the usual problems, frustrations, and even pain, including the occasional author's block.

It was accomplished quite simply by clearing my thoughts while focusing on an image until everything else faded away. I usually focused on the Lotus blossom and eventually felt quite removed from it all.

"What the devil...?" Brodie exclaimed, as he returned and found me quite mellow, not to mention almost pain free.

"Are you unwell?"

When I explained that I had been meditating to get rid of the pain, he looked at me as if I had sprouted another head.

"It's really quite effective," I told him, eventually standing and returning to the chair quite relaxed and clear of thought.

"A Yogi in India on my last visit taught me. He was quite revered among his people." I angled a look at Brodie. "And there are those who find it quite helpful in managing anger."

He chose to ignore me with one of those typically Brodie sounds that could have been interpreted as a snarl.

However, for his part, he was surprisingly solicitous and tolerant, ignoring my short-tempered moments. Not to mention my impatience, my meditating, and my pacing across the office from desk to blackboard, then back again as icy rain kept up a noisome patter against the window glass.

Shortly after midday, Mr. Brimley arrived to check on his 'patient.'

My previous experience with a gunshot wound had been my father by his own hand, a gruesome experience particularly for a young child. When Mr. Brimley peeled away the bandage, I was somewhat surprised at the small size of the wounds at the front and back of my shoulder that had been neatly stitched.

I was informed that the wound at the back of my shoulder was only slightly larger, the caliber of bullet having obviously been small, no doubt meant for close encounters. I was fortunate that I had been a few yards away when Resnick fired the pistol. It seemed an odd thing to be grateful for.

Mr. Brimley announced that there were no signs of infection, proceeded to spread some sort of noxious concoction on the two wounds, bandaged me up once more, and then tied a sling about my neck.

"That will keep your arm immobile so as not to irritate the wounds. I'll leave the salve. The bandages are to be changed every day, and you're to keep to yer bed for the next several days," he smiled congenially. I felt trussed up like a Christmas goose.

Brodie grinned.

"I'll see to it that she follows yer instructions."

And pigs fly.

My deliverance from absolute boredom and frustration, arrived the following afternoon in a message from Templeton.

"*We need to meet.*"

I scrawled a hasty note back to her explaining that I was presently confined to the office due to lack of suitable clothes, and the suspicion that I might smell as bad as I felt, having not bathed in as many days. I also mentioned the ever-watchful eye of Brodie, unless he was out and about.

And there was still no word from Mr. Conner about his inquiries among the cabmen and hired coaches that had traveled Charles Street the night of the attempt on dear Bertie.

I received no note in response, nor had I expected one in view of Templeton's scheduled performances at the Drury. Her answer, when it came, was in typical Templeton style in the arrival of Templeton herself the following morning, as she put it, *to rescue me*.

Her timing was perfect. Brodie had left earlier after making certain I had sufficient breakfast and coffee, installing Mr. Dooley as guardian.

To say that the poor man was quite flummoxed by Templeton's appearance, was an understatement. Apparently he was quite enamored of her in spite of the fact that he was a married man—and Templeton put on an incredible performance.

She flirted outrageously with the poor man until he was beside himself and completely outdone as she *rescued* me in her waiting coach.

Any objection the Mudger might have made as we escaped was silenced by one look from my companion. Then we were off, Templeton in a cloud of purple and red feather boas, with me holding the front of my jacket together over my blood-stained chemise. I could only imagine how we looked.

That thought rose again as our coach passed very near Regent Park, then around a corner in the Marylebone District and slowed to a stop at a side entrance of the Langham Hotel.

"Come along."

Like an excited child, Templeton reached for the door handle as the driver opened the coach door and assisted her. A hotel footman stood at the entrance, his expression, or lack of one, much like that of the palace guards.

"It's all been arranged," she explained. "Trust me."

Always dangerous where Templeton was concerned.

"I can't go in like this," I protested with visions of the two of us being escorted from the hotel as I was fairly certain that the Langham was not accustomed to receiving guests with blood-stained clothes.

Templeton motioned to the footman and requested his jacket. He removed it and handed it to her. She then motioned to the driver, who assisted me from the coach with only a subtle glance at my present garments. Templeton wrapped the footman's coat about my shoulders.

"There," she announced. "Quite presentable now, even though there will be no one to see you." She flashed that trademark smile.

"Trust me."

There was that word again.

Quite *presentable* was subject to one's interpretation, I thought, as she wrapped an arm about my waist and we entered the hotel, and I discovered there was indeed no one to see me in all my blood-stained glory.

The side entrance was removed some distance from the main entrance, possibly for employees or those who wished to come and go discreetly from the hotel. Perhaps the Prince of Wales's mistress as well? I thought.

The entrance turned to a short hallway where another Langham attendant appeared who led the way to the lift. We entered the cage. The gate was closed and the attendant engaged the lever. Not a word was exchanged, or apparently needed. It appeared that Templeton was well known by hotel staff.

The lift eventually slowed to a stop and we stepped off into a private lobby, then proceeded down a hallway.

There were only a handful of doors rather than the usual number I would expect to find on the floor of a hotel, and no room numbers. There was only the royal seal embossed in gold leaf over the entrance to the door we now approached.

The Langham was exclusive, the grand opening years earlier attended by the Prince of Wales. Rumors swirled that it was here that he kept company with exclusive *guests.*

Bloody hell! What was Templeton up to?

I had visions of stepping into the room and meeting the Prince of Wales, complete with my blood stains—not exactly a good impression to make.

"I don't think this is a very good idea," I protested, backing away from the door.

Templeton fixed me with that mischievous gaze that was reported to have enthralled the Prince and kept him captive. She opened the door and waltzed in.

The room was everything one might have imagined for a full suite of rooms fit for the man who would one day be king. And it was obvious that Templeton was quite familiar with them.

"You may, of course, continue standing out in the hall," she told me. "Unless, of course, you would like a bath."

Bath?

Templeton was joined by two women, one quite

young, the other substantially older, introduced as Mrs. Hawthorne. Much like the others we had encountered since arriving, their expressions were quite... expressionless.

"What is this all about?"

Templeton waited until the door had closed.

"Bertie insisted."

And that explained everything.

"You look quite exhausted," she added, and pointed toward the sitting area with two exquisitely upholstered, high-back chairs that sat at an elegant table with a chess board inlaid in what I assumed was gold leaf. So much for casual games of dice at the Old Bell.

"This should explain everything." She handed me an envelope with the royal seal.

The letter was carefully handwritten, no doubt by the Prince's equerry. It was apparent Bertie was not one to sit before a typing machine and peck out the royal correspondence himself.

The Prince of Wales expressed his enormous gratitude to me over the events at Clarendon House. He hoped that I was well on my way to recovery from my injury, and as a gesture of his sincere appreciation I was to be accorded every accommodation by members of his staff at the Langham. It included the use of his private suite for as long as I chose.

He closed by saying that he owed me a debt of gratitude that could never be repaid, and if I was ever in need of his assistance, I had only to ask.

I looked over at Templeton. "A bath."

It was if I had issued a royal decree. Both of the other women immediately flew into action as Templeton smiled with satisfaction.

There was definitely something to be said for warm water along with an assortment of fragrant soaps and oils as a restorative. It much reminded me of my mother's preferences for lavender.

For the first time in days, I was content to languish in the claw-foot tub with steaming water up to my shoulders—one shoulder to be precise as I kept the injured one out of the water. I was even content to let Mrs. Hawthorne and the young maid in her charge wash my hair rather than struggling with it myself.

Then, only when the water had cooled for the second time—such a marvelous invention, hot water that came through the gold-plated pipes in the wall—and my skin had begun to take on the look of withered fruit, was I willing to relinquish the luxury.

I emerged from the chamber, freshly bathed with my bandages intact, with only a curious glance at my wounds by Mrs. Hawthorne, then wrapped in a flannel-lined dressing gown.

Templeton was seated at the table with a bottle and two glasses before her, enjoying a cigarette.

"There you are!" she exclaimed. "I was afraid I might have to send the footman to rescue you. He really is quite adorable."

Then as Mrs. Hawthorne and the girl emerged, she thanked them for their attention.

"I am quite capable of attending to Miss Forsythe from here. Thank you for your assistance."

When they had gone, Templeton informed me that she had arranged for garments to be sent to the Langham as well.

"We are near enough the same size, and it isn't as if you can wear those dreadful blood-stained clothes." She proceeded to pour wine into the two glasses.

"I have some things I brought back from my last tour that are perfect for you."

With everything that had happened so far, I

wouldn't have been surprised if Ziggy had come slithering out of one of the adjacent rooms.

She proceeded to show me the split skirt she had acquired after attending Buffalo Bill's Wild West Show as his guest. I didn't ask how she had come by it.

It was divided much like a pair of pants, but included a buttoned panel that could be unbuttoned when the situation warranted. Otherwise, it gave the appearance of a walking skirt.

Other than wearing a pair of men's pants, which I had on occasion, depending on where I was traveling at the time, it was most clever.

"Annie Oakley, the American sharpshooter, wears them when she's performing in Buffalo Bill's Wild West Show. Fascinating woman. She much reminded me of you."

Templeton assisted me into the divided skirt and a new shirtwaist, with another set of clothes folded nearby. My boots finished off the ensemble. Templeton stood back to admire her inspiration.

"Oh, yes, perfect." She refilled both our wine glasses.

"It was very kind of his Highness to make the rooms available," I commented as we sat sipping wine.

"Kindness had nothing to do with it, although Bertie can be very thoughtful," she replied and went on to explain.

"He was in a fit after what happened at the Clarendon. I've never seen him so beside himself."

She had that look. "It really was quite exciting though, aside from getting shot that is. That dreadful woman. And as for Charles..."

"I want to speak with him," I commented. "Do you think it might be arranged?"

Templeton looked at me with a thoughtful expression.

"According to gossip, he's been taken to the Tower," she replied. "I suppose that Bertie could make arrangements..."

By that, I was certain she meant the Tower of London. A place with a notorious reputation, where those who threatened the Crown in the past had been imprisoned, with a few beheadings thrown in along the way.

I needed to speak with Charles. He was obviously involved in all of this. But how? And what part did Marie Níkola and Kosta Resnick play in this?

At Templeton's suggestion, I penned my request and handed it to her. She promptly gave it to the attendant in the hallway with instructions that it was to be placed directly in the hands of the footman to the Prince of Wales and no one else. It was apparently a familiar arrangement.

"DO you want me to accompany you?" Templeton asked, as we arrived back at the Strand.

At a glance, it appeared that Brodie had returned, a light glowing in the office at the top of the stairs. Knowing his opinion of actresses—Templeton in particular—I thought it best that I face the situation on my own.

"The woman is a complete disaster... She keeps a lizard for a companion, for God's sake! And has had affairs to rival any of the women who earn their living on the street!"

I hadn't bothered to point out that Brodie had a great amount of respect for the '*women on the street.*' It was an argument that could not be won when one of the participants was a stubborn Scot.

"It will be all right," I assured her, stepping down from the coach with my additional clothes and a wrapped peace offering in a basket that the hotel staff had provided.

"If you're certain?" she asked.

"Absolutely."

Never underestimate the power of a woman, freshly

bathed and dressed in a split skirt, I thought. I felt like Annie Oakley as Templeton finally told the coachman to drive on. The only thing missing was my rifle.

The Mudger was in his usual place, a bemused expression on his smudged, bewhiskered face.

"He is about?" I asked, although the light in the office was proof of it.

"Aye."

"In a temper, is he?"

"The usual," he replied, with good humor. "Ye've a talent for twisting his tail, miss."

I took that as a compliment.

"Is anyone else about?" I asked, since Brodie had enlisted the assistance of Mr. Conner to make inquiries regarding the night of the attack, and the man had a habit of showing up unannounced.

The Mudger shook his head. "He was out most of the day, returned a while ago. Not pleased to find you gone."

Rupert the hound was particularly fascinated with the basket I carried, nose lifted to the air to make his own investigations.

Knowing that he had a taste for sweet pastry, I handed the Mudger the sponge cake that had arrived with our supper, compliments of the Langham Hotel and their most distinguished patron.

Templeton was forever watching how much she ate, with the excuse that she would not be able to fit into her costumes, and had declined dessert. I had no such hesitation and had consumed mine. There was still a good portion of the dessert the hotel had provided, along with enough Beef Wellington to carry both Brodie and me into the following day.

The Mudger thanked me heartily, licking the sticky liquor topping of the sponge cake from his fingers.

"Any words of advice on the coming campaign?" I asked.

He grinned. "Yer should have saved the sponge cake for him."

Sweets to sweeten the foul beast?

"Right. Onward," I announced, turning toward the stairway much like a field commander heading into battle, my weapon of Beef Wellington in hand.

"Where the devil have ye been?" Brodie demanded, as I had barely set foot into the office, my hand still on the door handle.

"Quite well, thank you, in spite of my injury," I replied, with deliberate aim at his surly disposition.

"And what the devil is that?" he demanded.

I was certain the comment was aimed at my costume. I chose to ignore it.

Brodie was quite beside himself, and made no effort to disguise his displeasure at returning to find me gone, and in what he described as the company of *'that woman'*!

"Templeton is well, thank you. She sends her regards." Not precisely the truth, but I couldn't resist poking the bear.

I let him have his temper. He vented in the manner I was quite used to by now.

"You might want to read this," I casually replied, which was much like adding coal oil to a fire.

I laid the note from the Prince of Wales in answer to my request, on the desk. Brodie eyed it suspiciously.

"What the devil is that?"

"A royal summons, in a manner of speaking."

"What 'manner of speaking'?"

"You've been appointed to accompany me to the Tower, so that I may speak with Charles. He has appointed you as escort, although he was quite hesitant at first. Something about the nasty business of previously working with a private detective."

I couldn't help myself. It was quite true that the prince had been concerned about it, as he'd had some experience in the past that apparently hadn't ended well.

"How the devil...?"

What, and now *how*. There were moments when Brodie could be most amusing.

"I sent a note to him. I thought it might be important to our investigation," I included him in this, even though it wasn't precisely true.

"The appointment at the Tower is for tomorrow morning at ten o'clock."

"Bloody Christ!" he cursed. "Ye are the most..." He stared at me, momentarily at a loss for words.

I quite enjoyed myself.

"And what the devil is that costume yer wearing?" he demanded.

"It's quite the fashion in the United States."

I didn't mention that it was mostly the fashion of circus and Wild West performers, and proceeded to unbutton the front panel. The frown on his face deepened in a most gratifying way.

"The next thing ye know, women will be wearing men's breeches," he snapped.

I merely smiled and didn't bother to explain that I already had, on several occasions.

"And what is that?" He eyed the basket.

"Supper. Templeton thought to send it for you." Not precisely correct either, but a little further stretch of the truth never hurt, especially when facing down an angry Scot. And it most certainly couldn't hurt to soften his opinion of Templeton and actresses in general.

I opened the basket. Brodie curiously eyed the Beef

Wellington, as I pulled away the linen napkin from the plate embossed with the name of the Langham Hotel.

"Try it, you might like it," I told him.

"What is the damned thing?"

"Beef Wellington."

"The man had a supper course named after him?"

It was a long story.

"It will only spoil if you don't eat it, and it is a fact that men live their lives between their stomach and their... knees." I edited what I could have said at the sudden direction his eyebrows had taken.

The aroma of the rich entree worked its magic.

From the basket he seized a knife and fork that the hotel had also provided.

"Is that right?"

"It's a fact." I watched with amusement as he proceeded to assault the Wellington.

It seemed that our partnership was safe—proof of my theory about men and their... stomachs!

The day had left me quite exhausted. Of course, a bit of whisky didn't hurt—a tonic to ease the discomfort in my shoulder.

Having polished off a good portion of the Wellington, Brodie proceeded to pour a bit more for himself. I held out my glass.

"Yer still recovering from yer wound," he cautioned.

I didn't bother to mention that Templeton and I had quite enjoyed our afternoon over two bottles of wine, and survived quite nicely, thank you. I simply continued to hold out my glass. He eventually conceded the point and poured a very small portion.

We sat in companionable silence.

There were moments I quite enjoyed our unusual partnership, and I was forced to admit that I'd never before experienced a relationship with a man quite like it.

True, there were moments when Brodie could be aggravating, stubborn, over-bearing. There were also moments when he was thoughtful, loyal to a fault, with an acute sense of facts, and most handsome, when he wasn't snarling at me. Or when he was...

He was certainly not polished, groomed to a high luster like many of my acquaintance—my brother-in-law came to mind.

Brodie was more like the men of the Wild West Templeton had described during our afternoon together —rough around the edges, uncompromising, refusing to be ordered about by another. Men who took risks, setting off on their own into dangerous places.

"Very much like your Mr. Brodie." Templeton had quite surprised me. *"I do believe Mr. Munro is much the same."*

Something to contemplate, when I wasn't quite so tired.

Brodie rose from his chair. "It's late, and ye've a meeting in the morning with Sir Charles."

I emptied my glass and set it on the desk most efficiently, I thought. I rose from my usual chair across the desk, also quite efficiently—however, the room did not cooperate, as it suddenly appeared to tilt.

"Come along, then." Brodie rounded the desk and steadied me. "Before ye injure yerself again."

I could have sworn there was a curse in there somewhere, but my thoughts were a bit fuzzy—two bottles of wine and more than one dram that I managed to persuade from him.

Brodie deposited me on the edge of the bed, then went to the stove and spent several moments stoking it with more coal until the fire caught.

Then, another curse as he returned to where I still sat on the edge of the bed. He knelt down and began unbuttoning my boots, then slipped them off and set them aside.

My shirtwaist with its dozens of buttons that Templeton had helped me with earlier brought another curse.

"Damned things."

I smiled as he unbuttoned the tiny buttons at the cuffs, and cursed again. I was quite enjoying myself.

"You missed one."

As it seemed that he might simply tear the buttons from the shirt with aggravation, I took over the ones down the front, more or less successfully.

"*Ye've* missed one." He brushed my hands aside and finished the deed, then seemed somewhat flummoxed. At least I chose to believe that he was, at the sight of a half-naked woman.

"I don't suppose ye thought to change the bandage at yer shoulder after yer foray at the Langham."

"It seems to have survived quite well from yesterday," I replied.

"Mr. Brimley said it was to be changed daily. Take the damned shirt off."

"I can manage the bandage myself."

"Aye, perhaps the one at the front of yer shoulder, but not the other at the back unless ye've perfected the skill of spinning yer head about."

I could have sworn he had just described the commonly held belief about evil spirits—that they had the ability to contort themselves in all manner of poses and disguises.

He went into the outer office, then returned with fresh bandages and the salve that Mr. Brimley had provided after stitching me back together. I watched as he carefully untied the strip of cloth that held both bandages in place.

I had taken care not to get them wet, however *the best laid plans of mice and men...* according to Robert Burns—a fellow Scot by the way.

He frowned as he peeled away the bandage at the front of my shoulder. I looked down at the neatly stitched wound.

"Apparently no gangrene," I commented.

He shook his head as he removed the bandage at the back of my shoulder, the expressions on his face most entertaining.

I liked the frown as he hesitated, followed by some other comment under his breath as he applied the pungent salve to both wounds, then covered them with clean squares of cloth.

"You've done this before," I commented, as he efficiently tied off the bandage, checked to make certain it wasn't too tight, then tucked in the ends. He seemed to be having some difficulty, fidgeting with the strap of my camisole. He gave up.

It occurred to me that his uneasiness with the buttons of my camisole might have nothing to do with inexperience. For all his gruffness and surliness, Angus Brodie was a most interesting man.

"Ye do what ye have to when you live on the streets," he replied. "Clean bandages were in short supply."

I imagined a young boy, orphaned after the death of his grandmother, making his way about the streets of Edinburgh at whatever odd job he could find. Then he had found his way to London, with all manner of adventures in between.

Now the man, who had no doubt fought and scraped, had made something of himself—someone who was respected, from the beggar on the street to the

Chief Inspector of Police. Though I suspected Abberline would never admit to that.

He gestured to my divided skirt. "Can ye manage the rest?"

It took some effort, and I was admittedly a bit unsteady on my feet.

It had seemed quite easily done when Templeton assisted that afternoon with the row of buttons down the front of the panel. They were considerably larger than the ones on the shirtwaist; however it was a slow process.

"Leave off," Brodie gruffly told me. "Ye should probably just sleep in the damned thing. At this rate, ye'll be at it 'til morning."

I smiled to myself as he brushed my hands aside and proceeded to unbutton the front panel. I was no doubt a bit into my cups, but laughter at the moment was very possibly not a good idea, and I smothered the giggle that bubbled into my throat at his efforts.

"Damned thing," he cursed, as his hands brushed my waist, then steadied me as I stepped out of the skirt, my other hand on his shoulder. When I was relieved of the skirt, I sat back on the bed, wearing only my bloomers and camisole.

As I slipped beneath the covers on a cloud of whisky haze, Brodie went to the small iron stove and added more coal.

"That should keep for the night," he announced.

I was vaguely aware that he pulled the wool blanket up over my shoulder and tucked it around me before dousing the light.

Whether it was the whisky or the beginning of a dream, something familiar peeked at me from the edge of sleep, like a memory that lingered just out of reach.

"Damned fool woman."

Twenty-Three

THE TOWER OF LONDON was originally a royal palace and fortress where the royal family lived in centuries past, built by William the Conqueror some nine hundred years earlier.

In the more recent past, merely a few centuries earlier, it was the 'residence' of Elizabeth I and her mother, Anne Boleyn, for a time.

It was said there were royal apartments inside the Tower, as it was never intended to be a prison. However, the walls that surrounded the Tower prevented any escape.

The Tower's gruesome reputation as a prison included the rumored imprisonment of two young princes on the orders of Richard III in a bloody game of politics. Their bodies were found centuries later in the walls. Then there was the imprisonment of several other notable persons, including Sir Walter Raleigh after he displeased Elizabeth I, and William Wallace of Scotland, before he was drawn and quartered. Messy business being drawn and quartered.

It was also rumored that the Tower was haunted, not the least by the ghost of Anne Boleyn who was reported to have been seen on several occasions wandering about the place. Templeton would have been quite excited to pay a visit and see what she might be able to tap into.

The outer walls also contained the apartments of the staff that now lived at the Tower, along with living quarters for the warders, who were posted throughout as we now saw as we arrived for my meeting with Charles.

We encountered no ghosts, only the black ravens that the Tower was quite famous for. A yeoman warder scattered seed about the main courtyard and they descended in a frenzied black cloud as we were shown to the office of the Captain of the Royal Warders, who also lived at the Tower.

The accommodations were not austere, but most surprisingly comfortable, with a fire in the hearth that filled one wall, desk and chairs. It was not at all what I had expected with the rattling of chains in my imagination. Although I did make note of the iron bars at the windows.

"I was informed of your visit," the captain commented, as he read again the note with that royal seal, advising that I was to be given every courtesy as well as the opportunity to see the prisoner, Sir Charles Litton.

"And Mr. Brodie?" he inquired, as he looked up. "It has been some time."

It appeared that they had met before. In Brodie's previous incarnation with the Metropolitan Police perhaps. Or possibly on another matter?

"I will be accompanying Miss Forsythe," Brodie informed him.

"Overstepping yourself again, Brodie?" the captain responded.

"Not at all," I informed the captain before he could respond, in what would most likely be a bit of attitude.

"Mr. Brodie is well informed on the matter, and quite necessary to the investigation of the particular incident that this involves.

"If there is some confusion in this, I'm certain his Highness can set the matter straight," I continued. "Although I would hesitate to bother him in this, as his note is quite clear that I am to be allowed to speak with Sir Charles Litton."

It was a bit of a stretch of the truth once more, perhaps a large stretch. But I was not of a mind to argue the matter further. And I have often found that one could be persuaded to my point with a few well-chosen words, especially those in government positions.

"I suppose there's no harm in Mr. Brodie accompanying you." He looked up at Brodie.

"Are you carrying a firearm?"

Brodie opened the front of his coat, indicating that he carried no weapon.

"Very well then," the captain replied. "I shall have to keep this," he indicated the official request from the Prince of Wales.

He motioned to the uniformed warder who had accompanied us.

"You will escort Miss Forsythe and Mr. Brodie to Beauchamp Tower. They are to be allowed to see the prisoner held there."

We followed the young warder in his very official royal uniform.

Beauchamp Tower was to the west of the green with a scaffold. I wondered how recently that might have been utilized.

My brother-in-law had always been one to make others aware of his position as Home Secretary, as well as being born to a title that had given him privilege and rank. Now he shared that '*privilege*' with others in history who had resided there awaiting their fate.

The Beauchamp was not what one might expect of a Tower prison. It had wood floors in the main room, an enormous fireplace that one could stand in, and arched windows of the Medieval period. However, like the captain's quarters, the windows contained iron bars that discouraged any hope of escape.

Various hallways with stone archways angled off from the main room. Charles was imprisoned down one of those hallways with its rabbit's warren of passages, cells, and other rooms.

We signed in, and another warder was summoned and told to escort us to the room where Charles was being held.

It was not far, the entrance to the cell in the same Medieval style, the door made of stout oak with an iron bar across. As the warder released the cross bar and opened the door, I exchanged a look with Brodie.

We had discussed the questions I wanted to ask on the ride across London, and he had prepared me for the possibility that I might not receive any answers at all.

"It's the way of some," he had explained. "Especially when their neck is in the noose, so to speak. Sir Charles is no fool. He knows that there will be serious charges brought against him. He may be angry, even violent..."

We entered the chamber, the door closed, and that iron bar was dropped back into place with a sobering sound.

I had mentally prepared myself, but I suppose one can never be prepared for the sight of someone imprisoned in that sort of imposing place.

Where the captain's office had been adequately furnished, the chamber that Charles now occupied was quite Spartan, barren of furniture and fixtures except for a narrow bed, a small table, and the most minimal of accommodations, with a single small basin at the table. The arched window, like the others I had noticed, contained those same iron bars beyond the glass panes.

In appearance, Charles was quite changed from the man I had met with over a week earlier at the Grosvenor. He was disheveled, wearing the very same clothes he had worn that night at Clarendon House, his shirt now stained, tie missing, the expression on his face quite haggard.

"Mikaela..." Whatever he started to say ended abruptly as he saw Brodie.

"It's good to see you..." he finally managed to add, then, "This place..."

His gaze slid past me.

"This is Mr. Brodie." I made the introductions.

"Brodie?" he replied with apparent confusion.

"Formerly of the Metropolitan Police, now in private investigations," I explained.

"He's assisting in the search for Lenore." I saw no reason to conceal anything, unlike Charles who had much to answer for.

"Lenore? Yes, of course," he replied.

"Where is she?" I asked, straight to the point, as I had no way of knowing how long we would be allowed to remain there.

"If I knew... I would have told you."

"Would you?" I made no pretense at politeness. I was far beyond that.

"Of course..." Charles stammered.

"Spare me." I took a deep breath. "What is Marie Níkola to you?"

He continued to stare at me.

"How do you know...? Now, see here!" He took a

step toward me, then immediately stopped as Brodie moved between us.

"Ye have a great deal to answer for, sir," he told Charles. "Who is Marie Níkola?" he demanded.

My brother-in-law took a step back, driving his hand back through his hair. "I don't know anyone by that name."

"She was with you at Clarendon House." I refreshed his memory. "With another man by the name of Kosta Resnick."

He looked at me. "How could you possibly know that?"

"I was there."

"I would have seen you..."

"You did, briefly, in the confrontation outside the Green Room."

"There was no one else there, except some woman who had arrived with Templeton." Confusion changed to disbelief.

"The old woman in the hallway...?"

"Not quite as old as you were led to believe. I went after the woman and Resnick."

He shook his head. "I had heard that someone was shot and... killed?"

"Very much alive, as you can see," I pointed out, then asked again, "Where is Lenore?"

He seemed to crumble as he sat down at the edge of that narrow bed, his head in his hands.

"I told you before, I don't know!" This time with growing agitation.

"I have her journal, Charles. There are some most interesting things in it."

He looked up then, a different expression on his face, that first hint of fear.

"I don't know what she might have written..." he

started to deny. "She was not the same after the loss of the child. Different emotionally, her mind..."

I knew exactly what he was doing.

"She was deeply saddened by the loss," I agreed. "She very much wanted to have a child. But I spent a great deal of time with her then. There was nothing wrong with her," I was most adamant.

"She was herself, sadder, but very much herself," I added.

To have even suggested that she might have become unbalanced was infuriating. I felt Brodie's hand on my arm, a reminder of our purpose for being there.

"Were you having an affair with Marie Níkola?" I then asked.

It was on his lips to deny it, but he stopped.

"Linnie had become distant after the child," he eventually replied. "We barely spoke. Marie was... We met at an embassy gathering.

"It was a mistake, I know that now," he continued. "But it seemed harmless at the time and Linnie was never to know. I would never do anything..."

"But you did," I replied. "And she knew. She also knew about the meetings with others that kept you away. There was something else that badly frightened her. She wrote about it."

There was far more that I was determined to know.

"What was it that frightened her? Was it something to do with the white-haired man who has followed me since we last met? Is that the reason Mary and the others were murdered, because of what my sister knew? Because of what was in her journal? Who is he, Charles?"

"I don't know. I swear, I don't know... I saw him once. When I asked, Marie said she didn't know him!"

Marie—his lover.

"What do Marie Níkola and Kosta Resnick have to do with this? Where are they now?"

He came up off the cot, his features filled with something else. Desperation? Rage?

"I told you! I don't know!" He took hold of both of my hands even as Brodie grabbed him by the arm. To do what? I thought. To stop me? By force, if necessary?

"Step away," Brodie told him in a low voice.

There was no mistaking his meaning. Charles immediately let go of me and stepped back. He drove a hand back through his hair as he paced back across the cell.

"You must believe me! I never realized...!"

Never realized what? That he was destroying his marriage? And any hope of family? His career?

Was he perhaps beginning to sense the very real difficulty he was in? That he had been duped, and was now left to take the blame for the attack on the Prince of Wales?

"Ye would do well to tell us everything ye know," Brodie told him, in that same way he must have told criminals in the past.

"It might help yer situation."

Charles looked from Brodie to me.

"You must believe me," he implored. "I didn't know anything about the attack on the Prince of Wales. I didn't know!" He repeated, his voice rising.

"It was only supposed to be a private meeting that I was asked to arrange. It happens all the time in my position..." He turned and paced back. He looked up at me then.

"You must speak to Lady Montgomery to end this absurdity! She has influence..."

That he would try to involve my aunt only infuriated me all the more. It only emphasized how very low he had fallen, how desperate... and how guilty.

"Where are Marie Níkola and Resnick now?" I again asked.

"I don't know. We met at the Grosvenor, then... Linnie was gone, and I..."

They met at Litton House? My sister's home? Then, at the Grosvenor Hotel, even as we met over Linnie's disappearance?

How could he be so detached that day, so remote? Almost indifferent? How could he...? The answer was there. Because there was someone else who offered him solace, and her bed.

I had only one more question, one I had asked before, and then I needed to leave, to get away, to breathe fresh air, and try to make some sense of all of it.

"Do you know where Linnie is? Something either Marie Níkola or Resnick might have mentioned?"

He shook his head. "No! I had no reason to think they were involved in something like this. It was just to be a meeting..." He had retreated to the cot once more and buried his face in his hands.

No reason...

I looked at Brodie. He shook his head, then went to the door to let the guard know that we were quite through.

Charles came off the cot with a new urgency.

"They've not allowed me to have contact with anyone. You must contact my solicitor on my behalf."

Pity, sympathy? I had neither. There was only contempt and I thought of those gallows on the green that we had passed.

I didn't bother to answer as the warder let us out, then set the crossbar behind us.

"*You have to believe me*!" Charles shouted through the door.

. . .

We found a cab for the ride back to the Strand. I felt even more helpless than before our meeting with Charles. I had hoped...

What? I thought. That he might know where Linnie was?

The rain had set in once more, and the driver closed the doors over the compartment. Protected against the cold and wet, I thought of my sister.

"Do you believe him?" I asked, as the driver angled the cab through midday traffic, slowing at first, then lurching on ahead. I felt rather than saw Brodie turn toward me in the shadows inside the cab.

It surprised me, my ease of familiarity with him, when I had no use for such things. But then Angus Brodie was different from other men of my acquaintance.

His reply was thoughtful. "I have found that it's often what isn't said that tells ye far more than the spoken word, a gesture, a look, the sound of one's voice.

"For what it's worth," he continued. "I believe he was telling the truth. He doesn't know where yer sister is. It was there in his mannerisms, the sound of his voice, and the fear. He's terrified at what has happened, and a man in his position knows well the consequences.

"He's facing charges for the assault on the Prince of Wales, and might well be facing the hangman's noose."

It was little comfort to know that Brodie believed him.

"Is that the end of it, then?" I was discouraged, and heard it in my voice.

He handed me a note.

"What is this?"

"There is another question that hasn't been answered," he explained.

"When he came round to check the wound at yer

shoulder, I asked Mr. Brimley to make further inquiries with people he knows in the scientific community regarding the substance under Mary Ryan's nails.

"The Mudger handed me the note from him this morning before we left the Strand."

Twenty-Four

THE FROG HAD LONG BEEN dead, of course. Yet it floated, suspended in liquid in the jar, alongside other creatures in their jars—a mouse, a bat, and what was clearly a severed hand. The fingers were slightly curled as if it had been holding something. Obviously not the knife that had severed it.

"I wasn't able to restore the hand to the poor fellow. That was beyond my abilities," Mr. Brimley said, looking at us over the top of his spectacles with a good-natured expression. "But one day we will find a way.

"The poor fellow said that I might as well keep it, so there it is," he added. "A marvelous thing, the hand."

Brodie and I exchanged a look. This was far more than I had experienced on my previous '*visit*', although admittedly, I was not my usual observant self, having lost a great deal of blood at the time.

Frogs, bats, and a hand. Oh, my.

"How is your shoulder?" Mr. Brimley inquired.

"Healing quite well, thanks to your care." I felt a compliment was in order.

"Ah, well, it isn't every day that I'm called upon to sew up a bullet wound in a pretty lady. And I must say, the image on your wrist was quite interesting. I've not encountered a tattoo on a lady before."

Brodie looked over at me. Mr. Brimley quite obviously wasn't the only one who wondered about the colorful art on my wrist. However, that was not open for discussion at the moment.

"About the note ye sent round," Brodie reminded him.

"Ah, yes. I had a most interesting conversation with a fellow brother in the practice of medicine, Dr. Pennington. We attended King's College together. He teaches there now." he explained.

"I was able to ring him up and had quite a conversation with him."

King's College was a well-known medical college. It was also a research college. My opinion of frogs and hands in jars was elevated substantially.

Brodie had previously shared some of the details of Mr. Brimley's associations and accomplishments, and I had to admit that he was quite skilled when it came to stitches. Far better than my own attempts in stitching up a hem or replacing a button in the past.

He would have made a fine physician. However, whatever twists and turns in life had brought him to the East End, I was grateful.

"Come," he motioned for both of us to follow him. "My assistant can manage quite well out here."

We followed him to the rear of the shop, past beakers and jars, along with an assortment of measuring devices and microscopes that I recalled from our initial visit.

The small room was dimly lit and vaguely familiar. It included a cot with a neatly folded blanket, and a table. He closed the door and motioned to chairs that sat at the table.

He proceeded to pour something from a beaker over an open flame into two cups. He handed one to each of us. Considering the contents of those other jars, I glanced hesitantly at Brodie. I was not at all certain if Mr. Brimley was offering up some experimental concoction.

"Afternoon tea," he provided. "There's no fire box or kitchen in the place. One makes do with what one has."

Not usually inclined to tea, I caught the faint scent of the brew and took a sip.

Brodie likewise drank from the cup Mr. Brimley had handed him.

"What did yer esteemed colleague in medicine have to say in the matter?" Brodie asked, as we were both anxious to know what he might have learned.

"He was familiar with the incident in Paris, as a half dozen of his students had attended that unfortunate event," Brimley replied. "He spoke highly of Dr. Huber and his experiments, though many condemned them at the time."

"What of Huber after he was forced to leave Paris?" I asked, recalling the few details from the newspaper articles I had read.

"According to what he told me, Huber had been working for years with a young fellow in the science of chemicals. The event in Paris was to have been the culmination of his work.

He shook his head and took a sip of tea. "The mixture of chemicals is always dangerous business."

"After the incident, the French government determined that it was too dangerous," he continued. "It ended the work of both men."

"What of the other man he worked with?" Brodie inquired.

"Johannes Dietrich—brilliant, according to Robert.

Dietrich studied under Huber at the university in Berlin years ago, and most interesting, he had applied to have his experiments exhibited at the Crystal Palace. However it was determined that it was far too dangerous, and his application was denied."

My aunt had attended the Great Exhibition at the Crystal Palace as a young woman. She had often spoken of the marvelous inventions and machines, including a printing press that could produce five thousand copies of a book in a few hours.

Considering my choice of career and the success of my novels, I was enormously grateful.

There had also been an earlier version of my typing machine on display, the telephone my aunt regularly cursed, and the innovation of hot and cold water piped into homes, along with flush commodes.

The Exhibition had filled the Crystal Palace at Hyde Park, an enormous glass and wrought-iron structure, where vast pavilions housed art, inventions, and technology from throughout the empire and viewed by millions of people.

It was said that it had changed the world forever.

Then, a handful of years after it opened, the Crystal Palace was deconstructed. It was moved to a sprawling park in south London and rebuilt, in an effort to deal with the overcrowding at Hyde Park. The congestion on nearby streets had almost brought the city to a standstill during major events.

It was there at the new location at Syndham Park in the south of London, that I had marveled at the enormous aquarium that contained species of fish and sea creatures from around the world. There were also exotic gardens housed in hothouses, a collection of exotic animals from throughout the Empire—Templeton would have been delighted at the reptile exhibit.

I had attended sporting events and concerts there as well, most recently Handel's Messiah during the Christmas season the year before.

The disappearance of two scientists, however, did not explain the connection to Charles's affair with Marie Níkola or my sister's disappearance.

"What about Dietrich? What did Dr. Pennington know about him?"

Mr. Brimley retrieved the beaker and warmed our tea.

"That Huber and Dietrich had set up a laboratory on the outskirts of Berlin, next to the house where Dietrich lived with his wife and two small children. A horrible fire broke out at the laboratory and spread to the house. It is said that only one of the children survived."

"An unfortunate accident," Brodie commented thoughtfully.

Brimley nodded. "The scientific community is small. According to my friend, there were rumors at the time that the fire was no accident."

"Deliberate?" I asked. "But who would do such a thing?"

"Vandals perhaps, or possibly those who didn't want the experiments known." Brimley suggested.

"That was a very difficult time politically. Germany's hold on the new territories was precarious. Such experiments might have been seen as dangerous in the wrong hands." He shook his head. "A tragedy, to be certain."

"What of Huber?" I asked.

"He was away at the time of the fire, and did not return, which only fueled speculation about the experiments they conducted, and who might have caused the fire.

"He arrived in Paris some time later, and took up his work there once more at the university in Paris. That was a dozen years or so before the explosion of his own experiment."

"A horrible tragedy for a child to go through, the loss of a family," Brodie commented as we left Mr. Brimley's shop. His thoughtful gaze met mine before looking to the street and waiving down a cab.

"I saw it on the streets of Edinburgh—a man stabbed to death in front of his son, just for being in the wrong place at the wrong time. A woman was crushed beneath some cargo that broke loose from a cart, her daughter only inches away."

And not unlike my own experience that day in my father's stables, a memory indelibly seared into my memory.

"Perhaps not unlike a young lad who made his way in the streets of Edinburgh," I suggested, recalling the few details I knew about his own childhood. Birds of a feather, so to speak.

"It changes a person," he admitted. "Who they are, the things that are important, sets them on the course of what their life will be from that time forward. Some good... and some not."

A driver had pulled to the curb, and Brodie assisted me into cab with a steady hand on my good arm.

"For others there is no way forward," he continued, settling himself onto the seat beside me.

"There is only that moment, and it becomes who they are."

"And yet you overcame a difficult beginning," I pointed out.

"There are times, though," he admitted, "when my thoughts go back to the streets and what it took to survive."

He looked over at me, with an expression of one who could just as well have ended up like the Mudger, living on the streets, surviving from one handout to the next. But he had not.

~

Mr. Conner was waiting for us when we returned to the Strand. He had picked the lock and made himself quite comfortable at Brodie's desk.

"Come in, come in," he greeted us.

There was a fire in the coal stove and a meal spread before him on the desk.

"Ye must do something about the Mudger," he commented, taking a long swallow of whisky, no doubt from Brodie's supply in the file cabinet.

"The man is dangerous. He very nearly ran me over with that damned platform of his, and then threatened me with the hound—nasty tempered beast. I was tempted not to share my supper with him."

Supper, it appeared, included the common street fare, 'bangers and mash,' that consisted of a mound of mashed potatoes with sausages on top. The potatoes were easily recognizable, a common dish found in most taverns and pubs. It was the sausages that gave me pause. They were disgusting-looking and smelled worse. The entire office reeked of the greasy fare.

I had experienced food in India, Morocco, Hungary, along with assorted street fare in my association with Brodie. However, I was not in the habit of eating something that smelled like an old boot.

"There is enough for everyone," Conner said, slicing through one of the sausages which caused it to explode, sending juice all over the desk and soaking the sleeve of his shirt.

"No?" he asked, looking from me to Brodie.

"I don't have my appetite back yet." I made my excuse, far more interested in what news he might have for us.

"Ah, well," he told Brodie. "There will be more for the two of us."

He scooped a portion of the bangers and mash onto another plate, then slid it across the desk toward Brodie.

By the expression on Brodie's face it seemed that bangers and mash were not his favorite fare either. And this from a man whose people ate the contents cooked in a goat's stomach.

"I should charge ye more for my services," Conner continued. "It took this long to find the chap, and he was not of a mind to cooperate," he added, emphasizing it with his fork.

"The driver?" I asked.

"Aye, the man who picked up a man and woman quite handsomely dressed at Charles Street, St. James, two nights ago."

"Marie Nikola and Kosta Resnick?"

Mr. Conner nodded. "The same. It took some persuasion, but the cabman eventually confirmed that they both had foreign accents and they fit the description you provided." He looked at both of us with smug satisfaction.

"It seems they were quite nervous about something. Perhaps an incident that had just taken place?" He was very pleased with himself.

"They were in quite a hurry and paid him well in place of another fare he had stopped to pick up."

Brodie pushed back his plate and poured himself a liberal amount of whisky.

"Were ye able to learn where he delivered them?"

"That bit of information required more coin. I could have purchased the horse and the cab with it," Mr. Conner replied, then a smile appeared.

"We bargained and finally settled on the sum. I'll add it to the fee for my services," he told Brodie, then sat back with a satisfied smile and downed the rest of his whisky.

"Where did he take them?" I demanded.

Conner's eyes glinted with satisfaction. "An abandoned house in Charing Cross."

CHARING CROSS WAS in a part of London frequented by merchants, with shops and restaurants amid old residences clustered cheek by jowl near Trafalgar Square.

I exchanged a look with Brodie.

I was aware that he had made inquiries with Abberline's office regarding the event at the Clarendon House without much hope of receiving information. We had not been disappointed in that regard.

It appeared that Brodie's efforts, along with assistance from Mr. Conner, had now obtained information the MP either could not, or would not share.

"Charing Cross," Brodie commented, as he approached the board with our notes. "What of the address?"

"They had the driver let them off at the square."

Brodie wasn't surprised. "They're being careful."

"Not careful enough," Conner replied. "There was no extra coin in it for the driver that night, for the additional distance that took them from St. James."

Cab fare was reasonable enough, but the distance between St. James and Charing Cross would have taken the driver from his usual route and the loss of other fares. However, it appeared the two people that night had not paid the driver additional fare.

Conner grinned, his expression sharp as a fox. "The driver made out to wait for another fare to make up for the evening's loss, and just happened to see the house where they went."

And like a fox... "Number 38, Charing Cross."

Brodie nodded. "I don't suppose ye've had the opportunity to go there."

Conner grinned again. "The house appears to be empty."

"It appears to be?" Brodie replied.

"Aye, there was a sign posted at the door by the Roadway Enterprise Service, with a notice that the building is on the list to be torn down."

I had read something about the Roadway Enterprise Service and a new project that was planned in the city. Old buildings were to be demolished and the roadway widened to accommodate traffic that connected different parts of the city. However, the new roadway had been in the works, so to speak, for at least ten years. The buildings still stood, and traffic at midday was still a nightmare congestion of cabs, coaches, and omnibuses. So much for government efficiency.

However, we now had information that might be useful.

"We need to go there."

Brodie looked over at me. "We need to make inquiries first and not rush headlong into a situation that could be dangerous."

"They may have information that could help me find my sister," I insisted. "And they were involved in the attempt to abduct the Prince of Wales."

Brodie shook his head. "It's too dangerous. I should

think ye would understand that after what happened. I'll make inquiries with the watchmen in the area. They may be able to tell us something before we go there."

I was not about to be put off. "After what has happened, they may leave the country." I was insistent.

"We will proceed with care, " he replied, equally insistent, then with a look over at Conner, "Find out who is on the watch in that area. I want to speak with them. They may have seen something that is useful."

"Do ye want me to go there?"

Brodie shook his head. "Best to know what those people are about first, and how many others may be involved."

Another look passed between them, one of those maddening unspoken thoughts quite obviously meant to exclude me.

"Time is critical," Brodie added.

Conner nodded and rose from the desk. "I'll take Dooley with me. He knows some of the men who work that district."

Brodie agreed, again in that way between men—a look, or a nod. I wanted to tell both of them what I thought of that.

When he had gone, I turned to Brodie.

"We need to know what they're about *now*! Every day that passes..."

I fully expected his usual response—all sorts of reasons why we would proceed as he saw best, disregarding my input to the situation, possibly even that temper that I had grown quite fond of. However at the moment...

"No," he said in that quiet voice, quite catching me off guard.

The look he gave me then was quite different—dark and brooding, as Jane Austen would have described in one of her novels, and something else that I had seen before. Although at the moment I let it pass.

"These people are dangerous," he pointed to what was obvious. "They have shown that they're willing to kill anyone to achieve what they came here for. By the grace of God, ye were only injured."

It was somewhat disconcerting to think that this brash, gruff man who'd made his way on the streets and had then become an inspector of police believed in a higher being.

"Ye are brave, intelligent beyond anyone I have known, man or woman," he continued. "But this has become too dangerous. Whatever Resnick and Marie Níkola are about is not finished, or they would have already left London. Ye must leave this to me now."

I couldn't believe what I was hearing. Well, actually, I could believe it. It was so very typical of him.

"We have an agreement," I pointed out. "And I have no intention of..."

He crossed the office and seized his coat and scarf from the coat rack at the door.

"Ye must return to Sussex Square. Ye'll receive far better care there, and Munro can be relied upon to make certain that yer safe."

"That is not for you to decide!" I protested, the argument too familiar between us.

"We have an agreement..." Quite flustered now, I was repeating myself. I had never encountered a man so stubborn, so pig-headed... so bloody Scot!

"It's done," he said in that same low voice, and I thought that I would much rather have preferred that he yelled and cursed.

He paused at the door. "I'll have the Mudger secure a cab to take ye there."

Then he was gone, leaving me with my temper, my objections, and no one to yell at.

Something had changed, although I had no idea what that was.

Concern that I had been wounded? It hardly seemed likely—that would require that Brodie had a heart. I was not at all certain that one beat within the chest of Angus Brodie. Bloody, arrogant man!

And he was not there for me to tell him exactly what I thought of his instructions, or him for that matter. Therefore, I did what I usually did in a situation. I considered my options.

One: We had an agreement. There were two parties to the agreement. He might think it ended. I did not.

Two: I was not willing to endanger my aunt by retreating to Sussex Square. We already had that conversation, and it was not open for discussion or negotiation.

Three: Mr. Brimley had declared that the wound in my shoulder was healing quite nicely—therefore I had no need of further care, other than the changing of the bandage.

Four: It was obvious that he fully intended to carry on with the investigation. He was not one to lie, and while I considered his reasons and trusted his expertise in such matters, I was not in agreement with how to go about it.

I made my notes at the blackboard, adding the information about the attack at Clarendon House and the information Conner had provided regarding the location of the abandoned house in Charing Cross. I then added the information Mr. Brimley had provided from his conversation with his colleague in medicine, along with the name of Johannes Dietrich.

According to Mr. Brimley, Dietrich had died several years before in that fire. Huber had continued with his experiments, banned after the explosion in Paris that killed several people, and had then disappeared.

Was he now part of some anarchist group, using his experiments as a way of striking back after his work was labeled too dangerous and he was driven out of Paris?

If Herr Schmidt at the gymnasium was correct, the goal of anarchist groups like the Black Hand, was to return the power to the people by attacking and destroying autocratic governments.

If such a plan was to succeed it would plunge everything into chaos and set civilization back several hundred years. A drastic scheme to be certain.

It seemed that the attempt to abduct the Prince of Wales the evening of Templeton's performance at Clarendon House, might have been part of such a plan. It had however, been thwarted.

Or had it?

Resnick and Marie Níkola had fled to Charing Cross, presumably where they had met up with others. Once their plans had been thwarted, the wise thing would have been for them to leave as quickly as possible for surely the authorities would be after them. But according to Mr. Conner, they had not left London.

Was the attempt to abduct the Prince of Wales part of some larger plan?

I need look no further than my earliest notes after poor Mary Ryan was found murdered, and the clue Brodie had discovered under her fingernails—a chemical substance that Mr. Brimley had identified, the same chemical substance that Huber and Dietrich had experimented with.

I connected the new information with what we'd discovered earlier, lines filling the board in a spider's web of dates and clues, then stood back to study it.

Some could not see the trees for the forest, as the old saying went.

The motive was there, and most certainly the means. And the opportunity?

That brought my thoughts back to the attack on the Prince of Wales. It had failed. But what if there was to be an attack on other members of the royal family? How might that be accomplished?

I thought of the political unrest over the past few years, including my own experience in Budapest.

Days after our departure, a demonstration in the streets had turned violent with several people killed.

How would Resnick and Marie Níkola hope to strike at the royal family here, including the Queen?

In that way that one sees something and then tucks it away, I realized that I had read about it only a few hours earlier!

I returned to the desk and grabbed the daily Conner had brought. On the front page was an article about a concert that was to take place at the Crystal Palace. The Queen, the Prince of Wales, and several other members of the royal family were to attend.

Motive, means, and opportunity!

If I was correct, there was going to be an attack on the royal family that very evening!

And the abandoned house in Charing Cross? A place where they might be able to plan and carry out their clandestine scheme with no one to notice.

It was now half past four in the afternoon, with the concert to begin at eight o'clock that evening.

As the minutes ticked away, I had no idea how soon Brodie might return. I scrawled a hasty note, then retrieved the revolver from the desk drawer and put it in the pocket of my skirt.

The Mudger was in his usual place at the entrance to the alley as I ran down the stairs.

"Right yer are, miss," he said, and waved down a cab from across the Strand.

The driver swung the cab about and pulled to the curb. I gave him the address at Charing Cross.

"Mr. Brodie said as how yer was to go to Sussex Square," the Mudger reminded me.

"There's been a change of plan," I explained, and handed him a note. "I need you to find Mr. Brodie and give him this. It's urgent!"

I ignored his protests as I climbed into the cab.

"The note will explain everything."

Twenty-Six

CHARING CROSS

IN SPITE of the extra fare I had promised, the trip to Charing Cross took exceedingly long, due to weather and traffic at the end of the day. We eventually arrived at Trafalgar Square and I quickly paid the driver.

I passed only a handful of people at the square, the fog, the cold, and the late hour of the afternoon, quickly sending them on their way. A poster wrapped around the base of a nearby streetlamp, ironically announced the benefit concert that was to be given that night at the Crystal Palace.

The streetlights came on, and I made my way toward the adjacent street and the house at Number Thirty-Eight with a new urgency.

What would I find there? Marie Níkola and Resnick? Possibly others? No one, if they had already departed to set their scheme in motion?

What then?

I had no idea when Brodie might return to the Strand, and time was most critical if I was correct about what I had discovered and what might happen that evening.

This part of Charing Cross had been designated for

the widening of the roadway, with the houses along either side to be demolished.

The street where Number Thirty-Eight was located was darkened, along with other houses down the entire length of the street. There was only an occasional street lamp glowing through the fog, then disappearing once more. It was like exploring the ruins of some ancient civilization.

I found evidence of the City's plans for the district, a flyer posted at the door of a darkened residence. A poster was attached to a wrought-iron gate at another residence, faded and smudged with soot and grime from the street. They announced that the work was to begin nearly two years prior, with the City of London's reputation for moving slowly. So much for progress.

I eventually found the house number. Like the other houses on the street, the windows were all darkened and there was no sign that anyone was about.

It would have been wiser to wait for Brodie, but I had no way of knowing if the Mudger had been able to find him, and I wanted very much to know what was inside the house.

I didn't approach the front door. In spite of those darkened windows, I didn't want to give myself away if anyone was about. Rounding the side of the building, I entered the narrow walkway that separated it from the residence next to it.

One of those hand-held lights the night watch carried would have been useful as I tripped over some broken stones at the walkway. However, that would surely have announced my presence.

I emerged at what had once been a small yard at the rear of the three-story house, startling a cat that suddenly darted across my path. In the gathering shadows as daylight faded and fog shrouded the building, I saw what the cat had been so interested in.

An ash can at the landing at the back entrance had been overturned. But instead of ash, scraps of food were scattered about. I had obviously disturbed the cat at its evening meal that included the remains of fish, along with rotting cabbage, crusts of bread, and remnants of potatoes and other vegetables. Whoever was in the house had obviously been there long enough for garbage to accumulate.

There were shades on the windows; however I caught a faint sliver of light at the edge of the window near the service door. I ignored Brodie's warnings about not proceeding on my own, and moved closer.

The sound came from behind me, and a warning went off in my head. Then another sound with the realization that someone *was* there. Then I was grabbed by the collar of my jacket and pulled off my feet.

I fought back. But it was almost impossible to land a blow on the giant who had hold of me and dragged me backwards, as several things flashed through my thoughts:

One—this was not the best of circumstances, and proof of Brodie's warnings about going off on my own. Not that I would ever admit it, if I was able to extricate myself from the current situation.

Two—three people were already dead and my sister was missing, and these people had proven that they were very dangerous.

Three—I needed to retrieve the revolver in my pocket, which seemed highly unlikely as I was flailing about.

And four—I had no idea what *four* might be, but I had always been able to think on my feet as I was dragged to the landing at the service porch, then into the house, pain sharp at my injured shoulder.

The giant of a man who had hold of me made some comment, something I didn't understand, and suddenly drew a knife. He smelled of foul body odor and fish, and at any moment I expected to feel that blade at my throat.

With one hand holding the knife and the other arm clamped around my shoulders, I took advantage of his struggle to subdue me.

I thrust my elbow back hard into the soft spot at the top of his mid-section at the same time I drove the heel of my boot into the toe of his shoe.

There was a curse and I found myself suddenly released. I took advantage of that momentary freedom, turned sharply, and thrust the heel of my right hand hard into his face, connecting with his nose.

My attacker grunted then howled with pain. Blood streamed from his nose as I made a dash for the door. I didn't make it, as I was grabbed by the hair and dragged back off my feet.

It would have perhaps been better if I was terrified. I wasn't. I was furious. If I was going to die, I wasn't going to go easily. The pain in my shoulder was forgotten as I fought to retrieve the revolver. The door was suddenly thrown open.

It was Brodie! And at least a half dozen constables, including Mr. Conner!

I thought of the stories Templeton had shared with me about her travels in the Wild West. It seemed that the *Texas Rangers* had arrived.

"Release her!" Brodie ordered, as the constables filled the small service room.

Whether he understand what they were saying or not, 'Bloody Nose' understood the weapons pointed at him. Not to mention several constables that now surrounded him. The knife clattered to the floor, and he released me.

"Search the rest of the house," Brodie ordered, sending three of the men including Mr. Conner to the task. Dooley and the other constables remained to stand guard over Bloody Nose.

"I'm not even going to ask," Brodie snapped, as he helped me to my feet, then proceeded to do a cursory inspection of my arms, and my shoulder.

"Did ye have a plan if we had not arrived when we did?" he asked, obviously quite furious in that quiet way.

He couldn't resist, and I would have been quite surprised if he hadn't commented on the situation at hand.

"Of course," I replied. "I intended to shoot him."

That dark gaze fastened on me. "I believe ye would have."

All of that aside, I explained what I had discovered at the notes I had made, and the daily Conner had provided.

"They've planned an attack for tonight, I'm certain of it," I continued. "The entire royal family is to attend the concert at the Crystal Palace."

For once, there was no argument.

"I read yer note."

Dooley was in the process of questioning 'Bloody Nose.' It appeared the man didn't understand a word he said, mumbling in a foreign accent. It was doubtful we would learn anything helpful.

There was, however, a noticeable reaction when Dooley mentioned the Crystal Palace. Bloody Nose shook his head, at the same time he looked around nervously.

Body language, as Brodie had once suggested?

Mr. Conner had returned and appeared at the doorway that led to the rest of the house.

"Ye need to see this."

I followed as Brodie went with him, since it appeared that Mr. Dooley had the situation with 'Bloody Nose' well in hand.

Mr. Conner had made a search of the ground floor of the house. Now the beam of his hand-held light swept across the floor of what had once been the front parlor.

It was in disrepair, with wall paper peeling on the walls and badly stained carpet.

"Over here." Conner crossed the room where a long table stood at the far wall, with several items, including an assortment of utensils, a measuring device, and a pair of thick leather gloves. Beside the table was a metal canister.

The table and the instruments had much the look of Mr. Brimley's apothecary, I thought.

Brodie examined the utensils then the container.

"Sulphur," he said, and took out a handkerchief and wiped his hands.

It was the same chemical that Mr. Brimley had identified in the residue Brodie had found under Mary's fingernails!

"Was this the only one?" he asked.

"It appears there were others here quite recently." Mr. Conner swept the beam of his light across the floor, and the scrape marks in the dust that had accumulated and on the stained carpet.

"Mr. Brodie?" One of the constables called out from the entrance to the parlor. "We've found something."

Officer Dooley joined us as the constable led the way up the stairs to the third floor, where we were met by another police officer.

"The room at the end of the hall."

A metal latch and padlock secured the door from the outside.

I exchanged a look with Brodie. A room locked from the outside?

To keep someone in? Was it possible? I dared to hope.

When I would have gone to the door, Conner laid a hand on my arm.

"Let one of the lads go first. We don't know what might be behind that door."

But I knew. It had to be...

Brodie gave the order for the constables to breach the door.

It took several blows with an axe, but the door eventually gave way.

I pushed past the constables and was through the opening into the darkened room before either Conner or Brodie could stop me.

The room was completely dark like the rest of the house except for the light from the hand-helds that streamed in behind me.

But it was enough to make out a small table and chair, the coal stove at the wall, a single bed at the far side of the room, and the woman in the stained dress. Her hair was tangled about her shoulders, an ash bucket for a weapon clutched in her hands.

"Mikaela?"

I ran to my sister as she slumped to the floor and burst into tears.

"I can't believe you're here!" Linnie cried. "How did you find me?"

I pulled her into my arms, not unlike that day so many years before, when our father took his life, and we had held onto each other.

"You're safe now," I told her, as I had that day.

I have no idea how long we sat there as Brodie and Conner searched the room, then helped support Linnie as we left the room that had been her prison. I couldn't help but think of Charles in his cell at the Tower, and loathed him all the more, for he had fared far better. So far.

Linnie was thinner from her ordeal, but otherwise unharmed as we sat at the table together in that servants' room in the house at Charing Cross, her hands clutched in mine. She hadn't known about Mary, only that she had not returned after she had sent her to retrieve the contents of the security box at the bank.

She was silent for long moments afterward as I told her what had happened.

"Poor, dear Mary. I shall never forgive myself."

"You're not to blame," I told her, stroking her hand. "You had no way of knowing what would happen."

Conner and one of the constables had returned from their search of the rest of the house. I saw the look that passed between him and Brodie, and the shake of his head that they hadn't found anyone else.

"I don't understand how you knew where to find me," Linnie said, her eyes filled with tears again.

"That's not important now."

She nodded, confused and dazed.

Brodie sat across from us. I had introduced him to her.

"Mr. Brodie, of course," she had replied.

Now he leaned forward, the expression at his face filled with compassion and a gentleness, and I wondered how many other victims of crime had seen that very same expression and had been comforted by it. I was quite grateful.

"I know it is difficult, but we need to know what

these people have planned," he said, his voice low and even, something calm to hold onto.

"How many are there? Anything that ye might have overheard no matter how insignificant it might seem."

"I had very little contact with any of them," she replied hesitantly. "Other than the man who brought me here, and then only when I was brought food and water." By the description she provided, we knew it was Resnick who had found where she was staying and had abducted her.

"Do you remember seeing a white-haired man?" I asked.

She shook her head. "There was a woman. She mentioned something about Charles. The way she spoke, I knew..."

Charles's lover, Marie Níkola.

"I have your journal," I told her.

She nodded sadly. "I couldn't believe that Charles would do something like this." She looked up then and her voice broke softly.

"Where is he? Does he know what's happened?"

I looked at Brodie. My first instinct was to protect her, as it had been from the beginning. But she would have to know sooner or later.

"It seems that he may have been part of this scheme from the beginning." I did not tell her that he was in the Tower, that there would undoubtedly be charges against him for his part in the event at Clarendon House. There would be time for that later.

She nodded, suddenly seeming much older.

"I know this is difficult," Brodie continued. "But we need you to tell us if there's anything else. Anything at all that you might have heard one of them say."

Her hand shook as she pressed her fingers against her forehead, then looked at me, all the misery and horror of the past weeks reflected in eyes so like our mother's.

"I don't know if it's important..."

"Please try," I encouraged her.

"Once when they brought food to me, I overheard one of them mention something about a clock. Then, the last two days it seemed as if something might have happened that changed their plans, something urgent, but I didn't hear what that was.

"Today, the house was empty. I didn't hear anyone about." She looked up at Brodie.

"Is that helpful?"

"Aye," he told her. "It is."

Brodie and I exchanged a look. Two days coincided with the incident at Clarendon House and the attempt to abduct the Prince of Wales.

"Now, we need to get ye out of here," Brodie told her.

He was concerned that some of Resnick's people might return. I heard it in the instructions he gave the constables.

"Do ye feel strong enough to travel to Sussex Square?" he asked her.

Linnie nodded, and he asked one of the constables to have a cab brought round to the house. We waited in that ground floor servants' room until Dooley let us know that a driver had arrived.

"Mr. Dooley and one of the constables will escort ye to Sussex Square," Brodie told her. He wrapped a blanket around her shoulders that one of the constables had brought from the room upstairs.

"One of them will go ahead to inform her ladyship."

Linnie looked at me with a worried expression. "You're coming as well, aren't you?"

I shook my head. "You need to go with them," I told her, as gently as possible.

"After everything that's happened..." she replied, tears starting again, "if anything was to happen to you..."

I laid a hand on her cheek.

"I'll be safe enough," I assured her. "I'm going with Mr. Brodie. I need you to be strong now, the way you were when it was just the two of us."

I knew by the look in her eyes that she remembered that day, and the way it had always connected us.

"Go now," I told her.

She slowly nodded and let one of the constables escort her to the cab.

"Ye should have gone with her," Brodie said, after they had gone.

I looked at him, but said nothing.

"Aye," he finally replied. "Let's be on our way then."

A police wagon had arrived to take 'Bloody Nose' to Scotland Yard, with a message for Inspector Abberline that explained the man's part in my sister's abduction. If there was more, it would be determined later.

Then the three of us, including Mr. Conner, stepped down from the police van at the Square, and watched as it disappeared in the fog.

Brodie was thoughtful. "What might be the purpose of several of those canisters?"

"By what ye've told me, there's the possibility that Resnick and his followers intend to set off an explosion perhaps with that chemical you found under the maid's fingernails. It would create an enormous gas cloud," Mr. Conner replied.

"The same as Huber's experiment in Paris that killed dozens of people." I added what we had learned from Mr. Brimley and those newspaper accounts of the disaster.

"Aye. And how would ye move several of those canisters about?" Brodie asked, as we crossed Trafalgar Square, very much with the feeling that we might well be going into battle of some kind.

"A cart would be too slow," Mr. Conner replied. "With the weather, it could take several hours even in light traffic."

"And if they needed to get to the south of London quickly?" I asked.

"That would have to be by rail, the Brighton main line," Conner replied.

"Aye," Brodie agreed, and waved down a cab.

The Brighton main line had rail service that ran on the hour to South London. We arrived at the railway station just in time to catch the next train to what was known around the world as the Crystal Palace.

Twenty-Seven

UPON OUR ARRIVAL, Brodie asked to speak with the manager of the Crystal Palace.

We were informed by the station master that he was at the Grand Pavilion, where a new art exhibit had just opened, and was unavailable. However, he could send round a message that we wanted to see him.

With information I had put together, Brodie and Mr. Conner were convinced that Resnick and his followers planned an attack on the royal family that evening during the concert. And the time on the enormous clock on the wall of the rail station indicated the concert was to begin in just over an hour.

"We have no time for this," Conner kept his voice low, and I quite agreed.

If we failed to find those canisters, along with that clock device that Linnie had overheard one of them speaking of before it was set to go off, the potential consequences were horrifying.

"Ye have police constables on duty?" Brodie asked the station manager.

"Yes," he replied. "They patrol the grounds regularly,

and more are always present when the royal family is in attendance."

"Do ye have a way to contact them?"

"There is a telephone inside the station office," he replied, with growing uneasiness. "Is there some difficulty?"

"Put a call through to them now. Tell them that it's most urgent. They're to have as many men as possible meet us at the entrance to the amphitheater."

He started to protest. "This is most unusual..."

"Do it," Brodie insisted "And tell them it's on orders from Scotland Yard."

I looked over at Conner with more than a little surprise. Chief Inspector Abberline would have had a fit and fallen in the middle of it if he'd heard that convenient lie.

"Do ye have a map of the property?" Brodie then asked.

"There's one just inside the gates for arriving guests."

We were directed to a map displayed on an overhead board that showed a complete layout of the Crystal Palace property, including the Grand Pavilion, various exhibit halls, and the amphitheater where the concert was to be held.

"What is this area?" Brodie asked the station manager, pointing to an area under the amphitheater.

"That is the maintenance area for the amphitheater."

A look passed between Brodie and Mr. Conner, that I was becoming quite accustomed too.

"Aye," Conner replied. "That is the place to start our search." Then he asked, "How many guests were expected for tonight's concert?"

"We were told to expect as many as four thousand people, by rail and coach, " the station manager replied.

"That's not unusual when there's a concert, particularly if the royal family is to attend."

Four thousand people! Including the royal family, all who very well might need to leave quickly!

How could it possibly be done, I thought, without causing panic and disaster with hundreds injured?

"We need to find those canisters before they're activated," Brodie commented. Mr. Conner agreed.

I knew that it was the only solution that might avert hundreds, possibly thousands of deaths.

"We need a carriage to take us there now!" Brodie told the station manager.

He directed us to the concierge area just inside the main gates where at least a dozen carriages were lined up to accommodate guests either arriving or departing after attending an event. Mr. Conner waved down one of the drivers.

A trip that might very well have taken a good hour by foot was accomplished in minutes, as Brodie ordered the driver to make haste as we crossed the grounds of the property, then cut through the park and onto the avenue that led to the amphitheater. When we arrived, several police constables were waiting.

Brodie immediately dispatched two of them to make contact with the royal guard that always accompanied the Queen and the other members of the royal family. They were to make them aware that they must leave immediately.

"Who authorized this?" the younger of the two constables asked, obviously uncomfortable carrying such instructions to the royal family without official authorization.

"Scotland Yard," Brodie replied. He said it once more with such authority that the young constable nodded and they set off. Most certainly whatever repercussions there might be for that would come later. If we lived through this.

On Brodie's order, four other constables accompanied us through a *private entrance* and into the massive area below the amphitheater that he had seen on that display board.

The area beneath the amphitheater was a web of stairways and lifts that took guests into the main theater above, along with a carriage concierge to take those in attendance back to the main entrance once the concert was over.

Above us were the sounds of the amphitheater itself —the usual creak and groan of metal stanchions and girders that formed the framework of the theater, with thousands of guests in their seats, and the sound of the musicians making their last adjustments to their instruments.

Then there was silence followed by a welcome greeting from Sir Harry Langston, director of the London Symphony, his voice echoing down through the open floors above us.

"What other facilities are down here?" Brodie demanded.

"There is a dressing room for the workers, a dining area that is closed now, and the supply room for the maintenance of the theater with exits here and here." One of the constables, who regularly worked the grounds, pointed out the layout of the amphitheater.

"Where is the maintenance room?"

The constable took out a small version of the layout we'd seen at the entrance to the property.

"Just here." He pointed to a space on the diagram.

"And these?" Brodie asked, pointing to an area inside the maintenance room marked with letters.

"Those are the boilers. They provide heat for the amphitheater during the colder months."

"How exactly?" I asked.

"Large electric fans at the top of these pipes pull the heat up into the theater."

The wonders of the industrial revolution, I thought. Electricity and fans, no doubt very much the same as the ceiling fans I had at my town house for warm summer months.

"That would be perfect for their plan," Mr. Conner said.

And I had to agree that it seemed the most likely place for Resnick and his followers to place those canisters. When their contents were released, those enormous fans would draw clouds of poisonous gas up into the amphitheater. It was ingenious, and terrifying.

"Where is the access to the maintenance room?" Brodie asked.

"Through this main corridor."

"Take us there, *now*."

The space beneath the amphitheater was a maze of hallways with overhead lights, and connected storerooms, repair shops, the maintenance area, and the boiler room.

We stopped at an intersection of those hallways, the constable who had accompanied us indicating that the hallway to the boiler room lay just beyond.

"Are the doors locked?"

"No, sir. It's kept open for workers while on their shift."

Brodie turned to me. "Yer to go no further." And before I could object, "Ye will cooperate, or I will have one the constables remove ye."

I caught the look Mr. Conner gave me.

"It's for the best," he added. "We don't know what we'll find in there."

They were willing to risk themselves, but I was to stay behind where it was safe.

It was a reminder of that double standard I had often encountered and found quite loathsome.

In the past, I simply ignored it, and continued on as I pleased. That was not an option now. I saw it in the set of Brodie's jaw. I could make all the objections in the world and it would do me no good, and only waste precious time.

I reluctantly nodded, and they moved down the corridor toward the entrance to the boiler room accompanied by two constables. A third constable was to remain with me.

I have no idea how much time passed, as the young constable and I waited.

He seemed no older than me, standing tall at his assigned position with a most serious expression. His gaze briefly met mine.

"It'll be all right, miss," he assured me. "There's none better than Mr. Brodie."

Which raised the question how he might know that?

No sooner had he said it than we heard shots fired from inside the boiler room.

I was no stranger to the sound, most particularly after being shot, and started toward the door. The young constable held up a hand to stop me.

"Stay here, miss," he ordered, then ran to the entrance as more shots were fired.

I retrieved the revolver from the pocket of my skirt as he pulled one of the doors open and ran inside.

There were more shots, and I ran toward those double doors. I reached for the door handle.

The blow caught me on the shoulder.

I was slammed back against the wall beside the entrance as the door was thrown back, and a man dressed in workman's clothes and a billed cap ran past.

I caught a fleeting glimpse inside the entrance to the boiler room.

The young constable I had been speaking with only moments before lay slumped on the floor. Another man in workman's clothes lay only a few feet away as the sound of a door slamming shut came from behind me in the hallway.

It was very likely one of the more foolish things I had ever done—along with chasing after Marie Níkola and Resnick after the event at Clarendon House—and no way of knowing who might be dead now, as I turned and went after the man who had run past me.

He had fled through that side door that led to a cart path. I hit the lever and went after him.

In spite of the rain, the park-like grounds were lit from the glow of thousands of lights in the glass panels of the Crystal Palace, giving it a surreal appearance as if it was almost daylight. And then I saw him.

He had cut across the park and appeared to be making his way toward the roundabout where coaches and carriages waited until after the concert.

I shouted as I ran after him, oblivious to the rain, to everything except the anger—for my sister, for Mary Ryan, Officer Thomas, even Spivey—when he suddenly stopped, then slowly turned around, much the same as that night at St. James's Park.

He stared at me, then raised his arm, an expression on his face that I would never forget as the light that spilled across the grounds glinted off the pistol in his hand, and he smiled.

I fired the revolver. Then continued to fire as I ran toward him and that cruel, mad smile. When the revolver was empty, I continued to pull the trigger, even after he fell to the ground.

I stopped and slowly walked toward him.

Shouts and cries of alarm went out across the park. Somewhere among them, I heard my name. But all I saw was the man on the ground.

I eventually felt a hand on my wrist, and a familiar voice reached through the anger as I stared down at him.

"It's over." Brodie said, in that same quiet voice as with my sister. "Do ye hear me, lass? It's over."

I slowly nodded as that dark void seemed to fade, and there was only the rain, and the sound of a constable's loud whistle piercing the night.

The cap had come off as the man fell, along with the wig he wore. A white wig! And Marie Níkola stared back at us with vacant, dead eyes.

Twenty-Eight

IT WAS OVER.

The plot against the royal family by Marie Níkola and Resnick, along with their fellow conspirators, had been stopped in time, and the royal family as well as those who had attended the concert were safe. Many of them were none the wiser to the scheme that might have caused thousands of deaths.

And in the way that things come back after a horrifying experience, the events of the last weeks played over and over through my thoughts.

The sight of Mary Ryan's lifeless body lying on that table at the police mortuary would remain with me for a long time. Her death was made to seem as if it was just one more murder by the madman who stalked Whitechapel, while Marie and Resnick set about their scheme against the royal family.

They had been after the journal my sister had kept, locked away in that security box at the bank, that would have exposed them and their plan. Mary had simply been an innocent victim, but the loss was profound for so many.

But as much as possible, there would be closure now

for Mary's mother. However, as I knew all too well, it was a loss that would never fully heal.

My sister had been abducted, then held prisoner against the possibility that she might thwart their plans with what she had discovered in the months leading up to their scheme.

I would never forget the terrified look in her eyes when we found her. For now, she was staying with our aunt at Sussex Square, to recover as much as possible from the terrifying ordeal.

Officer Thomas was a tragic loss for his mother, who had depended upon him and now would never see him again. Brodie assured me that a fund, set up to care for families of members of the MP, would see that she was taken care of. But there was no way to compensate for the loss of a son. Brodie's care and compassion moved me.

Dozens of innocent people had died in Paris, and perhaps countless others, victims of Huber's and Dietrich's experiments. There was no way of knowing how many were victims of the anarchists, and Marie Níkola's revenge for her father that we had eventually discovered. But for now there was some small measure of hope that the world was safe, at least for a little while.

Spivey had eked out an existence at the docks and had unwittingly become part of the anarchists' conspiracy. It might be said that Annie Flynn sorely missed him, but who could know for certain? As we discovered, she had replaced him rather quickly.

The royal family was safe with only the barest mention of *'an episode'* the night of the concert in the dailies. More than that was not reported. It was an example of the royal family 'carrying on,' as they say. The only outward indication of any change was an increase in the guard that surrounded the Queen and members of the royal family.

My brother-in-law, once the Home Secretary and duped into an affair with Marie Níkola in her scheme to assassinate the entire royal family, was now imprisoned in the Tower awaiting trial on charges of conspiracy. He no doubt faced a very long imprisonment, if he was ever released, or possibly an appointment with those gallows I had seen on my visit to the Tower.

And for what? Some crazed need for revenge by Marie Níkola, the child who was thought to be the only survivor of the fire that killed her parents and younger brother? Who had then joined the anarchist group known as the Black Hand, and whose plan was to topple the English monarchy and other governments across Europe?

What then? More chaos, and more death?

Marie Níkola and Resnick were both dead. Those of the Black Hand left alive were hunted down by members of the new investigative group that was part of Scotland Yard.

More revelations eventually came to light by members of the community, including Herr Schmidt, perhaps eager to deflect suspicion from themselves.

"Resnick was her brother," Mr. Conner explained, as he sat at Brodie's desk several days later.

"Contrary to newspaper accounts both children survived the fire, and were out for revenge against those they felt had destroyed their father's work, and resulted in his death. The family name was—"

"Dietrich." I recalled the name of the scientist Mr. Brimley had spoken of.

"Aye," Brodie replied. "And God knows, there may be more conspirators that haven't yet been found."

It was a glimpse into this new world we were entering, I thought, with the turn of the century only a few years away. It was a world of innovations, machines, and terrifying possibilities.

"It will give Mr. Abberline something to do," Conner sarcastically replied, "instead of running around arresting a boy for stealing a loaf of bread."

He stood and stretched his leg against the stiffness from the wound he'd received that night in the boiler room under the amphitheater at the Crystal Palace.

"You should have a doctor look at that," I suggested. I had grown quite fond of him and didn't want to see him paddling about like the Mudger.

"Mr. Brimley is a good hand with stitches. You're proof of that, miss."

My shoulder was no worse the wear for our recent misadventure, although I would have a scar to remind me of my encounter with Resnick and Marie Níkola. I might be able to hide it with a new tattoo.

"I'll be off, then," Conner said. He paused. "Best give me one of those biscuits. That damned hound has gotten an attitude when it comes to food, and I'm not of a mind to argue the matter with him. The beast never used to be that way."

I was to blame for that, of course.

He limped across the office and out the door, biscuit in hand to avoid being attacked at the bottom of the stairs. For my part, I stood at the chalkboard and began wiping it clean, now that the case had been solved.

"Leave it," Brodie said, as he came to stand beside me. "For a while," he added. "In case I've forgotten anything Abberline might need to know about other people who were involved."

I laid the felt eraser back on the rail at the bottom of the chalkboard.

It was all there. Every clue, each twist and turn we

had followed, along with the notes from Linnie's journal and my own notes written down from the beginning—the habits of a writer, much to Brodie's aggravation at the time.

I had already returned to the town house at Mayfair. There was a lot of cleaning to be done, not to mention broken furniture to be repaired, as we now knew it had been Resnick and Marie who broke into it, searching for the journal and whatever incriminating evidence it might have contained that threatened their plans.

"I suppose I should be going," I said, turning from the board. "Aunt Antonia has commandeered a work crew to assist in the repairs at the town house and sent her housekeeper to oversee everything."

"How is Mary's mother doing?" Brodie asked, reminding me again that, contrary to some who wouldn't have bothered to inquire, much less remembered her name, he was a most extraordinary fellow.

"She'll continue on. The Irish are a strong, stubborn lot." Not to be outdone by a headstrong Scot, of course.

"We've arranged for Mary to be buried on my aunt's estate, where she spent several years as a child."

He nodded. "And yer sister?"

"Good and bad moments, what with Charles's betrayal that very nearly got her killed, and the rest of it. It will take time... But she's really quite strong."

"Like her sister." Brodie added.

I smiled.

"We've planned a trip to Brighton when the weather is warmer. It will do her good to get away from all of this for a while."

"And then ye'll be off on another adventure?" he added.

"Perhaps. I want to make certain that she's recovered

as much as possible before I go off again. She's had too many losses—our mother and father, now Charles."

And the child she had hoped for, I thought.

"I've left an envelope in the desk," I continued. Payment for his services. "The bank draft should cover everything."

I had also included a note, along with a good sum for the use of the adjacent room, which I was certain he must appreciate having the use of once more, rather than sleeping on one of the overstuffed chairs in the office. There was also an amount to cover the various expenses I was certain that he had incurred.

"There's a sum for the Mudger, Mr. Conner, and Mr. Brimley as well."

"Have ye forgotten anyone?" he replied, with obvious sarcasm that reminded me that Brodie was quite a handsome figure of a man, when he wasn't growling at me.

Speaking of growling... "You might consider laying in a supply of biscuits for Rupert," I suggested.

"Unless I want to find myself missing a leg or two, like our friend downstairs?" he replied.

Friends. That is precisely what I thought of everyone, without whom we would not have been able to solve the case, and my sister might not be alive.

As for Brodie... I laid my hand against his cheek, his beard tickling my fingers.

"I do appreciate your assistance. I couldn't have done it without you."

"That must have been difficult for *Emma Fortescue* to admit," he replied.

What *would* Emma Fortescue do at a moment like this? I thought, with the case finally solved.

I leaned into him, and pressed my lips against his.

Surprise was most certainly there. I tasted it, and

then something more. Something deeper, something a little stubborn, a hint of cinnamon and a hint of something dangerous. When I would have stepped back, he held onto me.

"Yer a rare woman, Mikaela Forsythe." And he kissed me back quite thoroughly.

For once, I didn't argue.

Epilogue

AUGUST 1889, BRIGHTON

THEY SAY that time heals all wounds.

I would like to think that it does, as I watched my sister, knee-deep in the gently rolling surf, with a little girl who had escaped her mother as she changed clothes in one of the nearby bathing boxes lined up like colorful confection cartons along the beach.

It was good to see the color at Linnie's cheeks once more and hear her laughter, after everything that had happened and in spite of things yet to come.

Charles had been brought to trial for crimes against the Crown for his part in the attack on the Prince of Wales at Clarendon House, and his association with known anarchists and the plot against the royal family.

In spite of his position and title, and protestations that he had been as much a victim as anyone, duped by his affair with Marie Níkola, he was found guilty and sentenced to sixty-four years in prison. That would make him a very old man when he was released. If he lived that long.

He was also stripped of his title, and wealth that was subsequently petitioned to be awarded to his wife, along with the dissolution of their marriage.

Linnie was now a very wealthy, single woman, although it was poor compensation for the loss of her hope for a family. Still, there were moments when justice was most satisfying, I thought.

I adjusted my tinted glasses against the glare of the sun and turned back to my writing tablet, in the midst of a chapter for my next novel, quite ironically a tale of a wronged woman, the philandering husband, and a murderous conspiracy.

Linnie returned, glowing with a smile at her face.

"Good heavens! A beautiful day at the beach and you're under an umbrella writing in that damned notebook."

It should be noted that after her experience, I have become aware that my sister had acquired a penchant for swearing. Mild swearing, but swearing nonetheless. I took it as a good sign.

I looked at her over the top of the tinted glasses. "I'm overdue on my next deadline, and my publisher is adamant there will be no further extensions."

Linnie grabbed a towel and threw herself down on the mat beside me.

"And what is the plot this time? What adventure is Miss Emma Fortescue off on now? Intrigue? Stolen jewels, perhaps? An affair with a sheik?"

And then, "Good heavens, who would come to the beach in Brighton in a full-dress coat and trousers?"

Since it appeared that I was not going to be able to continue without interruption, I looked up.

"I do believe it is Mr. Brodie," Linnie exclaimed.

I had not seen him since the day we concluded our business and I walked out of his office on the Strand.

Although there had been a note from him, congratulating me on the success of my latest novel, released as we ran about London trying to find my sister and stop the conspiracy against the royal family.

Congratulating me! How that must have taxed that stoic Scottish demeanor.

"Thank you for asking. I am quite well," I had replied to that brief note, which was irritating in the least, very businesslike, with no mention of our parting at his office that last day.

And now, he was approaching along the sand, much to the astonished—not to mention admiring—glances of other women in their chairs and on their blankets along the beach.

"You cannot just sit there in your bathing costume," Linnie commented now, as she scrambled to her feet.

She turned toward the bathing box we shared, as any proper, well-mannered lady would do, rather than risk a scandal at being caught in her bathing costume by a man.

"He has seen me in far less," I commented, recalling the days after I was injured and he had attended my wounded shoulder. But I digress.

In that way that the air can shimmer about things on a particularly warm day, Brodie was momentarily caught in the sun's glare, and I thought of another day and another beach along the Aegean, and far too much ouzo.

I looked up as he approached and regarded him over the top of my glasses. It was there again, more than an impression, very near a memory, that I *had* seen Brodie walking toward me once before just so. It was much that very same way, his coat hung over one shoulder, his shirt open at the throat, sleeves rolled back, the wind lifting the edge of his hair, and that dark gaze fastened on me.

"Miss Forsythe."

Miss Forsythe was it now? So, it seemed we were back to that. Exasperating man.

"Mr. Brodie," I replied.

"I trust yer sister is well."

"Quite well, thank you." Two could play this game.

"It's a verra fine day."

"Yes, it is, "I replied.

"And ye seem quite recovered as well."

I continued to watch him over the top of my glasses. He was quite an admirable figure of a man, particularly with his hair ruffled by the wind, and my fingers itched to smooth it back.

"I'm told by Aunt Antonia's physician that there will be a scar but no lingering effects, thanks to Mr. Brimley's care," I chose to ignore the tingle.

"What brings you to Brighton, Mr. Brodie? A new case perhaps?" I asked with some humor, aware that I was being deliberately disinterested even as something tickled at my brain with him standing there with the sea behind him.

"That is precisely what brings me to Brighton, Miss Forsythe."

A case? What the devil was he talking about?

"It seems yer friend, Miss Templeton, has found herself in somewhat of a difficulty."

I took off the tinted glasses. "What sort of difficulty?"

"She's been arrested and taken into custody."

"Arrested? For what?" I imagined all sorts of things, given her somewhat eccentric habits—perhaps the errant wanderings of Ziggy, or possibly dismantling of a statue at the Drury.

"For murder."

Good heavens! What had Templeton gotten herself into now?

"Whose murder?"

"A certain important gentleman. It's a rather delicate matter, and it very much looks as if she's in an impossible situation."

Impossible situation seemed a rather odd way of putting something that appeared to be most serious. However, we were speaking of Templeton, celebrated actress of the London theater, and around the world.

My thoughts immediately went to the Prince of Wales, considering their past relationship.

"Dear Bertie?" I asked.

That seemed to pull Brodie from his thoughts. "No, no. Another gentleman of her acquaintance, a foreign man, and there's quite an uproar about it. He is, or rather was, the French ambassador."

Well, at least she had kept it out of the royal family this time.

"And the cause of his death?"

"That seems to be of some question."

"How so, Mr. Brodie?"

"Well, there was just the one item that was found."

One item? The murder weapon perhaps?

"I see."

"Not precisely," Brodie replied. "His foot was the only part that was found."

A foot? Good heavens!

Templeton was certainly known for her eccentricities as well as her roles on the stage. Cleopatra came to mind. It was the role she had played during our investigation into my sister's disappearance. And there were countless others, not to mention her rumored affairs, including the Prince of Wales, her claim to be clairvoyant, and regular communication with Wills—William Shakespeare—among others.

"How could they possibly identify someone by a foot? I doubt even Mr. Brimley is that skilled," I commented.

"It seems they were able to identify him by the color of the paint on his toenails. It is supposedly a color he was known to favor, along with a... tattoo."

Toenail polish and a tattoo? I found myself looking at my own plain, rather short nails that were much in need of attention. When I had time, which apparently wouldn't be any time soon.

I stood and brushed sand from my bathing costume. "Where is she being held?"

Brodie gave me a slow look that took in my hair loose about my shoulders, my bathing costume that ended at my knees, bare legs, and toes curling into the warm sand.

"For the time being, she is being held at Scotland Yard, but she's to be transferred to Newgate in a matter of days.

"And she asked for me?"

"Yer the only person she will speak with about it. She wants ye to take the case."

With a body, or rather a foot, and a somewhat colorful affair, it seemed the case might already have been solved no matter how much I hated the idea that Templeton had done someone in.

It just seemed so... unlike her. What might have been the motive? And a foot with a tattoo?

Motive, means, and opportunity.

I reminded myself of the three things I had learned while working with Brodie as we searched for my sister.

It certainly seemed that Templeton had the opportunity.

The means? That was open to all sorts of conjecture with only a foot as evidence.

That left motive. A lover's quarrel? Or something more?

"Ye will speak with her?" he asked.

"Will I be allowed?" I was after all, merely an associate of Brodie's. And a 'former' associate at that.

"It can be arranged."

It was a reminder of a particular aspect of Brodie's professional status that had come to light as we searched for my sister. He did seem to have an extraordinary influence with the Metropolitan Police in general, and Scotland Yard in particular.

"Of course I will speak with her. I'll make arrangements to return to London right away."

He nodded. "Yer staying at the Grand?"

By that it was obvious he meant the Grand Hotel.

Why was I not surprised that he knew exactly where Linnie and I had accommodations?

"We will need time to pack and make arrangements for our return to London."

"What of yer sister?" he asked.

"She'll understand. She's always been an enormous fan of Templeton's, and would expect me to help in any way that I can."

He nodded, his expression that typical Brodie expression, his thoughts already on other things as he turned toward the stairs that led from the beach up to the esplanade and the oceanfront hotel just beyond.

"Do ye always go about very near naked on the beach?" he asked over his shoulder.

I had donned the tinted glasses and gathered my notebook and pen, and looked up, a memory suddenly returning quite clear, of another a beach, warm sand on the island of Crete, crystal blue water, and a man who seemed to appear out of nowhere suddenly standing over me.

"Do ye always go about naked in the water?" And

that unmistakable way the accent wrapped around the words—part question, part disapproval.

"It's very much like a bath," I had replied at the time, quite indignant, at least as much as I could remember, considering the amount of ouzo I had consumed.

"I don't wear clothes in my bath!"

It was Brodie! On that beach in Crete almost six years before, come to take me home after my aunt learned of my... shall we call them indiscretions.

That explained Brodie's previous association with my aunt, someone I could *trust*, that hazy image of a handsome man with dark eyes, and that accent that had stayed with me long after the ouzo had worn off and I had returned to London.

Bloody hell!

Also by Carla Simpson

Angus Brodie and Mikaela Forsythe Murder Mystery

A Deadly Affair

Deadly Secrets

A Deadly Game

Deadly Illusion

Merlin Series

Daughter of Fire

Daughter of the Mist

Daughter of the Light

Shadows of Camelot

Dawn of Camelot

Daughter of Camelot

The Young Dragons, Blood Moon

Clan Fraser

Betrayed

Revenge

Outlaws, Scoundrels & Lawmen

Desperado's Caress

Passion's Splendor

Silver Mistress

Memory and Desire

Desire's Flame

Silken Surrender

Ravished

Always My Love

Seductive Caress

Seduced

Deceived

About the Author

"I want to write a book... " she said.

"Then do it," he said.

And she did, and received two offers for that first book proposal.

A dozen historical romances later, and a prophecy from a gifted psychic and the Legacy Series was created, expanding to seven additional titles.

Along the way, two film options, and numerous book awards.

But wait, there's more a voice whispered, after a trip to Scotland and a visit to the standing stones in the far north, and as old as Stonehenge, sign posts the voice told her, and the Clan Fraser books that have followed that told the beginnings of the clan and the family she was part of...

And now... murder and mystery set against the backdrop of Victorian London in the new Angus Brodie and Mikaela Forsythe series, with an assortment of conspirators and murderers in the brave new world after the Industrial Revolution where terrorists threaten and the world spins closer to war.

When she is not exploring the Darkness of the fantasy world, or pursuing ancestors in ancient Scotland, she lives in the mountains near Yosemite National Park with bears and mountain lions, and plots murder and revenge.

And did I mention fierce, beautiful women and dangerous, handsome men?

They're there, waiting...

Join Carla's Newsletter

www.ingramcontent.com/pod-product-compliance
Ingram Content Group UK Ltd.
Pitfield, Milton Keynes, MK11 3LW, UK
UKHW020625240925
8055UKWH00028B/281

9 781648 392610

Murder, mystery, and two people in a most unlikely partnership. She's an unconventional lady who has traveled the world, practices the art of self defense most excellently, and has an interesting tattoo in, ahem... a very unusual place.

He's a former member of the Metropolitan Police, now a private investigator, who grew up on the poverty ridden streets of Edinburgh and has worked the dangerous back alleys of London's notorious East End.

A vicious murder brings them together in a race against time that takes them from the sordid back streets of London into the elite private clubs of the powerful and rich, to find the killer before he strikes again and prevent a deadly scheme.

A scandalous affair, deceptions, and secrets will challenge what they know and what they believe.

Come along as the lady and the detective join forces in an amazing time of new inventions, startling discoveries, and unexpected revelations, where a young woman who doesn't rely on anyone is forced to trust the irascible Scot who is a tough as they come and just might learn a thing or two from her... if they both don't end up dead!

US $10.99
ISBN 978-1-64839-261-0
51099
9 781648 392610